God

Of Our

Fathers

Woodsong Publishing
Seymour, Indiana

WOODSONG
PUBLISHING

God Of Our Fathers

By Larry M. Arrowood

First Edition 2019

 This is a work of fiction. All of the characters, names, incidents, organizations, and dialogue in this novel are either the products of the author's imagination or are used fictitiously.

Woodsong Publishing
5989 Spring Meadow Lane
Seymour, IN 47274

www.woodsongpublishing.com

ISBN 978-0-9979146-9-6

Cover design by Vision Graphics
Seymour, Indiana

Printed in the USA

In Memory of Dad

"And he said, The God of our fathers hath chosen thee, that thou shouldest know his will, and see that Just One, and shouldest hear the voice of his mouth" (Acts 22:14).

Chapter 1

Christopher Stone awakened in a sprawled position, suddenly aware of pain throughout his entire body. Stunned, he fought for consciousness. He winced at the high-pitched sound piercing his ears. A misty memory left questions, which he strained to answer. What just happened? Where am I? Who is the enemy and what is their location? He squinted through what seemed an impenetrable fog. An acrid smell, permeated with dust and smoke, induced a coughing spasm that left him lightheaded. He shielded his mouth and nostrils with his hand, gasping for fresh air. Was it an explosion?

Visions flashed too quickly to be real: images of a mysterious past of scrambled events. Chris' faculties assumed a combative position, albeit a defensive one. Was this an accident? Or was it on purpose? But who and why? How long have I been lying on the floor before consciousness returned?

With the back of his hand, he wiped at the sweat that stung as it trickled into his eyes. He repeatedly blinked, trying to see through the darkness. An array of thoughts pin-balled his psyche. Am I blinded?

Memory slowly returned, but it was elusive. It was a fiery explosion. Had a gas line erupted? How could he not have detected a smell? Though natural gas is odorless, the gas companies inject it with the rotten egg smell of tetrahydrothiophene as a warning to the unsuspecting. He would have noticed. His mind raced. It was an explosion but not accidental, for he would have detected the signs. It was a bomb. That explained the smoke, dust, and lingering carbon smell of TNT. And the heat. The room had heated to an uncomfortable temperature in a flash. He could assimilate a mental scenario of what had happened from the evidence surrounding him, but the "who" and the "why" were not as obvious

The coughing started again. He rolled onto his belly, began to rise, and involuntarily grabbed his forehead from intense pain. His elbow scraped against debris. He slid his fingers across the object-littered floor. A book. He extended his reach: a bed frame. His senses sharpened. He had been in bed before the explosion, reading. He was home.

"Oh, no! Eden?" He winced at the excruciating pain that shot throughout his head. The coughing resumed. He clasped his forehead to reduce the sharp stinging. "Eden, are you alright?"

Silence.

"Can you hear me, sweetheart?"

Only his heavy breathing responded to the silence. He strained for the slightest movement. Nothing.

He struggled to his feet, reached across the bed and patted the mattress but quickly withdrew his hand from the smoldering blanket. Fumbling in the darkness, he searched for the lamp, stumbled against the overturned stand, and fell hands first onto the porcelain lamp shattered on the floor. A shard stung his index finger. He carefully extracted the sliver and clasped his finger, the warm dampness covering his palm offered concern.

He pushed himself upright and shuffled through the darkness, searching. His foot bumped a heavy object. He knelt. It was a body, obviously severely burned, the clothes still smoldering.

"Eden!" he cried into the darkness. Speak to me, dear. Can you hear me?" His mind exploded with the realization of his wildest nightmares.

Everything slowed as he cradled her limp body and rocked gently, enduring the pain to his hands from the scorched clothing. He fought against nausea as the smell of burned flesh penetrated the air.

"Eden, speak to me. I'm here, sweetheart."

Trembling hands searched for a pulse. Nothing.

He tenderly laid her body onto the floor and instinctively administered CPR, counting the pumps aloud, breathing into her non-responsive mouth, spitting out whatever it was that had clung to her lips and now to his: counting, breathing, methodically. He rechecked the pulse. Nothing. Her hand slid from his own, and he crawled through the debris toward the doorway. Bumping into the wall, he felt for the door, found it, and reached for the light switch. He flipped the switch on, off, on. Total darkness.

"Where is the flashlight?" He mumbled into the darkness, struggling for his bearings. "The nightstand?"

Staggering across the room, he found the overturned nightstand, jerked open the door and rummaged through the contents until he found the flashlight. He turned it on and quickly scanned the room. Its beam illuminated swirling dust and smoke and affirmed his worst fear: the charred body of his wife.

He collapsed against the bedpost and slid to the carpet. The flashlight slipped from his hand and rolled across the floor. It stopped to rest against a book that lay among the litter, illuminating the binding: *Reconciling the Three Monotheistic Religions of the World.* He had been reading the book before the blast.

His mind raced. "Who would have done this? Why? An attack against me, I understand, but why Eden?" He screamed into the silence.

The mind is a machine that needs no prompting, no instructions, and no operator. You don't turn it on, but you find it difficult to turn off, even when you want to sleep. It is creative beyond comprehension and so fast that a speeding bullet to the forehead goes into slow motion before the impact. Everything seems to slow because the brain is working swifter than the action around it. A dozen years zipped by in a flash. His apparent enemies didn't know where he lived. Or had they found him? Surely not? What about the familiar face in the crowd at the racetrack? Coincidence? Probably. His primary associations were his students, but would one of them have done this? He didn't hesitate to challenge their cherished, religious dogmas, but that was his job as a professor. Had he been too harsh? Did he have a religious fanatic in his class? Perhaps. Chris wanted to swear, to curse them, to curse their gods, to avenge Eden's death. He opened his mouth and tried to speak, but nothing came out. Tears streamed down his cheeks. He burst forth into a coughing fit of anguish. The coughing subsided, and he buried his head in his blistered hands.

Despair crept over his soul. He tried to stop it, but he did not have the strength nor the knowledge to do so. He knew the end result: life without hope. He'd seen it before in others, a sure and certain death, like a slow-flowing magma from a crevasse in the earth, destroying everything in its path and leaving a lifeless and hardened residue in its wake.

Sirens blared from the distance.

Chapter 2

Sherri Carpenter enjoyed her job at the Clarksville Applebee's, mostly because she loved people. For the past two years, she received employee appreciation certificates. Some of her customers were like family, many were repeat locals, and she never forgot a face, but the two young men huddled in a booth in the far corner of her serving section were total strangers. Subdued lighting hinted of Middle Eastern features: dark skin tone, black hair, trimmed beards. She assumed them to be Arabic, for they had both ordered iced tea, which they drank without sugar, but then she wondered if Arabs might drink hot tea instead. But their accent removed any doubt. Her inquisitive nature relented to a smile, but it was a smile to no one in particular. She would know them before they finished their meal. They would not leave as strangers.

She returned to their table carrying a pitcher of the unsweetened tea. Curiosity overtook her manners. "Y'all not from around here?" The words flowed from her lips like thick sorghum poured from a Ball canning jar: sweet and slow but intentional. It was more a statement than a question but spoken in a way as to induce an answer.

"No. We arrived here last year." The taller one answered. "We are from the Middle East."

"Thought such. We don't get many outsiders, except shoppers from the mall. Students?"

"Yes." The taller one answered again.

"Cat got your tongue?" She directed her question to the silent one as she topped his glass.

He stared at her but did not answer.

"That's colloquialism here in southern Indiana. Probably never heard that from where y'all come from."

"Actually, we have. Some think it originated in the Middle East." The tall one continued to be the spokesman. The silent one stared at her, his eyes dark and penetrating.

Sherri feigned a smile and wiped up the tea she had sloshed onto the table.

Another police cruiser rushed by, siren blaring and lights flashing.

"Them boys are awfully busy tonight. Where y'all studying?"

"He is studying religion at McAlister Seminary. I am a business major at U of L."

"There you go again, not lettin' your friend answer a word. I attended U of L a few semesters back."

Neither commented.

"Just kiddin' ya about you not lettin' him speak." She waved her free hand in the air as if to wipe away the statement. "Y'all need to lighten up a little. This here is southern Indiana, and we like to get to know our neighbors." She gave them her tip-inducing best smile and patted the silent one on the shoulder. "You'll learn English soon enough living in America."

He returned a half-hearted smile, but it concerned her the way both of them looked at her, distrusting and condescending. She somewhat wished for a hijab under which she could hide from the piercing stares. Was that why their women wore those full-length garbs, to shroud their emotions?

"Which side of the Ohio y'all live on?" Talking seemed to calm her concerns.

"Louisville." It was the tall one again who answered.

"Ready to order?"

"Yes," the quiet one said brusquely.

"So, you can talk. Just for that, you get to order first."

She listened intently as they placed their orders, hoping to impress them with her ability to remember the orders without writing them down. One thing she suspected was that they did not like her. Maybe they didn't like women, especially nosy American women.

"I'll get your order goin'. Let me make sure I got it right." She repeated the order, using her hands for emphasis and saying a word or two—that they struggled pronouncing—the same way they did. They seemed uncertain of her subtle humor. She smiled, retreated to the computer, and typed in the order.

She couldn't help but be suspicious of the two strangers, but she tried to serve them well. Since 9/11 she suspected all foreigners, especially from the Middle East. Friends called her androphobic, but she had her reasons. She eavesdropped on the two throughout their entire meal but heard nothing of a suspicious nature, which somewhat disappointed her. She glanced at their table just as the quiet one thumbed through a stack of bills, stuffed them into an envelope, and placed it inside his tweed sports jacket. That's when she noticed the missing fingers on his right hand.

How much money was in the envelope? Was he receiving a payment for something? Her mind raced. They're up to no good, them two. And what are they doing on this side of the river if they're students in Louisville? She'd never waited on customers that she didn't get their names before they finished. She grabbed the iced tea pitcher and headed back to their table. A credit card balanced on the edge of the table.

"More tea?"

"No thanks," the man with the missing finger said.

She swiped the card from the table and headed toward her checkout stand.

Chapter 3

The uniformed workers bumped into each other as they came and went inside the modest house where Chris Stone had lived the past three years: forensics, coroner, inspectors, police, fire, and medical personnel. Some had specific business, but some seemed more curious than purposeful. An evacuation of the curious, the part-timers, and the volunteers would have helped the overcrowding. It seemed anyone in Clarksville with a badge had access to his house.

Chris sat at the kitchen table and answered the usual questions and some he wasn't comfortable with, but he appreciated the concern with which the police officers treated him. The climate changed when a muscular built, plainclothes detective entered, followed by a young detective whose youthful appearance rendered him barely out of high school, but his six-seven frame demanded some measure of respect. He instinctively ducked as he entered the room. The previous sympathetic mood of the entourage abruptly changed to a down-to-cop-business attitude, and the caregivers eased into the living room to let the tough boys do their work. The detective scanned the report given him by a female officer and asked her a couple questions under his breath before approaching Chris.

"Mr. Stone, I'm Detective Tony Trapp, homicide. So sorry for your loss." He extended his hand.

"Thank you, sir." Stone noticed the unnecessary hard grip of this fiftyish looking man, his sideburns graying, but maybe he was a little younger than he appeared, as long hours of detective work can age one prematurely. His dark, steely eyes masked his emotions.

"And this is Dallas Rogers, my associate."

Rogers likewise extended a hand. "Sorry for your loss," he said, his brow furrowed. He was young enough still to display what seemed an honest emotion of sympathy.

Trapp bypassed the small talk and jumped into the investigation. "I need to ask a few questions. This shouldn't take much time."

"Sure."

"Christopher Stone. No middle name?"

"Correct."

"May I call you Chris?"

"Some folks do." Chris did not like him, not because of anything in particular about his person, but because of what he knew was coming. He disdained interrogation tactics, especially the good cop, bad cop approach. And this would not be a one-time, few-minutes investigation. First will come the "we care" approach, even the "we're your friends" approach. Once the guard is down, the "we know you did it" saber thrust to the heart always catches the novice off-guard.

"Do you drive the car parked in your driveway?" Trapp asked.

"Yes."

"How and why does a part-time, seminary professor, living in a medium income housing development, drive a new Lexus?"

Chris stared at him. Trapp had skipped over the "we care" stage. This detective didn't waste any time going straight for the jugular.

"I resent that question, sir, and I resent the tone with which you asked it." Christopher Stone was no novice to Gestalt tactics that bordered on police brutality. Though he well understood the significance, he preferred to be on the other side of the table.

"I'll ask whatever questions I want to ask and in whatever manner I wish to ask them. All I want from you are honest answers," Trapp said, his take charge demeanor rising.

"Then I have the right to remain silent." Chris knew this would settle Trapp down a few notches.

"And I'll assume your silence is an admission of some sort of guilt. Maybe drugs, as a starter." Trapp didn't budge from his Gestapo tactics.

"Assume whatever you want, Detective. I could care less about your assumptions but understand where I'm coming from. The love of my life has been murdered, and you have the audacity to come into my home, making insinuations against me by the type car I drive. I resent that." His voice elevated with each word erupting from his anguished soul.

"Then just answer the question." Trapp's tone softened somewhat.

Chris stared at him, considering his options, wondering what cards the detective planned to play next.

The detective methodically rubbed the stubble on his chin. He breathed deeply and slowly exhaled. "Mr. Stone, my job is to find out who killed your wife, not to become your friend. Don't stonewall me, Professor. You can either help or hinder this investigation, but I will find out who killed your wife, with or without your cooperation. However, I can do my job a lot better if you cooperate." He actually showed a hint of sympathy.

"I'll answer your question, but I still don't see the relevance."

"I understand you are upset. Perhaps I was a bit abrasive."

A bit abrasive? You're brutal, Chris wanted to say, but he merely stared at him for a long moment, then lowered his gaze to the shag, orange carpet. He planned on something better someday, not just the carpet, but an entire house. He had promised Eden such. She deserved better, though she never demanded anything from him.

She had lived lavishly before she married him. Had he done her wrong by—

"Mr. Stone?" Trapp interrupted his thoughts.

Chris slowly looked up. "It belongs to a repair shop at the Thomas Stein Lexus dealership in Louisville. My Taurus is getting repaired."

"You know we'll verify this?"

"Yes."

"It's just that we can't take anything for granted, Professor. You understand?"

"Sure."

"We'll return the necklace," Trapp said.

"The necklace?" The statement surprised Chris.

"The cross necklace your wife held in her hand," Trapp said.

"I didn't realize she still had the necklace … ." His words trailed off into the commotion that surrounded them.

Trapp placed a hand on his shoulder. "I'm truly sorry about your loss, Professor Stone."

"Thank you," Chris responded. He knew the ropes. The investigative officials vacillated from compassion to suspicion to neutrality in their assessments, these being more tactical than sincere. Years of working with criminals petrified the emotions. This investigation would take months, for Chris knew little, if any, evidence survived the explosion. The detectives would leave no stones unturned, and a good investigator sometimes returned to look under a rock the second time.

Trapp was certainly a seasoned investigator, and when Rogers finally spoke, it was obvious that he, too, though young, was quite sharp. The two worked in tandem, shrewd in their tactics, asking him the same question more than once, sometimes just asking it differently.

"I know we've asked a lot of questions, but maybe we've missed something," Rogers spoke up. "Would you mind telling us one more time everything that happened, Christopher, as many details as you can remember." Rogers' voice seemed laced with compassion.

Chris was tired of rehearsing the same information for the umpteenth time. "There's nothing to add. I was in bed, reading … that's the book laying on the floor in the bedroom … I fell asleep … then the explosion … I found Eden's body—"

"Let's go back somewhat," Trapp interrupted. "Did you go to bed at the same time as your wife? Or was she already in bed?"

The question sparked a memory, though foggy.

"I recall her crocheting before we went to bed … and … I'm sorry … I can't—"

"We're taking the body, Mr. Stone." It was the coroner with his assistants, a more sympathetic team, and his tone emanated concern, but no tone could soften Chris' suffering.

Chris did not know what to say, for he had never been here before. He nodded and wiped at the tears blurring his vision. He wanted to follow them but remained at the kitchen table, too broken to move. He noticed Trapp staring at him. Should I have shown more emotion? He wondered what they expected from him, but under the circumstances, he didn't care enough about what they expected from him to pretend anything. His body felt little more than numbness. They'd have to accept that.

Detective Trapp wasn't finished. Was it because of Chris' response, or lack thereof, to the removal of Eden's body? Trapp dug in and proved harsh with a couple questions. Chris knew the routine; he also knew his rights. He had cooperated in every way, answering all their questions and offering some information for which they failed to ask, except for one piece of information he assumed they did not know. He would not voluntarily give that up. They would have to figure it out. Were they that clever? He wasn't sure. Time would tell.

Chapter 4

Chris unconsciously reached for Eden but quickly recoiled from the reality. He willed himself to redirect the dream, to awaken again, only to face the same reality. After that, sleep would not come. Since their marriage three years ago, he had not stayed in a motel without her. In reality, they had never been apart for a single night since their wedding. "Two peas in a pod," that's what he told her, but he had to explain its meaning, for she had never heard that expression. Their enchanted life seemed forever. But the pod had been split apart, crushed by the unthinkable.

Chris' last day with Eden was also a first. Their first visit to the Kentucky Derby had been fantastic, an experience so chock-full of adventure that it would remain a highlight of a lifetime. And in a moment, that was all he had left: memories.

***

The mass of multi-colored hats swayed and bobbed in the infield. A century plus tradition had survived time and chance. An unlikely collage of college students, rowdies, and ten-cent gamblers crammed together, forming a short-lived alliance whose primary objective was to have a good time in spite of any circumstances. For a crowd that wasn't supposed to bring alcohol to the event, the bootleggers were the envy of some, clever enough to sneak bottles of bourbon inside the enclosure, avoiding at the entrance the scowling confiscation of such illicit booze.

Chris instinctively surveyed the raucous rabble a few yards below. Though a boisterous lot, this crowd seemed a relatively fun-loving group, nonetheless, all crowds bothered him: too much groupthink often ended in catastrophic results, while at the same time it offered concealment for a lone wolf with an agenda. Recent terrorists' activities affirmed that lone wolfers sought out the crowds. Though the intent of this crowd seemed innocent enough, and the event itself attracted a somewhat respectable clientele, that in itself made the event a likely target, especially the crowded area. They'd each paid a twenty-dollar bill to walk through the tunnel into the racetrack, somewhat bitter at the uppity-ups who received far better treatment from management. The establishment simply tolerated them, but that didn't deter their frolicking away the day with jokes and laughter, and even the incessant rain had not dampened their spirits. But some never really got their money's worth, as little as the entry fee was, for they couldn't see over the crowd to watch the race, even on the jumbotrons that lined the infield facing them, and a few, having indulged a little too heavily from the brown-paper bags they'd sneaked under the radar, never knew when the race started nor when it ended. Still, all were making memories and would someday, with delight, tell their grandkids that they attended the Kentucky Derby back in 2010, though they would leave out the minor detail of actually not seeing the race when it happened but watched it on TV after they got home. Such dieheart fans keep sports alive, and no overcrowded infield or damp and chilly weather would prevent them from attending the annual event that boasted the most exciting two minutes of world sports. Once the race ended, and their adrenalin dipped into their shoes, they'd gladly double the twenty-dollar bill they paid to get in if they could escape the slow-moving crowd trying to squeeze back through that same tunnel they'd so joyously entered. But with a few days to recuperate, at the end of the month, some would trek two hours north for the ninety-fourth running of the Indy 500.

Eden's face was partially hidden underneath the brim of her white, Crystalle Church Hat. A colossal bow, rather flashy for her typical attire, adorned the right side of the hat and brushed incessantly against his face as she reacted with excitement to the momentous moments preceding the main event. He'd paid under sixty-dollars for the hat, though he'd tried to persuade her to get a more expensive white with black polka dots Southern Belle beauty, but she'd insisted it was a waste of money and too flashy. If she knew his thoughts about the bow, she might have broken with tradition and worn her Cincinnati Reds cap. Since he'd gotten off cheap on the hat, he made sure they had good seats, paying a little over three-hundred dollars a ticket for their grandstand bleacher, pretty pricey but much cheaper than clubhouse tickets, and it was a far cry from the four-thousand dollars the rich and famous paid for their box seats. She noticed his stare and returned the gaze with a shy smile.

A wealthy man's sport, the Kentucky Derby separated the good from the best—horses, not men—of winners, though it took more than good horses to pull off a once in a lifetime win: it took great trainers and great jockeys. The owners had each paid twenty-five thousand dollars to enter their three-year-old registered thoroughbreds, and they had to cough up another twenty-five thousand for today's start. The stakes were high, with more than a hundred million dollars in wagers around the world on these horses, and probably much more unaccounted for money, as some folks make bets off the records on about anything.

Chris had placed no bet on any of the contenders; he merely wanted to give his wife a special treat and introduce her to this grand event, somewhat akin in excitement to the bullfights of her native land: especially the pageantry at the beginning of the event. Since moving to the Louisville metro area, they didn't venture out much, but their marriage needed few, if any, social events for fulfillment. Life was more about conversations, and books, and trying new recipes to satisfy their multicultural palates. And he stayed quite busy at his job as a professor at the McAlister Seminary in southeast Louisville. He was proud of his work ethic, for he seldom took a day off, but the semester was almost over, and they'd travel during the summer. But he broke from the regular routine, for he wanted Eden to experience the events surrounding the Derby week. He had taken off work the day before so that they could visit the Kentucky Horse Park in Lexington, and now they followed up with this exciting day at Churchill Downs and the one hundred and thirty-sixth running of the Kentucky Derby. She was accustomed to horses before their marriage, for her father had bought her a prized chestnut-colored thoroughbred, and he hired a private instructor to train her in the finer techniques of riding. She often spoke of those days, so Chris surprised her with this weekend outing.

They had enjoyed several of the day's races hunkered beneath clear plastic rain breakers, but the rain had stopped just when the main event was moments away. The crowd roared to life as twenty spirited Thoroughbreds made their entrance onto the track, in order of their gate post, and strutting personal characteristics: heads erect, some pulling against the lead pony, others aggressively approaching another Thoroughbred, or seemingly posing for a photo shoot, much to the delight of the cheering spectators. This diverse populace included locals who saved their money all year to attend, as well as the rich and famous who placed bets on every horse running—making sure they could boast of picking a winner. Wealthy oil sheiks from Saudi Arabia came with prospects of buying, and sheep farmers as far away as New Zealand came for this once in a lifetime trip to America. But no matter the diversity of the crowd, they all became an enormous choir that joined forces with the University of Louisville Marching Band to sing the traditional *My Old Kentucky Home,* written by Stephen Collins Foster, one of Kentucky's most famous composers. They were halfway through their rendition when the person seated behind Chris dumped a cup of mint julep inside his suit-collar. This traditional concoction of bourbon, syrup, fresh mint, and shaved ice sent a shock-wave down his spine. His immediate response wasn't pleasant, but the individual's sincere apology, and Eden's hilarious laughter, saved the day.

As a professor of religions, some folks assumed him to be religious, in particular, most assumed him to be a Christian. That assumption was incorrect, for he was not religious, nor did he desire religion, though he came from a practicing Jewish family. That was the only dissension in his otherwise dream marriage, for Eden was a Christian, quite knowledgeable of the Bible, and committed to her faith. Chris sometimes discussed his college lectures with Eden, seeking her input, but that seldom ended well, for she couldn't conceal her disappointment in his cynicism toward her faith in God. His primary classes at the seminary focused on the three principal monotheistic religions, but he claimed faith in no God, his cynicism bolstered by the acclaim given to some followers of the monotheistic faiths whom he considered evil. Yet all claimed to be representatives of the one true God, a God of love and benevolence. The accounts of these evil, religious men, and their dark, spiritual empires remained a stumbling block to any personal faith he might have had in their God. He couldn't excuse religions that left a history of the inquisitions, and took up sword against another religion and dared call it a Holy War. Nor could he condone the methods of conversion used by Muhammad, or the shenanigans of popes like Leo X or Urban II. And he had little, if any, respect for religions that would not admit their flawed pasts and repent in sackcloth and ashes. He had lost interest in the faith of his childhood, for why would a loving Yahweh desert his people to imprisonment and torture, and how could a benevolent God allow them to be taken into captivity by nations more wicked then they? And the holocaust seemed like total abandonment by the God who promised always to protect. And for a million and a half Armenians to be slaughtered, primarily because of their Christian status, seemed rather insensitive by a Divine sustainer, and for the slaughter to happen at the hands of a competing religion solidified his disenchantment of all faiths. And how many wars were over religion? And yes, most of this among the three major monotheistic faiths: the ones who were supposed to be the real deal. He had too many questions for which he had no satisfactory answers, so he refused personal association with all three monotheistic faiths. His religion consisted in being kind to others and in self-preservation, though he leaned toward the latter, for personal experience had taught him that no one would take care of you as well as you.

So how does an unbeliever in the three major monotheistic faiths become the teacher? He justified his right to teach about these faiths because he viewed himself as unbiased. He would stir emotions by challenging one of the religions, but just as convincingly, he would switch sides. Such tactics made for an exciting classroom, but only a couple students, who claimed to be atheists, approved of his lectures. Some left his class in tears, but he at least had gotten them to question their traditions.

It was refreshing to take the Friday off from class and visit the Kentucky Horse Park in Lexington: an opportunity to see and learn about horses from around the world, to touch their bulging muscles and feel on your face the breath of champions of yesteryear, their heads pressing against the wire-mesh gates of their stalls. All had earned their place in this retirement community by proving to be the best. And to see the delight on Eden's face was reward enough. For the past three years, they had participated in the annual week of local festivities preceding the Derby, but this was their first time to the Kentucky Horse Park, home of the past champions. Likewise, this was their first visit to the Derby, and how exciting to top off the weekend by snapping pictures of Churchill Downs' famed twin spires, with Eden's smiling face in the foreground. She must have thanked him a dozen times for the two days of adventure.

"Look dear, a rainbow," Eden proclaimed, pointing toward the arched wonder of light rays.

A steady rain had disrupted the better part of their two-day excursion, so it was quite refreshing when the sun broke through the clouds just before the race, though the wet field had not dampened the spirits of men or horses. The rainbow momentarily stole the attention of some, but the cheers preceding the expectation of the start of the race quickly reclaimed every soul of the adrenaline-drunken crowd. A momentary hush fell over the grandstand in anticipation of the gate opening and the announcer's proclamation: "And they're off!"

A thin layer of glassy water covering the track mirrored the multi-colors of twenty prancing horses and their rigid riders—clutching the reigns with trembling hands—as the starting bell sounded, and the gates simultaneously clanged open to the roar of the crowd of better than a hundred and fifty thousand standing spectators. The tightly packed Thoroughbreds thundered across the brown, glistening sheen of the eight inches of carefully sifted sand, silt, and clay. Three inches of proportionately mixed surface cushioned the horses' pounding hoofs. Each horse topped the scales at somewhere around eleven hundred pounds. Horses and riders jockeyed for positions the entire two minutes, much aware that the rain made for a treacherous track. And though the groundskeepers prided themselves in a perfectly smooth track, the horde left behind a sloppy mess that looked like a field of gopher holes. There were no favored horses, but a favorite jockey, a two-time Kentucky Derby winner, broke out of the fourth gate and quickly scrambled for the inner rail, a position he favored in previous races. But on this muddy track, with much uncertainty, by the time the pack reached the back stretch, his mount had fallen into seventh place and remained glued to the rail, seemingly trapped by the throng of rivals running more than thirty-seven miles an hour in a cluster of a hair-breaths distance from side to side and nose to tail. Win number three for the revered jockey seemed to vanish into the wind as the seconds ticked away. Hunched riders, in rhythmic sync with the horses whom they'd studied and bonded, furiously coached and cajoled their mounts, while combating airborne grime that plastered their helmets, shoulders, and legs from the knees downward. One could only wonder how they could see the track ahead and what kept them from colliding into a massive and pitiful pileup of horses and riders.

The familiar voice of Tom Durkin blared above the roaring crowd as he heralded the names of the horses that galloped at top speed toward the far turn. The numbers emblazoned on the horses' saddle blankets changed positions several times before the turn for home stretch. Coming out of the final turn, surprisingly, number four suddenly charged from the crowd, left the rail to pass one horse, then returned to the rail position, but this time he led the staggered pack.

Chris struggled to focus on the race—the race itself was not what had motivated him to endure this crowd—but observed, in cinematic slow motion, the love of his life leaping to her feet and tossing her hat into the air when famed Louisiana Cajun jockey Calvin Borel, in his mud-caked white jersey, glided atop the bay colt, Super Saver, as he dashed for the roses across the finish line. This made Borel an unprecedented third-time Kentucky Derby winner.

Amid the cheers of the exuberant crowd, and the moans of a few big losers—their worthless tickets now crumpled in their fists—whose faces reflected the despair of their hearts, Chris glimpsed for a brief moment a familiar face in the moving crowd. It was an image that reminded him of someone in his past, not a welcomed sight, but he was unsure if the distant acquaintance saw him. Then again, he wasn't sure it was the person he knew. Perhaps it was the twin we all have somewhere that we haven't yet met. For a split second he imagined the worst, but then he returned his gaze to Eden, to that unassuming smile that came so easily. Her virtuous face and her soft, almond complexion projected an innocence reminiscent of the first Eden before the mistake in the garden. She had returned to him the peace he had somehow lost while pursuing a career of adventure.

The crowd of unknown faces, and the adrenalin rush of the excitement, momentarily reminded him of a faraway place among another people, and he wondered in amazement how things had turned out so fantastic for himself. But he could not help but also wonder how it would end. He glanced again in the direction of the one who had caught his attention, but the face had vanished into the crowd.

***

Chris momentarily clung to the pleasant memories that were but a few hours old, still as fragrant as a freshly-cut bouquet of flowers. Strange how those memories now seemed like another lifetime.

In a whiff, the fragrance turned pungent, spoiled by neglect. Chris berated himself for being so careless. It was his fault Eden was gone. If only he had not become so complacent! Her death could have been averted. Did she suffer? He hoped not. How could he live with such shame?

Chapter 5

"Line one, Sir," Rogers called to Trapp from across the room. Dallas Rogers placed the caller on hold, yawned, and stretched his lanky arms high into the air. It had been a long night, and it was showing on his face.

Trapp took another sip from his third cup of coffee before picking up the phone. The windows rattled suddenly from a thunderclap, and Trapp's reflex spilled hot coffee onto his desk. "Is it ever going to stop raining? I thought April showers brought May flowers … not May showers bringing … Detective Trapp here. How may I help you?"

"My name is … Carr. Susan Carr. I heard your name on the news… a reporter gave it … regarding the killing of that young woman in Clarksville. I work at … a gas station part-time … and since you're needing leads from anyone who might have seen or heard something, I … ." She paused. "Is this call confidential?"

"Sure, Ms. Carr." He snapped his fingers to get Roger's attention and motioned to get a trace on the call. Rogers gave him a thumbs-up sign.

"I'm not sure if my information is relevant, but—"

"Ms. Carr, if you have any information, just share it with me, and I'll decide if it's relevant."

"I didn't want to waste your time, sir."

"I've got all day, Ms. Carr, and I'm all ears." He wondered if his irritation transmitted along the phone lines. He tried to remain patient as he doodled on a notepad.

"Well, the night of the murder, I waited on two men at the restaurant where I work and—"

"I thought you worked at a gas station?" Trapp interrupted her.

"I work two part-time jobs, the restaurant … where I saw the two men, but I also work at this other part-time job … where I am now … but like I said, these two men, with foreign accents, came in shortly after the time of the killing. I could tell it was around that time cause the sirens kept going by the … by the restaurant."

"What restaurant, Ms. Carr?" Trapp tapped his notepad with the eraser of a tooth-pocked pencil.

"Ah, I'd rather not say, sir, not just yet."

"Okay, I can accept that, for now. What about these two men?"

"Well, just that there were two of them, strangers to the store, and they seemed rather out of place."

"Out of place?" Trapp asked.

"Yes, like they were up to something."

"So, anything in particular?" Trapp asked.

"Don't know much about them," she said.

"How about age? Clothes they were wearing? Strange activities? Nervous gestures?"

"Oh, that, sure. Early twenties. Dressed regular, but what made me the most suspicious was one of them had an envelope, and it was full of a stack of bills … must have been hundreds … maybe thousands of dollars."

"And what was suspicious about that?"

"Well, like I said, they were foreigners, from the Middle East, they told me so. Of course, I could already tell that by the language they spoke and their skin color. And hair color, too. Dark hair and kind of curly."

"Dark hair and kind of curly? Okay, what language?"

"Arab."

"Do you speak Arabic?"

"No, but it sounded like what I've heard on TV."

"And that made you suspicious?"

"Well, not just that."

"What else?"

"One is a student at the University of Louisville, and the other is a student at the same college that the dead woman's husband works at. The reporter said the husband teaches at McAlister Seminary. Don't you think that's not just coincidental, the foreign student with all that money being a student at the same college the murdered woman's husband teaches at?"

"I'd say there are several hundred students at the college … at the seminary where the husband of the deceased works, and I'd also say a few were at a restaurant last night, Ms. Carr." Trapp patiently worked on balancing his number two lead pencil, eraser down, on his desk, but it toppled onto his desktop and flipped onto the floor.

"Oh, I guess you're right about that. Well, maybe I wasted your time."

"No, no … not at all. Can you think of anything else suspicious? Like, did you overhear anything they said? I'm assuming they spoke English, so you understood what they were saying." He retrieved the pencil from the floor.

"Yeah, with that Eastern accent, of course. Never heard them say anything suspicious."

"Anything else you feel I need to know?"

"Well, this might not mean anything, but one of them did all the talking. The one with the envelope of money, the other one, the student at the religious school was quiet and … ."

"And what?" Trapp took a sip of coffee.

"Two fingers were missing."

"And that made you suspicious?"

"Wasn't it a bomb that killed that girl?"

"It was an explosion of some sort." He didn't want to give out too many details on the case.

"Well, maybe he is a bomb builder, and he lost his two fingers in a bomb-making accident. Couldn't that be a possibility?"

"I see your point." Trapp had been second-guessed for his investigative skills by more people than he cared to count. It came with the job. Monday morning quarterbacks and citizen PI's all have their right to an opinion, without any consequences for their false assessment. Trapp shook his head in amusement, for that was what this call was all about. It was simply unjustifiable suspicion. And maybe motivated by some fear by a woman who perhaps lived alone. "Which hand?" It was in the details that eyewitnesses seemed to falter.

"Right … left. No, I think it was his right."

"By any chance did you get the names of these two men?"

"Yeah, the quiet one, I got his name."

"And what was the name?"

"I can't pronounce it, but I have the name from the credit card."

"Great! Spell it for me."

Trapp was instinctively skeptical of anonymous witnesses, but he couldn't help but be impressed that she got the man's name. Maybe this lead was going somewhere after all. He reached for his coffee. The phone went dead.

"Ms. Carr. You there? Hello. Ms. Carr." Trapp slammed the phone into its cradle. "Dallas, did you get a trace on that number?"

"Sure did. Landline. A phone booth in Louisville, around St. Matthews Mall area."

For a young detective, Rogers was very efficient. Trapp liked him but wouldn't say so to Rogers. His aloofness would keep Rogers on his toes. "Get over there and check for security camera footage at every service station in the area until we find our Ms. Susan Carr. She also works a second job in Indiana?"

"Where?"

"She didn't say."

"How do you know she works in Indiana?"

"Sirens, she heard the sirens the night of the murder," Trapp said.

"But she could live on the Kentucky side," Rogers said.

"Very possible. We'll have to co-op with the Louisville PD on this one, but it's our case and don't forget that the crime happened here, on our turf."

"I'm on it."

"I'm gonna visit McAlisters and check out any Arab students enrolled in Professor Stone's classes. You focus on the security cameras at St. Matthews. McAlister is probably closed weekends, so, I'll check things out first thing Monday. Right now, I'm going home and going to bed. Oh, we're also searching for a three-fingered foreigner."

"Left or right hand?"

"Either. But he has an accomplice. He's a U of L student."

"Name?"

"Didn't get a name but how many Middle Eastern students in Louisville?"

"Two more than we need." Rogers chuckled.

"You're a racist, Rogers. Gonna get you fired someday."

"I didn't mean it like that. I meant two more criminals than we need," Rogers argued.

"Like I said, gonna get you fired," Trapp retorted.

"Never got you fired, sir." Rogers chuckled.

"Touché," Trapp said as he tossed the pencil at Rogers but missed.

Chapter 6

A Monday morning trip to McAlister Seminary by detective Tony Trapp turned up the name for the only student of Middle Eastern descent, Abdul-Bari Razi. And not surprising to Trapp, his name meant "servant of the creator." He was Jordanian and in the States on a student visa. There were no marks against him as far as Trapp could tell, but Trapp suspicioned colleges tried to keep their reputation intact. He had ways of circumventing the administration if necessary, but he didn't want to push too hard, not just yet. For now, he would focus on the professor. That was his prime suspect. In Trapp's mind, Mr. Razi was a secondary.

"Our mystery woman, Ms. Carr, was right about Abdul-Bari Razi. He's of Middle Eastern descent," Trapp barked into his cell phone that he balanced between his left ear and his shoulder.

"Somebody should have shot whoever designed this … ." He stopped short of finishing his sentence. A characteristic he often did.

"What's that, sir?" Rogers asked.

"I'm stuck in traffic at the bridge."

Traffic had slowed to a crawl on the Kentucky side of the river near the Kennedy Bridge, which hosted the I-65, I-64, and I-71 architectural mishap.

"Sorry, sir," Dallas said.

"We need governors that can partner together for a change and fix this Kentuckiana nightmare … finish the by-pass they've been talking about for years."

"Don't think we count much down here, sir," Rogers said. "Too far from Indy and politics."

"I certainly expected more from Daniels … course he's more interested in a balanced budget … his ticket to the White House."

"Want us to pick him up?" Rogers' voice sounded like he'd been up most of the night.

"The governor?" Trapp chuckled to himself. He enjoyed teasing Rogers, who seemed a little naive but was always a good sport.

"No. I meant Abdul."

"Too late! He left Sunday for a visit back home. I've already confirmed with immigration that he flew from Louisville International to Washington-Dulles and on to Jordan. The school wasn't sure why he left, since the semester isn't over. We'll have to keep our fingers crossed that he returns. Gotta keep this under our hats, especially from the press, or he'll never step foot on American soil again."

"What about the second student?" Dallas asked.

"I'm on my way now. I assume he was on the same flight, but we'll need a name to verify such. Did you find anything at St. Matthews?"

"Just a jackpot! A security camera filmed two men approaching a phone booth. Time coincides with our Ms. Carr's phone call. The only problem, we don't have a shot of their faces. It was raining so umbrellas shielded their faces."

"How about the woman? Any identification on her?" Trapp braked hard as a car squeezed in front of his white, unmarked Ford sedan. He considered turning on his lights and pulling the driver over, but that might not settle well with Kentucky cops. He blared his horn instead. "Crazy Kentuckians. Where'd they learn to drive?"

"What's goin' on, sir?" Dallas asked.

"Just an inconsiderate driver. What about the footage of the woman?"

"Same with her. No image of her face, but the time on the security footage is the same time the woman made the call to us. The woman went with the two men, or at least it looks like she did."

"Then I think we know our killers, Rogers. We've just gotta find them. And now, maybe another killing, at best an abduction. I think we've got us a couple Arab radicals, the one offended by Professor Stone, and his buddy from U of L. So, they took it on themselves to avenge Allah's reputation by bombing the professor's home but took out the professor's wife instead of the professor," Trapp said.

"What's the link with the gas station attendant?" Rogers asked.

"They became suspicious of her at the restaurant, so they followed her and probably took her out also?" Trapp inched his cruiser left on I-71, across three lanes of bumper-to-bumper traffic and onto the bridge ramp lane to I-65.

"Seems to fit," Rogers said.

"Were the men aggressive in the video footage?" Trapp asked.

"Didn't appear so."

"Did the woman show any resistance?"

"Not really. But it's poor footage, raining really, really hard."

"We need to check out a motive for religious radicalism. This case seems too far-fetched a motive for a double homicide here in the Midwest. I'm gonna check out Professor Stone's lectures, but I doubt they provoked murder. For now, I'm gonna let the professor think religious fanaticism is the trail we're on, but I do have another theory."

"What's that?" Rogers asked.

"The two Arabs could have been assassins for hire?"

"By who? Why?"

"Professor Stone." Trapp did not struggle in seeing the worst in humans. He'd dealt with too many cases to rule out anyone. Lust, greed, and hate were all powerfully controlling forces in humans. Animals kill for food or in defense, but humans were a different lot. They'd kill because someone was in the line ahead of them. His last trip to the Kentucky Kingdom was a mild case in point. He never saw such scrambling just to be first in line.

"You mean the professor had his wife murdered? What motive could he possibly have?" Dallas asked.

"Greed. His story doesn't pan out. He's on an adjunct's salary at the seminary. He lives in a modest house not far from the projects. His Taurus is in the shop getting repaired, and he somehow ends up with a Lexus loaner. How does that figure? He's conned the dealership into letting him drive a fancy car because he's got a pride factor: an ego in conflict with being broke. He's got Champagne taste and beer money, Rogers. Happens all the time. That brings us to two things we're looking for about Professor Stone: a girlfriend on the side, that his wife probably didn't know about, or just found out about, and I bet he has a large life insurance policy on his wife. If we find either of those, we'll visit the DA. And I suspect we'll find both."

"So, you think he hired the two missing Arabs to kill her? That accounts for the cash the woman saw at the restaurant. Right?"

"Yep. And if they get caught, Professor Stone's alibi is they were just religious zealots, but we'll be a step ahead by pushing that theory. But I'm not buying it." Trapp braked hard when the car in front of him stopped suddenly, trying to get out of the turn-only lane at the end of the bridge.

"What about the girl … Carr … what's happened to her?" Rogers asked. He hadn't been on the force long enough to separate business from emotion. He still allowed his feelings to show.

"If it's related, not saying it is, but it seems to fit the puzzle, the assassins suspected her and trailed her."

"But if the professor was so poor, how could he afford hit men?" Rogers asked.

"Good question, Dallas. He'd need someone to front him the money, which he could if he knew he had money coming from a life insurance policy on his wife. So, he had to be associated with some shady loan sharks, or … ."

"Or what?"

"That takes us down another twisty path. I snooped around the seminary and found out a couple of things. Professor Stone was at the Derby, so he probably has a gambling habit. We'll need to check that out. Plus, he had a visitor last month, a young man by the name of José Santos. Does the name Santos ring a bell with you?"

"The Mexican drug family?" Rogers asked, surprise in his voice.

"Right you are, Dallas. Mexican cartel doing business in Louisville through a professor of religion. Quite the cover."

"But couldn't his meeting with José Santos suggest he was a target of the drug scene? Maybe he owed them money?"

"It could be, but witnesses say he and his guest ate lunch in the school cafeteria. Too friendly! More like business partners than enemies. I think he's working with them. I'm beginning to believe our professor is not a squeaky-clean religions teacher. He's tied in with the big boys. I suspect he needed a sizable amount of cash to make a deal with them … that's why I suspect we'll find he has a large insurance policy on his wife. Enough to pay off the assassins and enough to buy a pretty sizable cache of drugs. And the Santos family fronted him the money."

"But I thought the main leaders of the Santos family were incarcerated. Isn't the kingpin in a federal prison in Kansas?"

"Some are incarcerated but not all. You're right about Daddy Santos. He's serving two life-sentences, but you know how that works, another family member steps up and takes their place. I need you to get a probable cause warrant for us to review Professor Stone's bank accounts … at home and offshore."

"Will do."

"I still want to visit Stein's Lexus dealership. I think they might be able to shed some light on the mystery," Trapp said as he glanced in his rear-view mirror before turning on his blinker.

"But one thing troubles me about your theory." Rogers paused before finishing his statement.

"What?" Trapp somewhat lived on the edge of irritability.

"Professor Stone was in the house when it was bombed. If he was an associate of the Santos clan, why would they have almost killed him?" Rogers asked.

"He was in the house, Rogers, but only received superficial wounds, nothing more than a scratch. In itself that ought to tell us something. He's in the same room with his wife who's burned to a crisp by an explosion that rips the room apart, but he gets only a couple of scratches."

"You've got a point there, sir, but what about Ms. Carr's abduction? How does all this fit together?"

"Of course, we're jumping to conclusions about an abduction, but I'd say we'll probably find her body floating in the Ohio in a few days. Turn the surveillance tape over to Louisville PD. Detective Davis is a good contact there. He'll work with us. I suggest he check at the gas stations in the St. Matthews area until he finds her employer, that is if she was telling the truth about her name and occupation. We need to link her with having a conversation with two young Arabs. I suspect she got too nosy. They got suspicious, stalked her, and while she was on the phone with me they nabbed her. Call Detective Davis right away. He's a good cop."

Chapter 7

Jane Powers assumed something was wrong. She had tried to call her cousin's cell several times over the weekend. Sherri always let her know when she was going out of town. She hadn't shown up for work at either of her part-time jobs, even though she was scheduled for both. She scanned the phone book and opened her cell phone. Her fingers trembled as she pressed the numbers on the keypad. It surprised her when someone answered on the first ring.

"Louisville PD. How may I help you?"

"Is this where I call about a missing person?"

"Yes, ma'am. What is your name, please?"

"Sherri Carpenter. No, I'm sorry, that's my friend's name that's missing. My name's Jane Powers. I'm sorry … I'm just so upset—"

"It's okay, Ms. Powers. Is there a number I can reach you if we get disconnected?"

"Yes." She struggled to recall her number but finally got it right.

"Okay. And how long has Ms. Carpenter been missing?"

"I haven't heard from her since Sunday."

"Sunday of this week?"

"Yes."

"So, she's been missing maybe three days?"

"Yes, as best I can tell."

This is what I need you to do, Ms. Powers. You need to go to the nearest police station and fill out a missing person's report."

"Can't I just tell you over the phone?"

"You could, but you'd still need to go to a police station and sign a report. You need to bring all the information you can think of regarding the missing person: a picture, social security number, address, description."

"Okay, but wouldn't you know if any reports have been made, an accident or something. Maybe she's in the hospital. She hasn't shown up for work, didn't call in sick, and she's never done anything like this before."

"I don't have anything in the system on a Sherri Carpenter? I really need you to come in and file a report. It's important we get right on a missing person case."

"I've got to get to work right now, but I'll stop in on my lunch hour."

"May I ask one more question? What makes you think she's missing? Maybe she took a long weekend with friends."

"I don't think so. She left a rambling voice mail Sunday about that young woman killed over in Clarksville and some suspicions about two Arab men she met at the restaurant where she works."

"I'll need a copy of the message."

"Okay."

"I do have a bulletin about an incident at St. Matthews. We're coordinating with Clarksville PD on this. They're searching for a woman who made a call to them, but her name isn't Carpenter. We're dealing with it as a possible abduction."

"That's where Sherri works, St. Matthews, at least part of the time. She's working two jobs, trying to save enough money to go back and finish college."

"We think the name of that possible abduction is Susan Carr, not Sherri Carpenter. We really need to meet with you, Ms. Powers. Can we send someone to your workplace?"

"I work at the Humana building, fourth floor. My lunch break is at eleven. You can ask the receptionist just off the fourth-floor elevator for my office. We can talk in the cafeteria."

"Very good, Ms. Powers. Thank you for cooperating. You can expect Detective Scott Davis, noon, at your workplace. He's the one working on the possible abduction."

Chapter 8

Lights glistened off the pavement from the spring showers that had bombarded Kentuckiana throughout the day, setting off a series of tornado warnings that left the community on edge. Christopher Stone stayed in the right lane as he crossed the bridge from Indiana into Louisville. He eased onto the I-64 exit heading east towards the seminary campus where he had taught the last three years. At first, he hesitated in returning to the classroom, doubting he could finish the semester so soon after Eden's death. Something happened at the funeral that changed his mind, and he decided it best to return to the classroom.

Workers had finished cleaning his house, and he was glad to be out of the hotel and back home. He preferred being in his home to oversee the repairs. Though he had apprehensions about moving back into the house, concerns that the memories would overwhelm him, but he needed to be in a normal setting, away from the distractions of motel living.

Detective Trapp called him almost every day with information and questions. Always questions. He wondered if they were about to put the pieces together. Were they suspicious of him? What about the insurance policy? Had they found out? They would. Had they seen his recent banking transactions and located his out-of-state bank account? Things had certainly not worked out as he had planned.

He glanced at a billboard announcing the winner of the one hundred and thirty-seventh running of the Kentucky Derby. A split-second vision of Eden's face at the Derby's climactic finish brought a momentary sense of pleasure, but the pain which followed quickly dampened the moment. They had strolled hand-in-hand through the derby season's opening ceremony, Thunder Over Louisville, and they made memories with their trip to the Kentucky Horse Park, and the derby was the icing on the cake. But none of that mattered now. His mind remained preoccupied with Eden's death and the ongoing investigation. And revenge.

Revenge is a powerful motivator. At first, the overwhelming desire for revenge surprised him. He had seen enough carnage in his thirty-five years to abhor any form of violence. And Eden's absence seemed to awaken his past. Dreams from a former life haunted him, causing him to awaken in cold sweats, and he couldn't go back to sleep once awakened. Those days were a life he wished he could forget, especially the violence. He hated violence and sometimes used his lectures about the Crusades, and the new religious radicalism, to denounce such. Perhaps it was an unconscious act of personal penance, but since the death of Eden, something had changed within. The more he considered his loss, the more he justified the idea of vengeance—a vengeance that included violence. Such contemplation both frightened him and consoled him. Like a cup of hot tea that stings the tongue but soothes a sore throat, the end result mattered most. He mentally counted the cost of revenge, and what price he might have to pay for avenging Eden's death, but he determined that revenge soothed his emotional pain and invigorated his mind, and that was worth any cost. It took a few days to fully embrace the idea of retribution, but now he awakened energized by its potential.

The police might find Eden's killer, but the prosecution of her murderer could take years and may bring only a prison sentence. He had seen this too many times. The idea of a cold-blooded murderer being housed and clothed by taxpayers' money infuriated him. Eden's killer did not deserve to live another day, and a prison sentence, even life, certainly wasn't enough. He didn't care what happened to himself, so he would somehow see that her killer did not get off with a prison sentence. But how would he get revenge? Eye for an eye, the Old Testament way, was what he envisioned. If God permitted it in the past, why would he frown on it now, especially when one so innocent as Eden was so mercilessly snuffed from life? Once he found her killer, would his retribution be with abandoned recklessness by himself, or would he hire a professional killer who would slip into the area, do his job, and be gone on the morrow?

He thought of various ways to avenge Eden's death. After he arranged the execution of the murderer, he would attend the funeral and look into the mournful eyes of the grieving, shake their hands, and say, "I know exactly how you feel. Someone murdered my wife."

He wasn't sure how he would avenge Eden's death. He was only sure about his intentions. And what if the police arrested her killer before he could find him. He would still figure out a way to get at him. Jack Ruby did when he killed President Kennedy's murderer. Of course, that might have been for other reasons, maybe to cover up the tracks that led back to Russia, or Cuba's Castro. At least that's how the conspirator theorists view it. But his motive would be pure—an eye-for-an-eye justice.

Detective Trapp had some ideas of who the killer was and why he had killed. "I think it's classroom related, Professor Stone," Trapp had told him. "We have no other leads, and the evidence we have points to that."

But which student? Detective Trapp had zoomed in on Abdul-Bari Razi, asking a host of questions about him. Abdul had gone home for a visit and had not returned to class, certainly making him a likely candidate. Chris had doubts, for he had discussed religion one on one with him. He didn't seem radical. Abdul had shared a Christmas at his house, fulfilling Eden's request to make sure students who did not go home for the Christmas break enjoyed a Christmas meal in a family setting. Detective Trapp interpreted this as more evidence that Abdul had convenient access to the layout of their home and ultimately committed the murder with ease. The police would interrogate Abdul if he returned, but all the evidence was circumstantial. If not Abdul, who was the murderer? Why? Was it a student? Chris wasn't sure; he had some ideas. For now, he would go along with Trapp's theory, but he would also work his own plan, a plan to flush the killer, whoever he, or they, might be.

The intense desire to revenge Eden's death drove Chris back into the classroom. The plan slowly unfolded in his mind. If a student other than Abdul had killed Eden, he would expose him. Such a radical only needed provocation; he would furnish that with his end-of-semester lectures, in hopes the killer would strike again. After all, he was the target of the bombing, not Eden. He would provoke the killer to strike again, but this time he was prepared to catch the murderer. He had a camera security system installed at his home. He would be more careful than before. He had gotten lax since moving to the Midwest. He was somewhat to blame for Eden's death.

Of one thing he was confident, the bomb was intended for him: Eden was collateral damage. Though he had not intentionally provoked religious fanaticism, if that was the case, he assumed it was his fault that Eden was dead. But he seriously doubted the killer was one of his students. He recalled his opening lecture back in January.

***

The content of this lecture may surprise you, but I have designed this class for the laity of the three major monotheistic world religions: Christianity, Islam, and Judaism. My lectures aren't prepared as theological discourses for religious scholars. If you want that, you will need to enroll in one of the more advanced classes. Nor is this class structured to convince extremists of their errors, for I doubt any such extreme views exist in this classroom: maybe some bigotry but not extremism.

Conversely, this class is designed for those whose daily lives intermingle with others of different religious beliefs co-existing in the same neighborhood. It is intended to challenge mothers of different faiths to sit together on the same park benches while their children romp at the community playground. It is for all of us as we labor together in a common workplace. No matter the religious preference, most of our goals are similar: provide for the family, assist one's fellow man, be a good citizen, and prepare for retirement years. With so much in common about life, why should we be so divided by religion?

It would only be fair that I acknowledge I am an agnostic. That may explain why my lectures may appear a mite stilted at times. Still, I hope my talks reflect the command of the Christ some of you serve: "Love your neighbor as yourself." You recall the story in the Bible? "And who is my neighbor?" someone asked the teacher. At which point Jesus told the story about a very caring person who saved the life of a wayfaring stranger. Ironically, the stranger was a person who was of a different religion than His own. I find that quite interesting.

***

That was how he began his first lecture of the semester, and the following addresses maintained the same theme: that the three major religions should be religions of tolerance, not violence. He tried to recall the students' expressions: disagreement, anger, confusion, or contempt. Which student had he provoked to murder? He did not know. Detective Trapp felt strongly about this possibility, and he was pursuing leads and questioning many of the students.

Chris' new approach would set the stage for all the others. He would postulate ideas that could provoke a student to violence? If Detective Trapp was correct in his theory, there was a crazed student in his classroom? An intolerant zealot? There is generally an odd student in the crowd. But a murderer? He doubted such, but he needed to rule it out.

Trapp seemed a determined man, and he would consider all leads. Chris would follow the detective's lead, just in case he was right. He would make his lectures much more antagonistic, hopefully, to cause the murderer to strike again.

What if Detective Trapp was entirely wrong in his theory? Could Eden's death have been the result of an elusive past, a past which Trapp would have no knowledge? If so, would the murderer go free? That was a likelihood he had considered daily since Eden's death. He hoped it was not so. He could tell no one, not even Detective Trapp, about this possibility. His was a past he wanted to leave behind. And to dig up the former days would not bring Eden back, nor could Trapp pursue the killers if they were from his past. But he could. And if necessary, he would.

Chapter 9

The foyer reflected the high-class automobile it represented: solid, wood-paneled walls, with polished terrazzo flooring, recessed lighting in the sculptured, twenty-plus feet ceiling. Two huge, glazed-ceramic flowerpots containing bird of paradise plants soaked in the morning sunlight streaming through the oval-shaped wall of glass that revealed a bronze fountain highlighting a bricked courtyard. A variety of the latest Lexus models sat in a perfectly aligned row in the center of the massive foyer. Detective Trapp glanced at the nameplate setting on the receptionist's mahogany desk and flashed his badge at the young lady talking on the phone.

"Just a moment," she said into the phone, placed the caller on hold, and instantly charmed him with a smile that revealed perfectly aligned but overly-white teeth.

"Good morning, Candi. Detective Tony Trapp with the Clarksville Police Department. I need to speak with Mr. Stein. He's the owner, isn't he?"

"Yes. Just a moment, please. I'll see if he's available."

She ended the call—evidently with a boyfriend, mother, or close friend, for she was too casual for it to be a customer—and excused herself. Her long skirt caught repeatedly on her gladiator style sandals as she sashayed through the corridor that led to the back offices. She could have called Mr. Stein, but evidently, she needed to relay a message about this unannounced visitor that she wasn't comfortable saying in front of Trapp. He halfway expected to hear the back door slam and the screeching of tires as the criminals made their escape, but all seemed calm in the back offices. He wandered around the display room, running his fingers along the hood of a white with gold trim Lexus. He studied the sticker and emitted a whistle when he read the retail. Too expensive for his meager salary. That thought reinforced his theory: there was something funny going on with Professor Stone.

Candi soon returned with her same charming smile. "Detective Trapp, I'm sorry, but Mr. Stein is on the phone with a customer. Can you wait?"

"Surely."

She tried to conceal—with a smile—her disappointment that he was in no hurry to leave.

Trapp wanted to confront her, for he could tell from her desk phone that Stein's line wasn't busy, but he chose to change the subject. "I was just admiring the inventory. Wouldn't mind having one of these beauties, but it's a little too expensive for a detective's salary."

She probably agreed with him but politely declined comment with that same adorable smile with which she continued to use to her advantage. She wasn't much for creating conversation, but he wanted such, for that allowed for a slip-up. Early on in his career, he once did a routine pullover for a failed taillight at a stop sign, and the driver volunteered that she wasn't drinking from the unopened bottle of vodka in her purse. A breathalyzer test revealed she was not only sipping from the bottle, she was over the limit.

Trapp stuck his head inside the open window of one of the vehicles and took a deep breath. "Sure smells new. Do you drive one of these?"

"Very seldom … a loaner, sometimes … to run an errand for Mr. Stein."

"Do you know a Professor Stone … the man whose wife was killed in Clarksville … that's the case I'm investigating … he was driving a Lexus from here."

"Really?"

She seemed surprised, but then again, that could mean she was trying to hide something.

"Did Professor Stone buy the Lexus, lease it, or was it a loaner?"

"I wouldn't know, sir, I'm just the receptionist."

"Yeah, and I know what that means. You run the place." He gave her a thumbs up.

"I'm sure Mr. Stein will be with you shortly," she said, a smidgen short of snippy. And a I'm-done-talking-with-a-cop expression replaced her usual smile.

Trapp didn't appreciate the curtness of her attitude, but it somewhat affirmed his assumptions. He had touched a nerve, and he made a mental note to run a check on Miss Candi. Was she the unidentified girlfriend he suspected the professor to have on the side? The situation indeed seemed a perfect fit. With her favored position in a high-end-car dealership, she could well be the unknown girlfriend of the professor that Trapp was ninety percent sure he would eventually discover. She existed somewhere, and he would find her and expose the religion professor as a fraud. Miss Candi sure was a looker, and she wasn't wearing a wedding ring. He decided to pursue the odds.

"Are those your children in the picture?" He pointed to a small-framed photo on her desk. He needed to clarify her marital status, but he needed to tread lightly. If he ruled her out as a suspect, he still needed her on his team, not stonewalling his investigation.

"My nephews and nieces." She still did not warm to his questions.

Strike two, he told himself, still working hard on refraining from speaking his mind. I have to be careful with this one. She's as hard as her fake, fire-engine-red nails. Trapp started to make another attempt at conversation when a short, balding man about sixty years old walked toward him.

"Detective Trapp?" the man asked.

"Yes."

"Thomas Stein. How may I help you?" He extended a hand.

Stein's physical appearance was not what Trapp expected, but his firm grip hinted of toughness, contrary to his appearance.

"Thanks for seeing me without an appointment. I was in the area, so it was convenient."

Trapp could schmooze when necessary, but he never made appointments, for surprise was his weapon. He quickly sized up Stein, though initially surprised by his features. He had expected someone more dazzling, the debonair type. A Lexus dealership reflects a more suave ownership. He wasn't necessarily disappointed, just surprised. He was pleased that an ordinary looking guy could succeed. That gave him a ray of hope, like he didn't need to suck in his stomach just because Miss Candi was present.

"I'm investigating a case across the river." He quickly reeled in his momentary lapse into vanity and refocused. "Is there somewhere we can talk privately?"

"My office. This way, please." Stein placed a gentle hand on the receptionist's shoulder. "Hold my calls, please, Candi."

"Sure will, Mr. Stein." Her pleasantness had returned.

Trapp's momentary lapse into vanity returned. He mentally recanted any nice thought he had about Thomas Stein. The man probably inherited his fortune, never had to work at being successful, and used his wealth to charm the low of IQ blonds that drooled over his wealth.

Stein's office was stunning: much larger than Trapp's shared office, and a burgundy-colored, leather couch with matching armchairs finished it off quite handsomely. A huge wooden desk sat in front of a mural of Stein flanked with former president Jimmy Carter and Benjamin Netanyahu.

"Quite an impressive picture." Trapp nodded toward the wall.

"Two men who both want peace; one a bit naive and the other too enmeshed in politics to get the job done. How may I help you, Detective?"

"So, which is which?" Trapp nodded toward the mural.

Stein hesitated.

"Sorry, I withdraw my question. Again, thanks for seeing me without an appointment." He certainly didn't want to get off on the wrong foot with Stein by joking about his artwork. "I'm following up on a piece of evidence ... the murder investigation of a lady killed in a bombing in Clarksville. The Stone case?"

"Yes, the young Eden Stone." Stein's tone showed some emotion.

"You've heard about it, I assume?" He was surprised that Stein knew the name.

"Yes, I've watched on the news, but how might it involve me in any way."

"The husband was driving a loaner from your company."

Stein showed no emotion to this bit of evidence, nor did he offer an explanation, so Trapp continued. "I find that amusing that an owner of a Taurus drives a Lexus loaner when his car is being repaired. Don't you?"

"That's a good question."

Stein still showed little expression, and he certainly showed no signs of intimidation by Trapp's subtle insinuation.

"And the answer?" Trapp tried not to be abrupt, but abruptness was his natural inclination. It frightened some into a tell-all commentary, but others didn't like being bullied and went into defense mode. He needed to be cautious, for Stein hadn't risen to his status as a Lexus dealer by being pushed around.

"I'll need to find out," Stein said. He slipped an ink-pen from its expensive looking, bronze holder and scribbled something on a notepad. "I imagine the answer is simple, not that I approve of giving a Lexus loaner to a Taurus owner." He placed the pen back in the holder. "David Stone is probably a friend of one of my mechanics."

"David?"

"That professor, the husband of the young lady. Did I get his name wrong?"

"It's Christopher Stone?"

"Yes, I meant Christopher, not David." He glanced at his watch.

"I really appreciate your time, Mr. Stein. Just a couple more questions." Trapp made a mental note of Stein's error regarding the professor's name, but by Stein's demeanor, the error seemed innocent enough.

Trapp thumbed through his notepad, trying not to acknowledge any suspicion. But the slip of tongue by Stein concerned him. Why would he call Christopher Stone, David Stone? Was that an innocent mistake, or was he dealing with something much deeper? Did Stein hesitate with his answer? Why would Stone use this repair shop? Why not a shop in Clarksville?

"Do you know Professor Stone personally?" That was the best shot he had at Stein's jugular.

"I've met him … you know … seeing him here having his car repaired. We allow our mechanics to work on friends' cars, a fringe benefit that helps keep employees happy. And of course, we give them a reduced cost, unlike regular customers. And who knows when one of them might hit the lottery? He chuckled. A poor man's tax … the lottery … don't you agree, Detective."

"I hear you." Stein had changed the subject. Why? And Trapp wondered if his face blushed, for he had spent his fair share on losing tickets in the Indiana lottery since its onset twelve years ago.

"Christopher … Professor Stone isn't a regular customer, but he's been here off and on the last couple years. Come to think of it, him driving a Lexus at the McAlister campus is good advertisement for us. There are a few students out there who can afford a Lexus … makes a good graduation present from daddy."

Trapp forced a smile. For an acquaintance, Stein seemed to know a lot about Christopher Stone. "I appreciate the information.

Can I get the mechanic's name … just in case I have more questions?"

"Sure. I'll have Candi check the records. Give me a minute."

Trapp stared after Stein as he left the office, making mental notes of the conversation. Something dirty here. This guy knows way more about our mystery professor than he's letting on. But Trapp didn't want to tip his hand. He'd snoop around awhile before he made any accusations. He needed Stein to cooperate as long as he would before the hammer fell.

Chapter 10

Detective Scott Davis of the Louisville Police Department felt stumped. All his leads were dead ends. Sherri Carpenter was definitely missing but without a clue. After talking to Jane Powers, who was her cousin and who had made the missing person's report, he was sure a criminal act had happened, but he couldn't find a trace. Sherri had vanished into thin air, and none of her associates seemed to know where she might have gone, but then again, someone could well know, but felt it best to keep quiet. Since her automobile was missing from its parking spot at the apartment, he had placed an APB on the vehicle identification, but that had gotten no response.

She was last seen leaving her apartment on foot, so he did a door-to-door search that turned up some raised eyebrows, deadpan stares, and a few concerns, but no one had any useful information. He checked at her part-time place of employment at St. Matthews

Mall and found out she had been scheduled to work on Monday but had not showed up then or since. Phone calls from her supervisor to her home had tripped her recorder, but she had not responded to any of the messages the supervisor had left. A colleague from Clarksville PD, Detective Tony Trapp, had informed him that their department had received a call from a female, from a phone booth near St. Matthews. That call had abruptly ended, which certainly caused some suspicion on their part that something was amiss, but they had no clue as to where that person might have gone after making the call. That call happened around the same time a video surveillance recorded two men approaching a phone booth in the Saint Matthews area and leaving with a woman who had been in the phone booth. Detective Rogers, Trapp's associate at the Clarksville PD, had given him the footage of that surveillance. But that caller's name was Susan Carr, not Sherri Carpenter, at least that is how she identified herself when she called the Clarksville PD. But how ironic that the initials to the two people were the same. Davis was beginning to think there was a connection between Sherri Carpenter and Susan Carr, perhaps they were one and the same person. He needed to meet with Detectives Trapp and Rogers and share his theory, but he needed some concrete evidence first.

Chapter 11

Chris Stone was glad to be back in his home, but the fresh paint caused his allergies to flare up, and he could also detect the odor left by the bomb. A dozen, wadded-up tissues surrounded the wastebasket. He tossed another, which bounced off the wall, clipped the rim and dropped to the floor. He hoped the odor would not be a lingering problem, and he had voiced such with his Farm Bureau agent, Jonny Combs. Jonny had been more than a good agent, he had been his friend, calling him often, expressing his condolences, and genuinely offering his prayers. And both the agent and company were faithful to their promises made when he and Eden chose to go with them to insure the house. All the damaged furniture had been replaced. And the new carpet that he had promised Eden had been laid. That was one of the hardest decisions, deciding what pattern and color Eden would have wanted. The house had been painted throughout, but no matter how many coats of paint, his once safe haven had become a place of unpleasant memories. The walls were barren, except for nails that had held various, original paintings: nails which had been left by the painters, a small detail that for some reason irritated him. Such presumptuousness galled him. He wanted no one doing his thinking for him. And that was one of his quirks that Eden had tried to change about him but obviously had failed to do so. It seemed lately that every event always led to some thought regarding Eden, but he did not mind. He wanted to make sure he never forgot anything about her.

He had sent the paintings to an art restorer to be refurbished. The paintings had been Eden's possessions, and they were valuable. He now regretted there was only one picture of himself and Eden. They had purposely avoided decorating the home with memory pictures. He wondered why that hadn't raised a red flag with Detective Trapp. Or had it? Now memories were all he had of Eden, and he clung desperately to them with an unrealistic fear that they might vanish, like priceless paintings taken by thieves raiding an art museum.

He determined to spend the weekend studying his past lectures, identifying what might have provoked someone to discharge a bomb in his home. For numerous reasons, he was convinced Abdul-Bari Razi was not the murderer, so, if Detective Trapp's theory—that a student killed Eden—was correct, it was someone other than Abdul. He must flush out that now concealed murderer. Trapp seemed to be too tunnel-visioned to do so, for he had quickly narrowed his sights on Abdul. That seemed to be profiling at its worst, something he had not expected to see in a mature detective.

Chris determined to rework his lectures, making them more controversial, attacking each of the three major religions of the world, using accusations and sarcasm to provoke anyone who might have taken the life of his Eden. He would fine-tune the lectures to fit that purpose. The recently-installed video surveillance camera in his classroom would capture every emotion displayed by his students. He had done so without the administration's approval, for he dare not jeopardize its secrecy. And he did not have to worry about a judge disallowing evidence in court, for he would be the judge, jury, and the executioner. If one of his students had murdered Eden, with some provocation, they would show their true colors. This could take time, but time was what he seemed to have most of nowadays. He had awakened early, and unable to go back to sleep, he brewed a pot of chai tea, Eden's favorite. He had often teased her about the name. Since chai is the actual Hindi word for tea, he challenged her, "Why say, tea-tea?' Why not simply chai or tea?" She never saw the humor in his joke—or at least did not acknowledge such—which made it all the more funny. He poured a large cup half-full with tea, filled it on up with creamer and honey, and settled into his recliner. Dawn was an hour away, and he would enjoy the sunrise, but for now he wanted to get a jump on his upcoming lectures. He opened his notebook and began to read, making notations along the way, inserting jabs when possible, and rewriting his lecture as he read in silence, pausing often to reflect.

***

Three, primary, monotheistic faiths make up about half of the world's population. They share central beliefs, tracing their spiritual source to a particular figure and specific location: Abraham of the Scripture and the Middle East where he staked his tents for almost a century. Because of such commonality among the three religions, some scholars use the phrase "Abrahamic religions" in referring to Christianity, Islam, and Judaism. Although with major commonalities, core beliefs divide, leaving a history of hate and violence between followers of the faiths.

All three religions have deep roots in the Old Testament, and all three believe in the God of Abraham. Still, the three religious groups are alienated by their interpretation of the Old Testament Scripture regarding God. Judaism traces its lineage to Abraham via his son Isaac, while Islam traces its lineage to Abraham through his son Ishmael. Christianity traces the doctrine of "salvation by grace through faith" back to Abraham, although not through human ancestry; instead, it was a spiritual connection. God accepted Abraham because of his faith in God's promises, not because of his good deeds. Christianity assumed this mantra: salvation by grace through faith.

Though vastly different, is there a common denominator within the ancient Script that could bring the faiths together? Could the views that separate be abandoned for a more significant cause? Is there a needless doctrine that divides? Can differences be reconciled? And could this God of Abraham have imagined that each of the three religious systems would do harm to the other two? These are some of the questions addressed in this course.

Let's focus on a portion of ancient writing on which all three religions can somewhat agree: the book of beginnings, called in the English translation of the Bible, Genesis. All three religions are familiar with this book, and all three religions agree with significant lessons taught by this book. Further, all three religions are included in this book either directly or prophetically. The story of Abraham and his immediate descendants make up the greater portion of Genesis. And Christianity is indirectly referenced by various passages in Genesis: the crushing of the serpent's head; the sacrificial system of worship being fulfilled in the death of Christ at Calvary.

All of us are connected to the monotheistic God of Genesis by way of the creation: "In the beginning … God created." All three religions would agree that this singular God of the Bible is the creator of us all. And all of us are from a singular lineage that can be traced to the first man and woman: Adam and Eve. How interesting that molecular biologists tell us that any two people on the earth today are ninety-nine percent identical genetically, no matter the national origin or religion. So, no particular race is superior to any other. And certainly no race should be superior because of a specific religion. God favors no race.

All three religions profess a connection to Abraham and identify him as the father of the faithful. He is the biological father of Isaac, from which the Hebrew race and Judaism come. Likewise, he is the biological father of Ishmael, from which many of the Arab nations come and whose dominant religion is Islam. Further, he is the spiritual father of Christianity.

All three religions identify with the same geographical location: that alone has brought much contention. God directed Abraham to offer his son as a sacrifice on Mount Moriah. Interestingly, this mountain range is of profound significance for all three faiths: it is the area upon which Solomon built the first Jewish temple. The Babylonians destroyed that temple, and another temple was erected on the same mount when the Jewish people returned from captivity, but the Romans destroyed it in 70 AD, leaving the mount a trash-heap. The Prophet Mohammad supposedly ascended into the heavens from this mount around 600 AD, and the Muslim's Dome of the Rock now commemorates that spot. On the same mount, Muslims worship at the Al-Aqsa Mosque. All this is but a short distance from where the Messiah of Christianity was crucified, and the Holy Spirit descended upon the followers of Christ after His ascension.

Some two thousand years before Jesus Christ was born, Abraham acknowledged that God would provide a sacrificial lamb to substitute for the sins of mankind. The story of Abraham being willing to sacrifice his son, Isaac, implies such. When Abraham's son inquired about the absence of the sacrifice, Abraham replied, "My son, God will provide himself a lamb for a burnt offering."In retrospect, Jesus Christ referenced Abraham when He acknowledged Himself to be the Lamb of God and proclaimed, "Before Abraham was, I am." How could Christ precede Abraham? From a biblical perspective, in the foreknowledge of God, His plan from the beginning included the incarnation: God would become a man. The Prophet Isaiah proclaimed that Messiah would be called Emmanuel, the interpretation being, God with us. And how did the Christian Apostle Paul explain the incarnation? "God was in Christ reconciling the world unto himself." The God/man, Jesus Christ, would be a sacrificial atonement necessary to pay the debt for mankind's sin, or so says the Christian faith. Of course, this teaching is rejected by both Judaism and Islam, though Judaism still awaits a coming Messiah. Some think this will be some manifestation of deity, for God has appeared in some human resemblance several times in the Old Testament accounts of His dealings with Israel. But in contrast,

Islam rejects the incarnation taught by Christians. The Muslim faith teaches that God could never become a man.

***

Chris liked the house cool for sleeping, so a chill lingered until the morning sun did its job. He laid his notes aside and sipped from his tea, clasping his fingers around the cup to warm his fingers. After a few sips, he set the tea aside and began a deep massage of the back of his neck. He ended the massage by rotating his head clockwise, then he reversed, doing this multiple times. He stood and did a few knee bends, his hands resting on his waist for balance. After some stretching, he slid into his recliner, snuggled underneath a comforter which was Eden's favorite, and picked up his notebook.

In the past, he had spent little time reflecting upon the idea of God becoming a man. He knew the concept of the incarnation would be very controversial among the Islamic students and somewhat controversial among students of Judaism. So, he needed to focus on the idea that God became a man. The Jewish students were still expecting their Messiah, so they certainly rejected the teaching of Christ's incarnation, some accusing him of being a fraud. Others allowed for His historical existence but not as the Messiah. For Jewish students, at best, Jesus was a historical figure; at worst he was an impostor. For the Islamic students, Jesus was a good teacher or a prophet, but He was not God. The subject of the incarnation should muster much emotion from his students. That was what he needed: the turkey to stick up its head and gobble, and he would have it in his sights. After a long pause, he returned to his reading.

***

All three religions trace their monotheistic teachings back to Abraham. That is their beginning: one God who is the designer, creator, and sustainer of His creation. Though different in many ways, we readily see all three religions directly linked to Abraham. With this in mind, could the three major faiths be closer in their beliefs than they dare profess?

All three major religions acknowledge the life of Abraham and hold him in the highest regard. Though a history of four millenniums past, we are able to read and comprehend the Bible story by way of translations of the Bible into almost every language. Therefore, during this lecture, I will focus on Abraham's life by referencing the Bible as the primary source for this lesson. In so doing, our faith in the God of Abraham should cause us friendship, not animosity, unless we have a distorted perception of who the God of Abraham is and what he desires of us. Anything less than peaceful coexistence is radicalism and does not reflect the view that Abraham had regarding God, for Abraham was a man of peace.

***

Chris' heart suddenly thumped and his body tensed. Had he seen movement outside the window? He quickly turned out the lamp. Eden enjoyed this community because of the serenity: tree-lined sidewalks, dead-end street, family atmosphere, and quiet. Few unfamiliar cars even entered their street. But Chris' tranquility had vanished since the bombing. He had grown wary of neighbors. Likewise, in the classroom, he studied the faces of the students more intently as he lectured. He eyed their backpacks and monitored their attentiveness, or lack thereof, to his lectures. He could read faces like he read a book. After all, he was trained in the psychological techniques of warfare. That's how he survived in a strange land being friends with the enemy.

Something slammed into the front door. Chris' notebook fell to the floor, scattering loose pages as he dropped to his stomach and hugged the carpet. Silence, except for the fan that oscillated from across the room, ruffling the papers. He waited. Nothing. Rising slowly to one knee, he managed a smile as he peered out the window and saw the shadowy image of the paperboy pedaling his bike down the street.

He picked up his notebook, collected the scattered papers, kicked back in his recliner, and continued his reading. His hands shook slightly from the adrenalin rush.

***

This less than scholarly approach to the three major faiths should not minimize the significance of the course. I suggest less than academic in that my final lectures will primarily refer to the first book of the Jewish and Christian Bible, instead of lectures from the textbook. This, of course, could be considered an unfair approach by you who are of the Muslim faith, but you should have purchased the textbook from which you should read, for only the contents of the textbook will be included in the final exam. We will leave the Bible for the theological students to study.

***

Chris paused from his reading. These lectures would throw some pretty tough jabs at his students, but he was playing for keeps. Personal feelings no longer mattered, no matter how delicate the students' emotions. His wife was dead. Someone was responsible, and he intended to find out who it was that killed her, and he … . He refocused his thoughts to the notebook that contained his lectures.

***

And for those of the Muslim faith, you should recognize that you play a role even in Jewish literature, for the record of Ishmael, the son of Abraham, is recorded in the first book of the Torah of Judaism. Albeit, Ishmael played a secondary part, for he was not considered the child of promise. And the first-century Jewish scholar turned Christian, Paul, affirmed such in his writings to the churches. So, as a religion, you entered the race a mite too late to claim equality, some twenty-five hundred years after Judaism—if we count from Abraham—and some six-hundred years after Christianity.

***

If the last line didn't raise some eyebrows among his Muslim students, nothing would. He laid the notebook aside and rubbed his eyelids with the tips of his fingers. He wanted to provoke animosity in any radical element in his classroom, and that statement would be a tough piece of jerky for his Muslim students to digest. He tried to recall if there were any previous classroom discussions regarding the idea of Isaac and Ishmael and their roles. He could remember some, but they lacked hatred, but he had broached the idea much more delicately before Eden's death. No particular face stood out to him as he reflected upon the day he discussed this thought regarding the age of each of the religions. But he would hit it harder in his upcoming lectures. Chris returned to his notes.

***

I will use few resources other than the Bible in these final lectures, but you are responsible for reading the textbook. My reason for using the Bible? It is a book that is studied on all educational levels: studied, quoted, enjoyed, and understood by those of various ages and social settings. Its teachings are used in kindergarten classes as a moral compass in storybook form, while it is used as a college resource in archaeology. Adults, for personal guidance, apply the teachings to their lives, and those same adults use the character studies as instructional material for children in both religious and secular settings. We are our brother's keeper, no matter if it is trying to get someone to heaven or helping that same person cross the street. Who among us has not heard of the garden disobedience? Cain and Abel? Noah and the ark? And of course, father Abraham? The first book of the Bible, the Book of Genesis, though old, transcends all boundaries of age, ethnicity, generations, and cultures. It has spanned the changes of time and distance. Scientists still marvel at the creation of the universe and search diligently trying to put together the puzzle of its origin.

All monotheistic believers wander back to the book of beginnings and ponder the story of creation by God and God alone. The "big bang" theory may have some merit, but who pulled the trigger? And all explosions I've witnessed left destruction, never a creation in harmonious motion.

All three religions insist on the Creator God of Scripture. And all three monotheistic faiths claim the Creator's servant: Abraham. The three religions have their differences, but Abraham is their common denominator.

***

Chris highlighted specific lines and scribbled notes. He realized his lectures were no longer about religion; they were tools in psychological profiling. Who in his class fits the description of a religious fanatic who would bomb a professor's home in retaliation for a lecture? If such student existed, he would find him before the semester ended. Further, he would not share his quest with Detective Trapp, for he wanted personal revenge. Trapp had acquired what he thought was his lectures, but Trapp did not have this updated version, the one with provocations. His TA had acquiesced to Trapp's demands for a copy of his lectures, but she was loyal to a fault to him, and she said nothing to Trapp about the planned revision. So, Chris was still a step ahead of Trapp.

But Abdul had not returned to class. Was that a sign of guilt? If Abdul was guilty in any way regarding the bombing, he would find him if he had to cross the Atlantic to do so.

Old impulses quickened. The hunted was now the hunter. And Christopher Stone was not trained in the art of running from an enemy; he was trained to seek and defeat.

Chapter 12

A slight groan caught the attention of nurse Nancy Stamper as she checked the monitors of the young female patient the nurses called Jane Doe. She turned quickly to see her eyes twitching and her bandaged head moving slightly from side to side on the pillow.

"Hey, Ms. Doe. That's what we've been waiting to see." She bent over the patient. "Can you hear me, dear?" Nancy placed her hand inside the partially cupped hand of the battered patient. "If you can hear me, sweetie, squeeze my hand."

Nothing.

Nancy paused from her technical duties and gently rubbed her patient's rigid hand. Who was this young woman? An ambulance had brought her in: the state police had found her bruised and broken, with no identification, lying alongside one of their curving West Virginia interstates. The hospital anxiously awaited a police investigation as to who she was and what had happened to her. How does one end up this way, alone and unknown? And why hadn't someone called in a missing person's report? "Poor child," she muttered to herself. "Lord help her, and Lord help us help her," she whispered.

The quietness of the room gave room for reflection. What an isolated and thoughtless society we are becoming! The whooshing of the ventilator and the rhythmic beep of the monitors were the only sounds: no loving voices of kin, no minister for prayer, no one to care. Nancy turned her attention back to the monitors, then typed some comments on her laptop. She glanced once more at Miss Doe, turned off the overhead light, and gently shut the door as she quietly exited the room.

Chapter 13

"I would advise that you not allow your son to return to the United States. Some rumors among my friends at the State Department say he is a suspect in the murder of the wife of one of his professors. He will be questioned and may be arrested and interrogated." Mohammad Ismail Hajbi was adamant in his argument.

He was no pushover by adversary or client. Ismail had graduated from Yale Law School before returning to Amman. His Jordanian roots, coupled with his legal contacts in American, gave him a host of wealthy clients, many of them parents of pampered offspring. Ja'far Sa'ad Razi was not only a client; he was married to Ismail's neice.

"I have spoken with Abdul. He has assured me he had nothing to do with that woman's murder, and if he does not return, it will elevate suspicion," Razi argued.

"There is already enough suspicion to have him arrested, uncle." Ismail thumped his forefinger against the file laying on the table. "It's all here, reports from my American contacts."

"But are we not breaking the law if we know he is a suspect, and we deliberately protect him from those doing the investigation?"

"We are not breaking the law by using our legal rights, as citizens of Jordan, to protect ourselves from the long reach of the American strong-arm," Ismail countered.

"But what about our moral obligations? Aren't we obligated to a higher authority than man, to the one, true God who demands we walk in truth?"

"I am your lawyer, uncle, not your conscience. You can take up those issues with the clergy. But I do know how the legal system works here and how it works in America. You are much safer in your homeland, under the protection of those of your kind. And the animosity in the States against Arabs is quite high. Your son would never get a fair trial in America; to the contrary, he would get a lynching."

"But America is a Christian nation. Its laws are derived from the Mosaic principles. They afford us the opportunity to clear Abdul's name. To clear the name of the Razi family."

"But America's lawyers have long discarded principles, and they are not meek like Moses. As your lawyer, I am leading you through the dangerous wilderness of the legal system, not Moses' and the Bible's spiritual wilderness. But I will pray for Allah's guidance through this wilderness. Trust me on this."

"I would prefer having Moses lead me," Razi said, his humorlessness visible.

"And I am warning you that, as a Christian in a Muslim country, you have neither Moses nor Allah on your side. I am your best advocate."

"I have my Heavenly Father."

"There is some confusion as to whom that may be, uncle."

"I am not confused, Ismail."

"Be as it may, what is your final decision?" Ismail asked, his frustration apparent.

Ja'far Razi hesitated. He closed his eyes as if in prayer. "And what about the other suspect, Gamali?"

"Gamali Hadidi is nothing more than an exchange student at the university. His family is less than—"

"He is a soul, Ismail. And a good friend to Abdul." Razi's elevated voice cautioned Ismail.

Ismail gathered his files. "We have some time. Think about it, uncle. And while you do, remember that your wife has brothers who are not of your Christian persuasion. They will be very disappointed if you send her only son to the abattoir. And it will be a slaughterhouse. An Arab in the United States penal system hasn't a chance."

"Should we be more privileged than our Lord? He was led as a lamb to the slaughter … he accepted his fate."

"I have already received my sermon for the week, uncle. The mullah tends to lean more toward jihad than pacifism." He clicked his briefcase shut.

"And because of his doctrine of violence, we may all eventually die by the sword."

"Then at least I will die fighting, and you will die praying."

"And I will pray for you, Ismail, with my dying breath, that you will find the Prince of Peace."

"Don't waste your prayers on me, uncle. Pray for Abdul, especially if you send him back to the infidels."

"Abdul and I will discuss your advice. We will decide. Be well, my nephew. *Assalaamu 'alaikum.*"

This age-old greeting had lost its sincerity among many Muslims, but Razi, now a Christian, still used the phrase. However, it wasn't necessarily received with enthusiasm by Ismail. But for Razi, the proclamation, God's peace be upon you, was spoken with genuineness.

Ismail stood and bowed slightly. "*Wa'laikum Assalaam,*" he responded, but his words lacked the oomph that a true believer manifested. He feared something other than peace was headed toward the Ja'far Sa'ad Razi family, but he had spoken his mind. His conscience was clear, but his heart was heavy. And angry.

Chapter 14

Over multiple years the Leavenworth, Kansas penitentiary has gone through significant additions and renovations. Only D-Cellhouse maintains the original design. That has been the living quarters of Fernándo Leoncio Santos for the past three years. The US Justice Department transferred him to the prison five days after a jury found him guilty of a long list of crimes and a judge announced his sentence: life without parole echoed throughout the mostly empty courtroom. At his sentencing, due to his advanced age, he was to be sent to a new minimum-security prison in Central California, but the recession had delayed opening the facilities. So, the Big House in Kansas became the temporary housing for Santos. The Santos family couldn't shoot or buy their way out of this jam. In the meantime, they settled into some long-range possibilities that would take strategic planning. They anticipated the soon transfer to California.

Leavenworth started as a military prison in eighteen seventy-five, but after twenty-five years in operation, Congress transferred it to the US Department of Justice. It has housed its share of infamous criminals: James Earl Ray, Machine Gun Kelly, Gus Hall, Frederick Cook, to name a few.

James Earl Ray had spent four years in Leavenworth—in the late fifties—for mail fraud. His was a long history of crime, once escaping from prison, and he spent many years running from the law. Quite a resourceful guy, he posed as a film director in Mexico, campaigned in California for presidential candidate George Wallace, and crossed international lines on multiple occasions. Of course, all those were before assassinating Dr. Martin Luther King Jr. He escaped the death sentence by pleading guilty for the murder of Dr. King instead of facing a jury trial.

Kelly was a gangster from the prohibition era and had been a part of the kidnapping of businessman Carl Urschel. His gang collected a $200,000 ransom. Hall was a four-time presidential candidate representing the communist party in America. Cook was quite the personality, having claimed to reach the North Pole a year before Mr. Peary's team. That claim was eventually discredited. And his claim to have climbed to the summit of Denali was also disproved. He was ultimately found guilty of fraud related to some Texas oil deals, and the judge sentenced him to Leavenworth for fourteen years and nine months.

Fernándo Leoncio Santos now joined the roster of inmates, and he was among the more infamous. From his nickname, Chico, you'd not perceive him as belonging in Leavenworth. He grew slowly as a child and stopped growing altogether at five feet. He never tipped the scales above one hundred pounds. So, the name Chico—meaning small—had stuck.

Chico's saintly mother saw him differently. She had grand expectations at his birth. Fernándo means "ardent of peace," and Leoncio means "lion-like." Her aspirations expired over time, for he was not a peaceful man, nor did his stature conjure up lion-like qualities.

He stayed out of trouble through his formative years, but things got off-track when he turned eighteen, shortly after two rival drug gangs gunned down his father in crossfire at the Mercado El Popo. The death of his father left Chico as the eldest of seven brothers and a heavy sense of responsibility to take care of them and his mother. He sought a means to support the family, and he simultaneously sought revenge for his father's death. He found the opportunity for both—support and revenge—in the ever-growing world of drugs. Being of small stature and youthful facial features, authorities never suspected his frequent trips across the border, peddling a cart loaded with religious figurines which he sold at a roadside flea market that attracted tourists. But some of the figurines—filled with cocaine—were set aside for particular customers, who came by often. He started as a runner, then through a series of calculated risks, he worked his way up the ranks of the cartel, and when the timing was right, he assumed organizational control by a coup that left fifteen dead, including two of his own brothers. With four remaining brothers, he lived the good life, until an undercover operation infiltrated his organization and sent him to prison.

Chico's brother Luis had escaped prosecution, and he assumed the operations of the family business when Chico went to prison. Luis had to complete a host of forms before the warden approved his meeting with his brother. He loved Chico and always looked up to him, but he was apprehensive about this meeting, for multiple reasons. Their mother was ill. The business was definitely struggling since Chico's arrest. Further, he did not have good news about the kidnapping, and events were progressing slowly. This would anger Chico.

Luis brought along his son, Alberto. Chico had favored him over some of his other nephews. And Alberto genuinely liked Chico. That might defuse some of Chico's anger.

Chico, aided by a guard, shuffled into the visitors' lounge, his dimming eyes scanning the room. Luis waved to him and caught his attention. Chico thanked the guard who helped him. He could be gracious when it favored him.

"Good to see you, *mi hermano,*" Chico said.

"And you, Chico. How are you?" Luis clasped Chico's shoulders and pulled him close. They embraced long. It bothered him immensely to see his older brother broken and deteriorating. The three years had not been kind to Chico.

"*Estoy muy cansado.* Very, very tired." Chico closed his eyes and exhaled slowly, then half-fell onto the bench and placed his forehead in his palms, elbows resting on the table, as he sat at the end of the bench.

"I wish I could take your place," Luis said.

"No, you don't, Luis, but I … forgive me, *hermano*, for I should not have said that. You have come far to visit me. Anyway, I would not allow it if you could. Now, no more about me, let's talk about the *familia*. How are things with you, Alberto? You are looking well."

"I am well, uncle Chico. It is good to see you." Alberto bent down and embraced his uncle.

"And good to see you, Alberto." Chico pressed his forehead against Alberto's. "My, you have grown up since I last saw you."

"I am nineteen next month." He smiled.

Chico struggled to get his legs underneath the table. Alberto assisted him.

"Thank you." He patted Alberto on the shoulder. "You have been kind to your old uncle. You will be rewarded someday. If not by me, then by him." He tossed a glance skyward.

Luis and Alberto sat across from Chico. He leaned toward them and lowered his voice. "Any news about our missing *familia*?"

"Nothing," Luis answered.

"You must push harder." Chico slammed both fists onto the table.

"I know how you must feel, *hermano*. Please believe me when I say we are doing all we can to find them." Luis placed his hands on Chico's clenched fists.

"Three years without progress is not doing enough." Chico's elevated voice aroused the attention of the guards.

"Please, brother. I beg patience, for we are truly trying to find them."

"Do you really think they are still alive, uncle?" Alberto asked. "They've been missing ever since you were—"

"I believe they would have told us if they had killed them," Chico interrupted him. "They would have made a scene and gloated at our pain."

"But who are they?" Luis asked.

"I am not sure, but it seems obvious it is a competitor. That narrows the field. One thing I know, captives are of no use if they are dead. So, they will call, soon I believe, to make some deal. Why would they go to the bother of kidnapping them if they did not have a plan to use them to their advantage? I believe they are holding them for a bargaining tool." Chico spoke from years of experience, most of the time being the one holding the winning hand and therefore making the deal.

"If we hear from them, we will do our very best to get them back safely, brother." Luis placed one hand over his heart and the other on Chico's hands resting on the table. "I promise with my dying breath."

"Do whatever it takes. You and the rest of my *familia* are my only reason to live, so you must understand my pain … we are all *familia* … we stick together … rotting away here and not being able to do anything to acquire their release is killing me. Promise me *hermano*, you will do whatever it takes."

"I understand your pain, brother. They are my family too, and it hurts me also."

"Forgive me, Luis, I know you care. It's just that—"

"I promise, on our father's grave, and for all of us, we will find them," Luis said.

Chico stared long into the eyes of Luis before he spoke. "And the gringo? You have taken care of him?"

"*Si*," Luis answered.

"How?"

"A bomb."

"You are sure he is dead?"

"No one could have survived the blast."

"I did not think anyone could deceive me so, but he did," Chico responded, his facial expression revealing his anger.

"We sent family to do the job. Carlos."

Chico did not respond.

"He showed us pictures of the house after he bombed the gringo's bedroom," Luis added.

"Good." Chico paused, staring across the room. "How is our man doing with the assignment out west? Who did you send for that?"

"I chose Juan for the job. He is getting everything in place. He is very efficient," Luis said.

"I like Juan. He has been very loyal." Chico placed a hand over his heart. "He is a good man. And *familia.* Promote him in the ranks."

"Absolutely," Luis agreed.

"How long before any action? I can't live forever, you know, but I don't want to die in prison. I want to die with the sky over my head, the sun shining on my face, and a Cuban cigar between my fingers."

"Things have gone slower than expected." Luis slowly rubbed his fingers back and forth against his open palms.

"How much longer?" Chico's voice elevated.

"Any day now. The prison should open soon … the recession—"

"And *Madre*?"

"She grieves much, especially for her *nieta*."

"I must get out of this hothouse, *hermano.* I must find those kids and comfort *mi Madre*."

"I know. We are doing all we can. Our plan is set. We must wait for your transfer. That part is not in our hands, but we believe it is soon. We are headed to Mendota after we leave here."

"They cannot … ." Chico scanned the room before continuing. "You are sure they are not tracking you?"

"We are being careful. It is an enormous challenge, but we have planned well. We had our man inside. It cost much, but I know you understand. I believe you will be home soon."

"And where will home be for me?"

"Where no one can find you. I dare not even speak it for fear this room is bugged."

"Good. You have done well, *mi hermano.* Now, if you can only find my children, we can all be together soon."

"We will keep looking. I promise you if my life depends on it."

"Visiting hours are now over. Please exit … ." The muffled announcement blared across the speaker. Additional guards hastened into the room to make the transition.

The calloused sounding voice over the loudspeaker brought momentary silence to the room, then final goodbyes and hugs, and some tears. Chico struggled to rise from the table. Alberto assisted him.

Chico embraced his family before shooing them from the room. They stopped at the door, turned, and waved to him as he shuffled back across the room where a guard waited to assist him to his cell.

Chapter 15

Detective Tony Trapp wasn't a religious man. Sometime during his college days, he had decided that cops and religious creeds didn't harmonize. He walked away from eighteen years of Sunday School attendance: a bronze medal with a string of annual bars—tucked away in his mother's memory box—showed the years of perfect attendance. His decision regarding religion broke his mother's heart, but at least he wasn't deceiving her, a principle he'd learned in Sunday School. He limited his church attendance to wedding and funeral occasions. The funerals were mostly to honor fallen comrades and their family members, or to offer condolences to the families of homicide victims whose cases had been assigned to him. But tonight was different, for he was interested in religion: at least Professor Chris Stones' religion.

A thick, black notebook of the professor's lectures rested on his lap. He wanted to know what these lectures were like, so he had acquired a copy from the professor's assistant, albeit she was reluctant to share them. Trapp pulled off quite a performance expressing his concern for the professor's safety, and ultimately the safety of the teacher assistant, before she consented to his request, without a subpoena. He popped the tab of a Diet Coke, sat it on the table beside his Lay's barbecue potato chips, and settled in for a weekend of indoctrination.

"I need to get inside the professor's head," he said to the deaf walls of a house he'd lived in alone since his wife of twenty years decided she couldn't take another day playing second fiddle to his mistress: police work. "And I'm gonna do that before the weekend is over." He opened the notebook and began reading.

***

Abraham. His name holds significance: father of a multitude. It was a long time coming. He was not always called Abraham; initially, his name was Abram. One year shy of his hundredth birthday, God spoke to him as in the past, renewed a former covenant, and changed his name from Abram to Abraham. Why the name change? Why so late in life?

We are not sure of Abram's age when God first spoke to him. We discover his age, seventy-five, when he is departing the city of Haran, continuing a journey begun sometime before from the city of Ur. The call of God came to Abram at a time when idolatrous worship was the norm among the people of the Mesopotamian Valley. God's call to Abraham was two-fold. First, it was a call to leave his homeland, a region rife with pagan practices. Second, it was a call for service to the one and only God of heaven. And the call came with a promise: Abraham would become the father of a mighty nation.

His recorded life began in Ur of the Chaldeans: a biblical city along the Euphrates River, about one hundred miles southeast of the ancient city of Babylon. The land is known today as Iraq. Abram's obedience to God's call would eventually remove him from the polytheistic culture of his ancestors. The moon god, Sin—the guardian deity of the city of Abram's birth—was the head of the pantheon dominating the Euphrates Valley. Abram, along with Terah his father, and his nephew Lot—Lot's father was Abram's brother, who had died in Ur—migrated to the biblical city of Haran, associated by some as Harran (known by different names during different periods), an ancient town in northern Mesopotamia, now the country of Turkey. If the biblical Haran is the same Harran of history, it was an outpost city of Ur, linking Ur's trade route to the Mediterranean, and like Ur, Harran had as its principal deity the moon god, Sin. Abram would eventually leave this town and seek out the place that God would show him. That promised land would someday be called Israel, after Abraham's grandson, Jacob, whose name was also changed by God, from Jacob the supplanter or usurper, to Israel, in recognition of his desire to obtain the blessing of God. And that is why the small strip of land bordering the eastern shore of the Mediterranean Sea is now called Israel, and that is why the nation of Israel still claims to be the legitimate owner of Palestine. Jehovah, the God of Abraham, gave them the land over four thousand years ago.

***

"Hmm." Trapp contemplated the last line. He made a mental note regarding this assertion that Israel was the legitimate owner of Palestine. That might have created some emotions among the Arab students, especially Abdul-Bari Razi—whose name meant servant of the creator. His name alone suggested he was very religious, and Trapp assumed he was both of Arab descent and of the Muslim faith. He paused, folded his hands behind his neck, and stared at the ceiling. Trapp twisted his neck back and forth a few times, and the popping of vertebra relieved his tense muscles. He rubbed his eyes with the tips of his fingers before continuing his reading.

***

It is no marvel that Abraham's God called him to separate himself from the idolatrous practices which dominated the lives of the wealthy valley inhabitants. In revealing Himself to Abram as the one-true God, it was as if God started over with His creation, with a single family, with a single religion, in a land far removed from Abraham's birth: the land of promise, called Canaan and Palestine, after its inhabitants. This call of God to Abram, and his lifetime as a Bedouin, are recorded in the Book of Genesis.

Abram left Haran, journeying southwest into the land of Canaan, now modern-day Israel, as mentioned previously. Here he wandered the earth in search of grazing and water for his herds. Circumstances took him south into Egypt, but eventually back to God's chosen country, Canaan, to establish and perpetuate monotheism.

The name, Abram, designates him as a patriarch: head of a large group, including his nephew, Lot and his family and a host of servants that he lorded over. Abram and his wife Sarai were childless, and therefore, the promise of God to make him a mighty nation seemed highly unlikely. Though a large clan, his nomadic lifestyle was no match against the occupants and professed owners of the land, for these tribes were entrenched over many years. He was the outsider, a former city-dweller, now living in a portable city of tents among strangers.

When drought forced him to seek refuge in Egypt, he became fearful the more powerful locals would kill him and take his extraordinarily beautiful wife, Sarai, as their own. So, Abram concocted a plan: he asked her to say that she was his sister. This was partially true, for she was the daughter of his father, Terah, but not of his mother. Sarai, being his half-sister, and being in subjection to her husband—a rare quality for today—went along with the plan. Just as Abram had been concerned, the Pharaoh did selfishly take Sarai into his harem. Assuming Abram to be Sarai's brother, and probably wanting to obtain her favor, since she was basically a sex prisoner and unhappy with the arrangement—though Pharaoh never got around to defiling her—Pharaoh treated Abraham favorably and gave him much livestock and servants. Abram kept his fingers crossed that somehow this deception would work for his good. There seems to be mostly self-interest in his plan, but we were not there, and we can't quite comprehend such culture. So, it is difficult for us to conceive of these circumstances unless one lives in a country where the women are still treated as chattel. Oddly, in a supposedly civilized world, such atrocities still exist.

***

Trapp made a star by the last line and traced over it a couple times for emphasis. He was an avid reader, especially history, so he was aware that the Arab slave trade was an age-old practice. The Arab trade alone displaced as many as ten million people from the Swahili coast, many of those being women taken to Saudi Arabia, some as domestic slaves and others as nannies. And many ended up as sex-slaves in the harems of those in authority.

The famed missionary, Doctor David Livingstone, had written in his diary of the atrocities of the Arab slavers who invaded his beloved Africa and devastated entire communities and even entire regions. Some historians contend that Dr. Livingstone's sense of duty in trying to deter slavery's devastation of the African people kept him in Africa, separated from his family, far longer than he intended. He ultimately tired of the barbarity, and the slave trade broke his heart; moreover, the barbarousness broke the backs of many African tribes, leaving families decimated and their villages in ashes. America wasn't the only country with the blood of millions crying out from the ground: men for their wives, mothers for their children. And though slavery is a term of antiquity, many cultures still treat their women like items of possession. His thoughts wandered to Eden Stone. Was she just a pawn in the hands of evil men? Trapp contemplated the possibilities before returning to the professor's notes.

***

In spite of Abram's fearfulness and deceptive practice, God protected Sarai by causing disease among Pharaoh's clan. The truth of Abram's deception surfaced, Sarai was sent home to Abram, and the Pharaoh immediately deported Abram from Egypt back to the land of Canaan. Ironically, Pharaoh did not demand a return of the gifts he had given to Abram, who shamefully returned to Canaan, along with additional wealth and servants.

Through the years, Abram's wealth and fame grew, his sprawling tent city dotted the Canaanite landscape for miles. His clan probably numbered into the thousands, for he once led three hundred and eighteen armed men of his household into battle. He did so to free his nephew, Lot, who had been taken captive during a revolt in the southern Jordan Valley where Lot had foolishly chosen to reside. Abram and Lot had separated because the explosive growth of their Bedouin community, especially the flocks, created dissension among their servants. In a most generous gesture, Abram allowed his nephew to have the first choice of the land. Lot chose the fertile valley stretching toward the south of Canaan. Abram accepted what was left: the more rugged terrain of Canaan.

When Abraham first entered the land of Canaan, he was the patriarch of a company made up of family and servants, though he had no children of his own. His influence extended only throughout his camp of tents sprinkled across the landscape. At that time, local tribesmen owned the land, and these men, more powerful and influential, permitted Abram and his clan to wander the area in search of grazing land and water for their livestock. During these years of wandering the land of Canaan, Abram dug wells for his clan's survival and built altars for them to pray to the one-true God. From well to well and altar to altar, Abram prospered. He grew in wealth, he grew in his relationship with his God, and his clan grew numerically. On a moonless night, their campfires looked like fireflies dotting the hillsides.

Abraham's life was filled with tough challenges. With each difficulty, he learned to trust and obey God. The name change—from Abram to Abraham—represented a new status he acquired from God in response to his faithfulness. God affirmed His promise of making Abraham's descendants a mighty nation. During twenty-five years of nomadic wandering, Abraham's skin leathered, and his hands calloused, but his heart remained tender toward his God.

We understand that the descendants of Abraham include both the Jewish and Muslim people. But how does Abraham relate to modern-day Christianity? God's promises are conditional. They were conditional with Abraham, and they are conditional regarding Christianity: obedient faith is the essential ingredient in the work of grace. Strangely, modern Christianity has removed any concept of obedience being linked with faith. This idea is akin to what Bonhoeffer called cheap grace and challenged pro-Nazi Germany to return to a biblical concept of obedient faith. Likewise, such cheap grace often exists in our Western society, and this concept is in opposition to the response of Bible characters such as Abraham in the Old Testament and Paul in the New.

Abraham believed God for the promises God made to him; further, he walked in obedience to the direction of God for his life. These, however, were acquired over time, for he had failed in both faith and obedience. More than once his faith faltered. As before mentioned, he feared the more powerful local ruler would kill him to take Sarai as a wife, so, on at least two occasions, he connived with her to say she was his sister.

Further, Abraham did not wait for God's promise of an heir but gave in to Sarai's plot for them to have a surrogate child, a child that God rejected as the legitimate son of inheritance. He had laughed at God's promise of a child in Sarai's old age, thus showing his faith possessed cracks. Though considered the father of the faithful, at times he seemed contemplatively slow in obedience, stopping in Haran until his aged father, Terah, died. It seems God would not fulfill his promise to Abraham so long as his father, an idolater, tagged along. Abraham needed a clean break from such. Initially, instead of separating from his father and doing as God had directed, Abraham took Terah with him. But Abraham finally met God's conditions, at which point, God reaffirmed His promises. Then came the change of his name from Abram to Abraham. The name-change assured Abraham that God had not forgotten His promise of making Abraham's lineage a mighty nation, not just another oversized family. But it would be many years before the completion of the promise.

God's promises often precede our acts of obedient faith. Abram was seventy-five years old when the promise first came. He was ninety-nine years old when God reaffirmed the promise and changed his name to Abraham.

The name change occurred at least twenty-four years after God's original call and promises. During the twenty-four years from God's initial call to Abraham, numerous events challenged his faith. On some occasions, he fared poorly, but he remained true to his belief in the one-true God. Though he made some poor decisions regarding his personal life, he never failed in building altars to worship the one-true God. Not once did he participate in the idolatrous practices of the people around him. Because Abram remained true to this monotheistic faith in the God of creation, wherever he journeyed, God showed Himself faithful to bless and protect him.

Abraham. That is what God eventually called him. God's message was clear. The name change revealed God's approval. Abraham had not faltered in his monotheistic faith. The condition for receiving the promises had been met. Abraham would be more than a Nomadic figure, leading a wandering tribe and their herds. He would be a father of an entire nation. And this nation would be followers of the one-true God of Creation.

An important message we learn from the life of Abraham is that God recognizes our human frailties, and in spite of these, God is faithful. Still, we learn from Abram's experience that God has expectations for us regarding how we should live. While God's promises are conditional, he is patient while we acquire faith and learn obedience. There is, however, one condition upon which we dare not wavier, on which God does not excuse our behavior. It is in the worship of the one-true God. In this, we, like our father Abraham, hear the same call that Abram received: "… I am the Almighty God; walk before me, and be thou perfect." Perfect? Humans perfect? How? The only area in which God can expect mankind to acquire perfection is in being perfect regarding an absolute belief in the monotheistic God of creation.

***

Trapp highlighted the last paragraph. He paused as he pondered the thought process of Professor Stone. He scribbled a note alongside the section. *The chink in religion: room for mortals to commit sin and remain in God's favor.* But murder? David committed murder and stayed on the throne. And he committed adultery. And somehow, he escaped the penalty for both, even though the Bible demanded death for either.

"My years of Sunday school are paying off after all," he murmured. "The professor evidently believes the end justifies the means."

His thoughts turned to the Lexus parked in Christopher Stone's driveway. And he contemplated the expensive, diamond necklace he personally removed from the charred hand of Eden Stone. From his lectures, the professor's idea of religion leaves room in all lives for some weakness of the flesh, some flawed performance, some godless desire. And Stone's flaw? Greed. Which led to murder. And sin always demands a cover-up. He's another King David personified, and his Bathsheba is hiding somewhere, and when she is found, she will certainly help solve the case.

Trapp's cell phone rang. He laid aside the notebook and checked the number before answering. "What's up, Dallas?"

"You wanted me to check out Professor Stone's financial status?"

"And?"

"The judge reluctantly gave permission, saying it'd better produce a strong case."

"Did it?"

"I'll let you decide. The professor has a few bucks in a local savings account but check this out. He withdrew ten grand from that savings a week before the bombing. He also has an offshore account of around two-hundred and fifty-thousand. He gets four-thousand a month from a not yet identified source, deposited monthly like clockwork for the last three years, into a checking account."

"Bingo, Dallas. This is bigger than I thought. So our modest-living professor is faking. I was only half right when I said he has champagne taste and beer money; he has champagne taste and he also has the money to buy it."

"And that's not all. He has a million-dollar life insurance policy on his wife."

"Has he collected?"

"Not yet."

"Get in touch with the insurance company and forewarn them that he's a suspect in the murder of his wife. Let's stall payment as long as we can. We don't want him to get the upper hand on us, money to flee to wherever he wants … to some island where we can't touch him. And the insurance company is going to love this. That's how they get their fat pockets … unpaid claims."

"I'm on it. And there's something else … ."

"What?"

"Every month there's a check written from his account to some outfit in Mexico."

"How much?"

"It varies … couple hundred … five hundred … ."

"To whom?"

"I haven't been able to trace that."

"Find out ASAP. Sounds like the puzzle is coming together nicely. I think I can forgo the rest of my reading project for the weekend. Let's nail him before he slips out of Haran."

"What's that?"

"Put surveillance on him twenty-four-seven."

Chapter 16

They had been in communication for days and finally rendezvoused at Frisch's Big Boy Restaurant on Louisville's south side: Tony Trapp, Dallas Rogers, and Scott Davis. Davis shared his missing person's investigation of Sherri Carpenter and inquired about the phone call by the mysterious Susan Carr. Trapp obliged him with as many details as he could recall.

"I have an idea." Davis seemed all business, unaware of the tartar sauce on the corners of his mouth, producing a clownish look.

"What?" Trapp asked, respectfully refraining from announcing the tartar sauce adorning Davis' face. He needed to stay in good graces with the Louisville PD.

"I have a theory," Davis said. Between bites of his Big Boy sandwich and fries, he explained his speculation. "My missing Sherri Carpenter and your missing Susan Carr are one and the same person. Your Susan doesn't work at a gas station; she works part-time at Dillards in St. Matthews Mall, and she works a second job in Clarksville.

"A restaurant?" Trapp asked.

"Right you are. She works at Applebee's," Davis said.

"If she had told me the restaurant in the first place we'd be days ahead in this investigation," Trapp said.

"True. Let's go on the assumption your Susan and my Sherri are one and the same person. This is what I know. She lives on Louisville's east side and is looking forward to going back to college as soon as she can afford it. She works at Applebee's in Clarksville. That's where she saw the two Arab men she suspicioned. But now she's missing."

"You've been a busy detective, Davis, but where's your proof?" Trapp picked up a sweating glass and slurped the last bit of tea from the crushed ice.

"I know it's speculation but … ." He picked up a fry and dabbed it in ketchup.

"That's for sure," Trapp said, "but I'd have to say it's pretty good speculation. But we don't have a body. No witness to identify the two as being one and the same person. No definite identification for the phone call we received or any proof that your missing person has actually gone missing." Trapp held up his empty glass to get the attention of a passing waitress.

"Hear me out," Davis said, "before you shut me down … ." His statement trailed off as the waitress approached with the tea.

"We'll consider it, Davis," Trapp said. "That's enough Miss." Trapp grimaced as the waitress over-poured iced tea into his extended glass, ran down his hand, and up his arm, leaving a wet stain half-way up his shirtsleeve.

"I'm so sorry," the waitress said, and she continued to apologize profusely.

"No problem, ma'am," Trapp said as he waved her away.

"Nothing a little soap won't fix, I hope," she lamented.

"My fault, ma'am," Trapp said.

She continued to apologize and announced she'd get a napkin to wipe up the mess.

Trapp's impatience showed more color in his face than the ice tea stain on his shirt. Davis waited until the waitress returned with a towel, wiped the table down, and left, before continuing the conversation.

"Like I was saying, Sherri Carpenter's cousin told me that Sherri, whom I suspect to be your Susan Carr, also works at Clarksville's Applebee's. So, I did some snooping in your neck of the woods, and a couple waitresses are sure Sherri Carpenter waited on two young men of Middle Eastern features the same night Eden Stone was murdered."

"How can they be so sure it was the same night?" Rogers asked, wiping tartar sauce from his chin.

"It was an impressionable night with the blaring of sirens. It was late, and the restaurant wasn't crowded, just a handful of customers. Sherri waited on them. Another waitress I interviewed remembered one of the men had some missing fingers. 'Kinda creepy' is how she described his missing fingers. Just like your Susan Carr said in her phone call to you." Davis paused and picked up another fry, twirled it in ketchup, and plopped it into his mouth. "I'm afraid when we find our missing person, we'll also have another murder case on our hands. And I somehow think it will be connected to the professor's wife's murder. Two homicides instead of one, but both linked."

Trapp scratched his graying, burred head and stared out the window as if distracted, but a silent Trapp meant he was seriously giving consideration to a hunch, no matter how ridiculous. A no-nonsense detective, he didn't waste time, especially his own. So a long pause had merit.

The Louisville International Airport runway ran parallel with the expressway, just south of where they were eating, so there was constant activity of planes from their window view. Trapp had been a pilot during the end of the Vietnam Conflict, which he was quick to correct anyone who called it a conflict. "It was a war," he'd scold anyone who tried to be politically correct, "no matter what the politicians called it." A Boeing 727, almost a million pounds of metal, fuel, and cargo, glided effortlessly alongside I-65 south. A distinctive logo identified it as a UPS aircraft. Since around 1980, the company had found a home at the Louisville airport, bringing a good many jobs to the south-side area. Louisville's mild weather and strategic location had brought the company to the city.

Just as abruptly as Trapp seemed sidetracked, he returned his attention back to the table. "I think you could be on to something, Davis. But there are some missing pieces to the puzzle." He paused, looked out the window again as if concerned about the jet's low-level flight pattern.

"Like what?" Davis asked.

"For starters, why did our Ms. Carr lie to me on the phone? And if she lied about one thing, how much more about her is a lie?"

"I don't think she lied, other than to keep her identity anonymous," Davis challenged. "Maybe she's scared to get involved. I don't think there was any criminal intent. If your caller is Sherri Carpenter instead of Susan Carr, she has no police record, and her credit's good except for an unpaid student loan. Rent was paid up through the month. Friends have the highest regard for her. And by-the-way, I've done a search on every Susan Carr I can locate in the area, and I can't find a one that admits to the phone call, or as far as I can tell, that fits into any type of profile for making an anonymous phone call to report on Eden Stone's murder."

Rogers cleared his throat and repositioned himself on his seat, as if wanting to get in on the conversation but not wanting to usurp authority over his boss. His lanky body didn't quite fit under the one-size-fits-all table.

"You got something to say, Dallas?" Trapp asked.

"My question is how do we link the two men in the restaurant—with Davis' missing Sherri—as being the two men who approached our Susan at the phone booth. If it was the same two men that we have as suspects, by our timeline, that was the same evening of their flight back home, so they had to be on their way to the airport. And why would they take the time to track down someone who just might suspect them of killing Eden Stone and risk making it to their flight out of the country and to safety? Does that make sense?" Rogers typically spoke his mind with a question.

"Good question, Dallas," Trapp said. "Let me add a question for you, Davis."

"Sure."

"When you checked on your Sherri Carpenter, did anyone affirm her arriving home the night of our Susan Carr's abduction?"

"I didn't make a thorough attempt to track her movements other than the fact she was seen leaving the apartment. She was probably going to work, but the timeline for her leaving the apartment was a bit iffy. I'll make a note to check a specific time she left from work ... and if anyone thinks she returned home." Davis had seemed to impress them up to this point, but he had definitely dropped the ball on the details. "Could the two women, Eden Stone and Sherri Carpenter, or Susan Carr, as you know her, have something in common we're overlooking?" Davis asked. He needed to recover his fumble.

"Like maybe one was married to Professor Stone and the other dating Professor Stone. Where did Carpenter attend college?" Trapp asked.

"U of L," Davis said.

"Did you find her to have any connection at all with the professor?" Trapp asked.

"None that I found. Of course, I wasn't trying to link her with Professor Stone. I'll investigate that angle." Davis scribbled more notes.

"And one of our missing Arab boys was a student at the University of Louisville. That's interesting. While you're checking out our missing Carpenter's link with the professor, check on any connection with … what was his name?" Trapp asked.

"Gamali," Rogers said.

"And since you're the king of onomalogy … whatever that word is, I wonder what Gamali means in English, Rogers? Probably identifies him with some kind of religion."

"The word's onomastics, or onomatology, or linguistics, whichever you prefer," Rogers said, grinning. "Gamali actually means camel."

Trapp laughed. "Who would name their kid camel?"

"Maybe the same kind of people who name their son Todd," Rogers said.

"And what's so strange about my son's name, Rogers? I'll have you to know I like it." Trapp argued playfully.

"It means fox."

"Okay, Mr. Smart Guy. Now I'm wondering what my name means?" Trapp asked.

"Tony means … ." He smiled mischievously. "It means invaluable."

"You're full of it, Rogers. Making half of that stuff up, I bet." Trapp tried to keep a straight face, but a grin slipped out the corner of his lips.

Scott Davis stared at the two partners. "You guys do this very often?"

"Like I said, he's just making stuff up as we go, Davis, to taunt me for all the overtime I make him work. Aren't you, Rogers?"

"Afraid not, sir.

"Oh, whatever. Let's get back to our investigation." Trapp shook his head as if in disbelief of Rogers' expertise.

"I'll see if there's any connection with Sherri and Gamali," Davis said. "And Abdul," he added as an afterthought.

"You do that," Trapp said. "In the meantime, we should find out if our two Arab students have returned stateside, or if they're planning on returning at all. Rogers, check with INS and see if our boys might have sneaked back into the country. Also, see what kind of extradition agreements we have with Jordan."

"Will do."

"Also, I want to pursue another angle." He touched the tips of his fingers together and gently tapped to some silent rhythm, arthritis beginning to show in some of the knuckles. "Davis, have you heard of the Mexican Santos family?"

"The drug cartel?" Davis asked.

"Yep. One of them visited Professor Stone just before his wife was murdered. He was in your jurisdiction, at the professor's college.

There might be some drug activity funneling through the seminary campus."

"You sure about that?" Davis asked. He sat back in his seat and crossed his arms. "That's quite a twist of events."

"The same week they met, Stone withdrew ten thousand dollars from a savings account. Rogers got a judge's permission to check Stones finances. So, I have a theory. It's starting to fit together rather nicely ... especially if our Susan Carr mystery caller is your Sherri Carpenter missing person. By the way, can we have access to your files on Sherri Carpenter?"

"Sure. What's your theory?" Davis leaned forward and rested his elbows on the table.

"I believe Stone hired the Arab boys to murder his wife. That's how they had the cash Ms. Carpenter saw at the restaurant. That took part of the money Stone withdrew from his savings, and he used the rest as a down payment on a drug delivery from the Santos family. He'll come up with the rest of the payment with the insurance money from his wife's death. And someone in Mexico is receiving money from him on a regular basis. Have you figured that out, Rogers?"

"No, sir. That's still quite the mystery. Needing to brush up on my Spanish."

"Stone is into something big. I'd say drugs. We need to do a thorough background on him. Passport check. Where's he been spending his summers the last five years? Mexico? Jordan? Where's all his money coming from? Certainly not his professor's salary. Where is his money going? This may be bigger than we've thought ... not just crossing state lines, but he could be a kingpin to an international drug ring." Trapp turned to Rogers. "We've got some homework to do, not like we haven't been working overtime. But too many unanswered questions about this guy. I felt he was hiding something from me the first day I met him. We need to find out what, if any, his association is with the two Arabs? Is he their source for foreign drug deals? I know the Jordanian government is tough on drug traffickers, but that hasn't stopped the influx of drugs into their country. They'd gamble losing a hand before they'd miss an opportunity to get rich. In fact, they've become a conduit to some of the other Middle Eastern countries. Of course, they need a supplier, and I think Stone could well be a key player … Mexico … Louisville … the Middle East. I doubt it's coincidental his association with those fellas. I won't be surprised if we discover the Arab boys killed Eden Stone, and maybe they killed Sherri Carpenter. We know they had contact with her … at the restaurant … and maybe at the phone booth."

"But why kill the Carpenter girl?" Rogers asked.

"My question, too," Davis said. "Of course, we're not sure she's dead."

"Carr, or Carpenter, whoever she may be, has simply gotten in the way. I imagine we won't find her alive. The professor may not know she exists, but then again, she may be his girl, and the assassins wanted to remove her as a witness … maybe she knew too much. That's why they went to the restaurant. And maybe Stone needed her removed just in case we sniffed out his trail and picked up her scent on his suit jacket."

"You think he's that cold-hearted?" Davis asked.

"He's got the name for it: Stone. How long have you been on the force, Davis? Trapp asked.

"Ten years," Davis said, a question mark permeating his boyish face.

"Another ten and your blood will turn to ice." Trapp looked him square in the eyes. "In our business, we deal with too many criminals to have faith in the human race."

"You think?" Davis folded his hands together on the table and stared at them.

Trapp smiled at Davis. He probably was the typical altar boy back in the day, he thought. "I know … it's hard to accept, but Professor Stone's criminal mind will hasten the process in your loss of faith in mankind."

Davis' facial expression challenged Trapp.

"Tell me I'm wrong in a year or two, Davis," Trapp said.

"Umm … I'd like to think it's different with me," Davis protested.

"It's tough to accept, but mankind is capable of any crime imaginable. The way I'm beginning to see Stone, he's capable of killing his wife and his girlfriend without blinking. Anyway, he can afford any girl he wants since he's due to collect a million bucks from a life policy on his wife. He'll add that money to his two hundred and fifty thousand offshore account and cut a deal with the Santos family that will put him in The Fortune 500."

"But didn't you ask me to give the insurance company a heads up?" Rogers asked.

"Yes. Have you done that?"

"Not yet. Got that on my list."

"Good that you haven't done it. I've changed my mind. Let's back off and allow Stone to collect the money, then we'll monitor his activities with the Santos family and nail him on multiple charges. The insurance company needs to pay anyway, they're too fat as it is. And Stone won't be able to spend it anyway, at least on himself, since charges associated with the drug cartel will cost him plenty for lawyers. And a conviction for murder will not just send him to prison, it will put nails in his coffin." Trapp's balled fists slammed against the table, rattling the tableware.

"Let's nail him in Indiana for the murder," Davis said. "Kentucky's too lenient on murderers. You're up on us twenty to three on executions since 1976."

"Your blood is beginning to chill a little already, Davis. I told you so. I don't think we can nail him on murder just yet, but we'll give it our best shot. Course Indiana has gotten soft on murderers also, fifteen on death row now," Trapp said.

"But Kentucky's still softer. We've got thirty-five on death row. Let's make sure we convict him in Indiana." Davis folded his hands as if in prayer.

"But how do we link the two murders, assuming our missing person is dead?" Rogers asked.

"That's what we're going to find out, gentlemen," Trapp said. He paused, reflecting on their meeting. "As much as I hate to, we may have to call in the Feds. We've got tax-evasion, probably a tax-evasion conspiracy, drugs, and murder."

"Not to mention crossing state lines," Davis injected.

"That, too," Trapp replied. "But we'll focus on the murder case … our jurisdiction. Rogers, get us an appointment with the DA to see if they'll contact the American Embassy in Amman and tell them we're offering immunity to the suspects in a double murder for their sworn affidavits of assassins for hire. I hate like crazy to let them off the hook, but it'll take years to extradite them, so we'll settle for our best deal: their testimony to implicate our squeaky-clean professor. Then we'll put the CIA onto the actions of the Arabs. They may well nail them for something else. They're bad to the core, so they'll mess up again. They always do."

"And if they won't cooperate?" Rogers asked.

"Threaten extradition and prosecution for the brutal murder of two female, American citizens. And remind them of how angry Americans still are about 9/11. That ought to make them want to bargain for a plea deal." Trapp gulped the last of his tea and crunched hard on the crushed ice that plopped into his mouth.

Chapter 17

A huge sign situated along State Route 180 welcomed visitors to Mendota, California. A couple trail bicycles lay abandoned along the roadside, while their suntanned owners splashed in a fountain that spewed water into arid space. With a population of under ten thousand, Mendota is just another Central California, farming community. Its current claim to fame is being the Cantaloupe Center of the World, or at least that's what the sign boasts.

Juan Santos had spent the late morning shining his black, heavily chromed Kawasaki and reading a book he had borrowed from the local library. Both tasks were done underneath the shade of a pistachio tree near the welcome sign. He nonchalantly observed each vehicle that entered the city, watching for one car in particular, and he eventually saw it in the distance. As the black SUV—a Jeep Cherokee with Nevada plates—passed by, Juan started the engine to his Kawasaki and headed toward the designated rendezvous. He fought the impulse to pull alongside them as he kept a reasonable distance from their vehicle. The SUV slowed as it turned left onto Seventh Street, then right into the parking lot of Los Amadores Motel. Juan passed by the motel, circled the next block, and drove back to the motel. It surprised him how much he had missed his family, but caution seemed prudent. They could have been followed, and to be seen with them immediately could blow his cover, something he had worked diligently to establish. The Sonora Mini Mart across the street from the motel seemed a practical place to stop. He cut the engine of his Kawasaki and pretended to check something gone wrong with the brakes.

Juan blended well into the surroundings. In a town of ninety-four percent Hispanic, he was not suspect. His unemployed status raised no red flags, for above forty percent of the inhabitants of Mendota were unemployed, and of those who were employed, over forty percent lived below the poverty level. He despised his squalid apartment, but it was prudent that he do nothing to reveal his connections. And intentions.

Juan peered through the Mini Mart window at the local newspaper. The headlines caught his attention: *Federal Prison to Open Soon.* It had been a long wait. Juan smiled. He sauntered to a sidewalk bench and sat down, occasionally checking his watch as he kept an eye on the motel entrance.

Juan initially hated this assignment. He missed his familiar surroundings from his hometown near Mexico City. But after a few weeks, he had resigned himself to the task ahead and settled into a routine: a pickup soccer game at one of the four local parks, lunch and dinner daily at the Chvelas', and evenings at the local library. Always listening. Watching. Questioning. Gathering all the information possible for his upcoming mission.

Over time, Juan took a liking to the community: The laid-back environment, with friendly locals, gave him a break from his usually stressful assignments. He had not expected the assignment to take so long. Who could guess the recession would delay the target date for the opening of the federal prison?

The Joaquin River Valley especially intrigued him. With more time than he knew what to do with, he read every book the library had on the history of the valley. He spent weekends exploring the natural surroundings. His camping excursions were a reprieve from the routine. Each weekend he ventured deeper into the valley, following the course of the San Joaquin River, fascinated by its history. Locals were sometimes taken aback by his knowledge of the valley, surprised by his questions about times gone by, dating back hundreds of years.

In the latter part of the nineteenth century, Mendota, located in Fresno County, thrived as a Southern Pacific Railroad town. Later, a series of state water projects facilitated the growth of agriculture in the Central California Valley, giving it a far-reaching significance.

The town grew up near the San Joaquin River, which has its source high in the Sierra Nevada Mountains and flows for three hundred and sixty-five miles on a westerly course through the valley. Near Mendota, it takes a northwesterly turn and continues until it empties into Suisun Bay, San Francisco Bay, and the Pacific Ocean. Juan daydreamed of the Native Americans who canoed the river through the valley, perhaps all the way to the Pacific, sometimes envious of their adventurous opportunities.

In bygone days the Miwok and the Yokut tribes trudged through the muck of the swamped riverbanks and droppings of the millions of migratory birds that darkened the sky. They fished from the banks of the river swarming with as many as three hundred thousand spawning salmon, a natural phenomenon lost by man's modern ingenuity of dams.

Rich in wildlife and vegetation, the native nomadic tribes favored the valley. This ended when the Spaniards, who had their own ideas for the valley, forced the indigenous tribes into missions. Once addicted to the security of the missions, they depended upon white man's aid for survival. Welfare controls the mindset of the masses, and it weakens the resolve of its people. And the people are the strength, or the lack thereof, of any hamlet, city, or nation. A dependent people leaves opportunity for despots. In retrospect, the indigenous tribes succumbed to accepting cheap handouts in lieu of liberty.

Juan pulled a book from his knapsack and scanned the cover: *Jedediah Smith and the Opening of the West* by Dale Lowell Morgan. This first American to roam the valley both intrigued and challenged him. Jedediah Smith, the famous mountain man and entrepreneur trapper, had come into the valley in eighteen hundred thirty-three while Juan's people still controlled California. Smith was arrested by the protective Spaniards but eventually released, after being threatened within an inch of his life. But he was of a more Pollyanna tendency, not easily discouraged. The temptation to trap wildlife in the valley was greater than his fear, so he secretly remained in the valley for some time, hunting and trapping. Shortly after Smith left the territory, tragedy struck. As many as sixty thousand Native Americans died when smallpox and malaria swept the region in the early eighteen hundreds.

After the Mexican-American War, the United States acquired California and thus this valley, just in time for the gold rush of forty-eight. The population of the valley quickly swelled to as many as eighty-thousand, and the bank accounts of some increased proportionately, but most settled for any other means of income they could find, busted and terribly disappointed.

When the gold depleted, farmers settled into the region to take advantage of the natural hydrologic resources: a fancy description of fertile soil. But they, too, were defeated by the annual flooding of the San Joaquin that inundated their crops and crushed their hopes. In the twentieth century, the numerous levees and dams built along the river facilitated agriculture, and farming resurrected, especially the cultivation of cantaloupes. But cantaloupe alone was insufficient to keep the populace employed, so the newly built federal prison created high hopes, and such expectations created immigration, and immigration more unemployment, and unrest. But the atmosphere was changing, for after many months of postponement, the prison was about to open, that is if Congress will stop fighting and pass a budget that can release the needed funds to run the prison. California politicians were pressing Congress, and the response was optimistic.

The new prison was the only reason Juan was in Mendota, not to work at the prison, but because of someone who was to be housed within the prison. Any day that should happen, and his lazy days would abruptly end. He hoped for a good outcome.

Juan checked his watch: three o'clock. An hour had passed since his boss and the boss' son had entered the motel. He was a Santos, but there was a pecking order he knew to follow, and following orders kept his name high on the list of the organization. They would meet him at ten, probably with some new orders. He wondered what information they carried for him. He was eager to share his latest findings and plans.

Chapter 18

Juan stepped inside the dimly-lit restaurant at precisely ten o'clock. They were already there, sitting at a corner table near the back exit. He removed his Oakland Raiders cap and tossed it onto a wall hook, ran his fingers through his curly black hair, and sauntered toward them. A smile lit up their faces as he approached, and they quickly stood and embraced him. It was an emotional meeting after these many months.

"My relatives from Mexico," he explained to the waitress, "Luis Héctor and his son Alberto. How are you, Maria?"

"Fine, thank you, Juan. And you?"

"Doing great! Especially tonight. I am at my favorite restaurant, my *familia* is here, and you, ever so beautiful, are waiting on us. What more can I ask for? Life is good. No? And thank you for serving us, Maria." He slid into the booth beside Alberto.

"It is always a pleasure, *senõr.*" She swiped at a strand of hair dangling over her forehead in an attempt to conceal her blushing. "What would you like to drink, *senõres*?"

"I'll have my usual Diet Coke, and my family … ." He gestured to them.

They both ordered iced tea.

"I will get your drinks, and then you can order from the menu, *senõrs.*" She smiled at Alberto.

"Maria is cute, no?" Juan said to Alberto.

"*Muy bonita.* Is she married?" Alberto asked.

"No. She came to the States two years ago. She lives with her *familia.* She works here every day, long hours. I think she has to provide the living for her *familia.* She is a very nice young lady."

"You dating her?" Alberto asked.

"No, but she is very nice to me. We talk a lot when I come in … she is lonely I think … but stays busy at the restaurant, serving, sometimes cooking … and she is beautiful. No?" He jabbed Alberto with his elbow.

"How are you, Juan?" Luis asked, reaching across the table and placing a hand on his shoulder.

"I am okay. It has been a lonely assignment, but I have adjusted."

"How is progress?"

"The prison will open any day."

"How are you doing with the contacts?"

"I got a job with the HVAC company that will manage the prison … but I can't work until they open. They gave me papers describing the entire system so I could study it. How convenient is that? I am learning much about the prison operation. I should start work at any time. And—"

A customer walked by to go to the restroom.

"And?" Luis asked.

"I've been inside the prison for orientation of the facility. I've seen the blueprints which maps out the entire complex."

"You have a copy of the blueprints!" Luis said, surprised.

"No, we could only view them with supervision, but it is all here." He tapped his forehead with his index finger. "I have drawn some diagrams that I keep hidden."

"In your *apartamento*?" Luis asked.

"*Si.*"

"Be careful that no one sees them. That could raise suspicion," Luis cautioned.

"I am cautious. I know how important this—"

"What about the *securidad*?" Luis interrupted Juan.

"The facility is minimum security. We can easily—" Maria approached the table with their drinks.

"A Diet Coke for *Senõr* Juan and two iced teas for his friends." She placed the drinks on the table. "Are you ready to order your meal?"

They placed their order, making casual conversation, hoping Maria would view the meal as simply a family gathering. When she left the table, they immediately resumed their business conversation. Juan laid out his plan, step by step. He drew diagrams on napkins with stick men as guards and X's as towers. He circled the recreation area and made a check mark where the helicopter would land. Héctor asked many questions. Juan confidently answered each, adding more info than Luis called for: both the positive and negative of such a plan.

"There is much risk," Juan cautioned, "and it will be very expensive."

"Don't spare any expense. We cannot let the old man die in prison." Luis stared at the diagram and finally gave his approval. "Now we will simply wait for the prison to open and Chico to be transferred."

As Maria approached the table, Juan casually wadded the napkins into a ball and stuck it inside his pocket.

"Anything else?" She asked.

"Do you have any *tres leches*?" Alberto asked.

"Yes, especially for you. A good choice."

"Three large slices." Alberto smiled.

"Is this a celebration?"

"Yes, a celebration" Juan said, smiling. "We celebrate our *familia* being together again. Thanks for waiting on us, Maria, for you have made it extra special."

"My pleasure, *senõres.*"

"Sorry for taking the table so long," Juan added.

"No problem. It is not busy this late. Please, take your time."

"*Muchas gracias.*" Alberto smiled at Maria.

"*De nada.* I will get your dessert." She gathered their plates and walked away.

"How is the search going for our missing *familia*?" Juan asked.

Luis hesitated. "We have not heard from anyone. We do not believe they have been killed for that would serve no purpose to our enemies. We are still searching, but it has been three years. That concerns me." His taut facial expression affirmed his concern. "Chico feels confident they are still alive. He is pushing us, but we are doing everything we know to do. It's mostly to wait until their captors call. It'll be a high ransom they will ask for. Maybe more than … ." His words trailed off.

"You know I care much for her and for him?" Juan said. He slammed his hand onto the table.

"We are doing our best to find them, Juan," Alberto said. He grabbed Juan's hand and held it tightly. "I promise you, we will find them," he added.

"Thank you. And Chico? How is he doing?"

"Chico's health is much worse than I expected. He grieves for his family, but he receives some satisfaction in knowing his deceiver is dead," Luis said.

"The gringo?" Juan asked.

"*Sí.*"

"That is fantastic! How did we locate him?" Juan asked.

"It was by accident. One of your distant cousins was making a shipment and by chance saw him … ."

"Which cousin?"

"Carlos."

"I don't claim him," Juan said.

"Can you believe it? Verco Drew found at last," Luis said.

"What luck!" Juan said.

"Too much luck. We do not always trust Carlos, but he was convincing. I doubt he would lie to Chico, then again, we are concerned the whole story was fabricated just to make money. Your cousin has some expensive habits. I think he has sold his soul to *Diablo*." Luis lowered his voice.

"Your cousin, too. Remember? I never trusted him." Juan did not attempt to hide his concern. "The hit was not verified?"

"It was a contract bombing by someone Carlos hired to place the bomb in the bedroom. The hitman presented Carlos a picture of the smoking house, with a window blown out of the bedroom. The hitman collected on the contract, and your cousin probably collected a kickback from him. No, it was never really verified, just the hitman's word and a picture of the smoking house, but why would Carlos lie and risk Chico's wrath? It's highly unlikely that Drew escaped. I trust the whole thing was not a farce by your cousin just to collect money. If it was, his life is on a short noose." Luis sipped from his glass of iced tea.

"Why do you keep calling him my cousin?" Juan's tone showed his disapproval.

"For I do not claim him," Luis said.

"Nor I," Juan affirmed.

"But we assured Chico that his enemy is dead. And I did not want him to die in prison thinking his enemy was still alive. Lately, I am having second thoughts about the whole story. You know, how can we be sure when we allow Carlos to hire someone to do an important job? So, while you wait for the prison to open, I have a little trip I want you to make. Are you up to that?"

"I would appreciate the break. Where?"

"Midwest. Southern Indiana."

"Who?"

"Verco Drew, if he is still alive," Luis said. "And this time, with verification."

"With delight." Juan smiled, but it faded into a devilish grin, satisfied that revenge could finally be realized.

Chapter 19

Chris Stone decided to play all his cards. His lecture today would flush the quarry, if any existed, and his sights were set and ready. He tossed his notes on the lectern, and the abruptness seemed to surprise some of the students. He opened the notebook and began in a deliberate manner, observing every expression, and wondering why the student in the far right of the room refused eye contact.

"There is an area for grave consideration regarding the three major religions of the world: the violence that has permeated the history of all three religions, which have been at odds with each other for centuries. Conversely, the Christ of Christianity proclaimed a non-violent faith, and both He and his disciples practiced such, albeit some of them had to learn to control their emotions—I'm speaking of the man to whom was handed the keys to Christ's Kingdom. Yet the religion they started, over the centuries, became a political machine that used tactics of persecution as debased as those used by the Romans in their attempt to stamp out the religion. And as for Islam … ."

The student who had avoided eye contact glanced at him. Why? Chris continued, "Some current scholars of the Koran teach that the prophet Mohammad expressed non-violence, while others hold to the justification of jihad. However, for scholars to insist that original Islam was a peaceful religion is contradictory to its history, for many individuals, even entire cities, were coerced to accept Islam through violent force. Extremists of Islam today are in total opposition to the teaching of non-violence, for they interpret the Koran as promoting the destruction of infidels (that includes anyone who does not convert to Islam)."

The student to his far right had gone from momentary interest to an all-out attempt to keep his dog-drooping eyelids open. His head nodded like a bobblehead in a windstorm. Chris could cross him off the list of suspects.

After a long pause, Chris transitioned from the podium to the side of the room with windows, allowing time for the students' emotions to catch up with his confrontational lecture. He glanced out the window and surveyed the multiple areas from which a sniper could sight his target. Why did he feel so exposed? He had never experienced such before on this peaceful campus.

"And as for Judaism? One of the lofty Ten Commandments is etched in stone. 'Thou shalt not kill.' Yet the conquest and retention of the Promised Land by the Israelites was with such violent acts that it is difficult to comprehend the commandment's intentions. Further, the Jewish religious leaders of Christ's day blatantly acknowledged their disdain for non-Jewish believers, considering Gentiles (defined as those outside the lineage of Abraham and who are nonbelievers in Judaism) as dogs. And it was the Jewish leaders who demanded Christ's crucifixion, not the pagan Romans. Did not Pilate seek an opportunity to release Christ? And his own wife pleaded with him to have no part in Christ's death. But the Jewish leaders prevailed. And what crime did Jesus commit? He did things contrary to their way of thinking; therefore, He was a sinner that deserved to die. These attitudes still exist today—though somewhat masked with political correctness—among the three major religions. Apparently, there are exceptions to the rule. So, my questions to all of you—whether Christian, Jewish, or of the Islam faith—need consideration. How can your religion be right when it has been so wrong in its dealings with your fellow man? Why would I want to become a part of your faith? Why would I want to align myself with religions of such violent pasts? Would anyone venture an answer?" He paused. "No one? Why? Because you don't have a logical explanation."

Chris studied the students' faces, quickly eliminating the females. He looked for the stone-faced sociopath indoctrinated by an imam, or rabbi, or priest. Then again, what about the televangelist who coaxed the last dollars from the widows' checkbooks, monthly, promising untold dividends in return for their seed money. He looked for an angry reaction, a sneer, or just a twitch. The antisocial behavior could be cold and calculated, difficult to detect, but Chris Stone had met them before: and prevailed. He had more at stake this time. It was more than a job; it was personal. He must chop away at the root, challenge the life source. Even the most hardened have an Achilles heel, and he must find it.

"And Judaism, in its conquests of Canaan, seemed but a prelude to the later spread of Islam, when their holy wars dealt with infidels from Asia and across the Middle East and into Africa. Like Judaism in conquering Canaan, the history of Islam is rife with aggression in making converts."

For a Christian seminary, his class included a rather diverse religious body: manifestly overbalanced with those of the Christian faith. He anticipated the smug expressions of those students when he castigated both Judaism and Islam, so he purposefully bore down on those with a cross dangling around their necks.

"And what about Christianity? How many of you are of the Christian faith?" A few raised their hands enthusiastically, while some hesitantly, and at least one, whether on purpose or in a nervous gesture, tucked his cross necklace inside his shirt. "Can anyone justify the slaughter perpetrated by the Crusades?"

Chris paused and scanned the classroom. A couple students in the back seemed to be asleep, while some seemed unattached to history. Most took this class because it was a required subject, so they simply endured. He was mentally dismissing most of them as having any potential for violence. A hand slowly raised.

"Yes, Miss Riley."

"But those you are referencing seem to be extremist, not true believers, whether in Christianity, Judaism, or Islam. The extremist shouldn't be the representatives of the true believers. I don't want them representing me."

"That's a good observation, but perhaps somewhat naive. Let's consider it for a minute. Take Islam, for example. All Islam, no matter what sect, is based upon the teachings of Mohammad. Do you classify him, the founder of Islam, as an extremist?"

"No. Mohammad seemed to be a good man that wanted the world to know God," she said, in defense of the prophet.

"Yet he waged war upon those who rejected Islam. That is extreme and wrong. Don't you think?"

"Well, yes."

"So how can a religion founded by an extremist, who used brutal force to make converts, be a true religion? Why don't all non-violent Muslims reject the prophet?"

"I can't speak for those of the Muslim faith, for I'm a Christian," the student continued. Her tone wasn't argumentative, and she seemed sincere.

It surprised Chris that no one came to her defense, or that none seemed defensive for his faith. He was readily drawing a conclusion, but he continued with the lecture.

"The ongoing strife between the major monotheistic faiths is a key reason to question the validity of the major religions then and now. Did Mohammad truly hear from God? Did the basic truth of the church even survive the second century? When Judaism rejected Christ, did they forfeit their elite status with God? Perhaps it is time all three religions take an inward look at their negative effect upon society, at the destruction they have caused throughout the centuries, and look backward to the father of the monotheistic faiths. Abraham. They need to make a comparison with his faith and theirs. He is exemplary in exhibiting a life of faith, but his faith was without violence."

Chris noticed his statement caused some attentiveness, not visible animosity toward him, just interest in his concept: a world of peace.

"We read of Abraham's journey into the land that Jehovah promised, but Abraham did not take the land by militant force; rather, he waited upon the promises of God to unfold. In the meantime, he lived in peace with his neighbors. He paid a fair price to purchase a burial plot when his wife died. Further, he gave preference to his neighbors in arguments over the use of the land. Ironically, the Christian missionary, Paul, in his letter to the Roman church, expressed that Abraham never received the Promised Land except in faith. He certainly did not take it by force. There is only one biblical reference in Abraham's entire life of him taking up arms. This, however, was a provoked action to rescue a family member, his brother's son, Lot, whom warring tribes had violently taken captive. Otherwise, Abraham lived his entire life extremely nonviolent in dealing with others. I believe all three religions need to revisit this concept of a non-violent faith. In so doing, they might repent for their crimes to humanity committed under the guise of religion."

Chris glanced at the clock hanging on the back wall. His time was up.

"Allow me to conclude. When asked regarding the greatest Commandment, Jesus, the central figure of the Christian faith, quoted from the confession of the Jewish faith: 'Love the God of Abraham with all your being.' Then he proclaimed that the second most important commandment is to "love your neighbor as you love yourself.' How clear! Further, the theme of Jesus' Sermon on the Mount promotes a non-violent lifestyle for believers. Similarly, some scholars of Islam express that the Koran teaches a non-violent lifestyle. If all would genuinely practice the non-violent teachings they proclaim, we could all live in peace with each other. If this had been the practice of the monotheistic faiths in the past, a host of wars would not exist in our history books. If it became the practice of today, numerous wars would cease.

"All three religions trace their existence to one source: The God of a peaceful man by the name of Abraham. All three religions claim allegiance to that singular God of Abraham. So why cannot the three major faiths co-exist without violence against each other? They can disagree without violence. Perhaps our traditions have a far greater influence over our daily decisions than our faith in, and our desire to truly know, the God of our fathers. Class dismissed."

Chris watched as each student filed out of the classroom. These were not extremists, especially not murderers. These were young minds trying to find their way in a complex world. None of these murdered Eden. Detective Trapp was barking up the wrong tree. The murderer was out there somewhere. He must follow his gut feeling, but he knew where that path led. And he knew the danger involved. He would continue his search for the killer. Should he confide in Detective Trapp? He wasn't sure.

Chapter 20

"Thanks for coming down to the station, Professor Stone," Detective Trapp said, as he pulled a chair out from the table and motioned for Chris to sit down.

"I want to do anything I can to help," Chris said, feigning sincerity. He didn't feel right about this meeting. Trapp seemed too eager. Detective Rogers seemed to purposefully busy himself on his computer. Another person, whom Chris had never met, sat across the room, scribbling something on a notepad.

"Scott Davis, Louisville PD," Trapp finally said, nodding at the stranger.

"Professor Stone, glad to meet you but sorry for the circumstances," Davis said, somewhat solemnly.

"You already know Dallas Rogers." Trapp nodded at Rogers.

"Yes, we met at my house the night Eden was killed."

Rogers seemed to avoid eye contact. Chris wondered why. The door opened, and two black-suited men entered the room. Chris knew immediately why the meeting seemed so awkward. These were the Feds. He had lived among them too long not to recognize their confident walk and smug features as they took center stage at the conference table.

Chris did not bother to register the introductions. His mind raced ahead. How could he avoid being arrested without uncovering his secret? What best approach should he take? Why were the big boys called in?

"Professor Chris Stone," the lead officer read from a portfolio, "husband of deceased Eden Stone, murdered in a house bombing. You know why we are here, so we'll cut to the chase and be done with it."

Chris knew the guy was just doing his job, but he still did not like him.

"We know that you are involved in some way with the Santos drug cartel," the federal officer said.

That statement surprised Chris. How did they know, and if they did, why would they be so quick to reveal such involvement? What did they mean by somewhat involved? He started to speak but thought otherwise. Don't redirect them. Hear them out. They might be fishing. On second thought, they are fishing. These fellas are locals with limited resources. They're still a step below the real deal.

"We know that the son of the ringleader met with you a few weeks back, and we also know you gave him ten thousand dollars in cash. We were wondering why a professor of religion would be involved in such odd activity?"

Chris did not answer. He tried to show no emotion.

"We can assume the ten thousand was a down payment for some kind of shipment. Was it religious books, professor?"

The comment drew some smiles, but Chris shook his head at the sarcasm.

"This activity seems strange to us, so we have tried to figure it out," the lead investigator continued. "You carried a huge life insurance policy on your wife, but we were wondering why would you think she might die so young? This all adds up to a bigger deal, a more complex deal. We figure you need a lot of cash for this bigger deal, cash you can't earn on a professor's salary. That is why you conspired with Abdul-Bari Razi and Gamali Hadidi, two Jordanian students, to murder your wife, so you can collect on the million-dollar policy. We also know that you have an offshore account for which you have not offered any explanation. Further, we assume that your dealings with the Jordanians connect you with the Middle East drug trafficking. But you didn't plan on a second murder. Or did you?"

"I don't know what you are talking about. A second murder?" Chris broke his silence.

"A second woman was murdered, all because she was connected in some way with the same two Jordanians. We haven't figured that out just yet, but we will. You can make it easier on yourself if you cooperate now, before we put the puzzle together on our own. Your partners didn't stop with the murder of your wife. Do you know a Sherri Carpenter, professor?"

"No."

The agent suddenly stood, rested his fists on the conference table, and stared down at Chris, his posturing supposedly to be intimidating, but his angry facial expression was absent of the normal flushing and tense veins of real anger. "You're lying, but we'll find the truth on our own, and you're going down with all the things we've got on you."

"We just need you to cooperate with us," the accompanying Fed said in a caring tone. "You be our friend, and we'll be yours."

The good cop, bad cop routine sounded pathetic, though Chris had used it a few times himself. Had he come across as translucent as these guys? He shook his head but did not respond.

The bad cop regained his composure and sat down. He cleared his throat before continuing, stalling to get his bearings. Chris assumed his own counter-tactics had thrown the scripted investigation off course.

The lead investigator finally continued but in a calming manner. "We're not too interested in the Middle East drug trafficking, at least not now. So, since we're trying to bring down the remaining brothers in the Santos clan, we're ready to cut you a deal, Mr. Stone, if … do you mind if I call you Christopher? Or Chris? Which do you prefer?"

"Call me what is comfortable for you. Christopher is okay, Chris … whichever is okay with me. But most professionals I deal with call me Professor Stone." Chris tried to resist the jab, but it slipped out. "I don't need a deal because—"

"Okay, Professor Stone, maybe our deal is not the ideal, but it's better than the alternative." His voice elevated. "Our deal is we're going to let you live if you cooperate."

"Now hold on," Trapp came unglued from his seat. "This man murdered—"

"Our call, Detective." He waved Trapp off and continued. "You'll get used to prison, Chris, for we'll find a nice minimum-security facility for you. And we'll be okay doing that because we'll have a notch on our belts for stopping drugs from crossing the border and killing our youth. You have one chance to get an awfully good deal."

"And if I don't accept your deal?" Chris asked, feigning contemplation of such.

"We're working right now on cutting a deal with the Jordanians, and if we do, we won't need your testimony, and we'll seek the death penalty for you."

"You and I both know they're not involved in any way with the death of my wife, so there's no way they're going to cut a deal with the US government." Chris shook his head in disgust. "You guys are bluffing with a weak hand. You know everything you have is circumstantial at best, and it's unrealistic. No Jordanian students were involved—"

"The Jordanians' testimony isn't circumstantial, Professor Stone," Trapp interrupted, but this time in a tone smothered with compassion for a fellow Hoosier.

"Then what have you offered them to lie? Turn your back on corrupt oil deals?" Chris snapped.

"You'd better listen to Detective Trapp, Professor. He's done a thorough investigation," the head Fed chimed in.

"You're all lying … you … Trapp … the Jordanians—"

"We're not asking them to lie, Professor, but to merely tell the truth about their connection with you. In testifying against you it will save their skin, and it'll save the taxpayers a lot of money an ongoing investigation will cost." The agent was on his feet, a fist on the table and a finger in Chris' face. "We're offering them immunity from prosecution for the murder of not one woman, but two women, both US citizens. Now that we have them in our crosshairs, we'll quickly find traces of their DNA all over the crime scene that happened in your home. They are willing to testify that you hired them to kill your wife. But it doesn't stop there. We have video footage of them kidnapping the second woman. We are going to trace that woman to you also, Professor. You want to deal with us or do you want to die for murder?"

Chris' mind raced. They'd pieced together his meeting with José, and they'd traced his finances. They'd soon realize he'd spent time in Mexico with the Santos family. If he'd just tell them the truth, they would stop the interrogation. But to tell them the truth would expose him to the revenge of his enemies, and he needed to stay alive. To acquiesce to any of the accusations they had made would cost him immediate freedom, for they would arrest him on the slightest admission of connection with the Santos cartel. And his bank accounts were certainly red flags. He had to avoid arrest, for he could not avenge Eden's death behind bars. His best defense at this point was to stall, to call their bluff, to circumvent this immediate danger of arrest. He had no idea how the other woman could be implicated with the death of Eden. That in itself showed they were fabricating their investigation. Right or wrong, he had to made a judgment call.

"You'd best talk to your Jordanian friends," Chris snapped. "This meeting is over unless I'm under arrest." He stood and pushed back his chair, which fell backward and slammed against the hardwood flooring, bouncing onto the foot of the Fed. Now they would probably add assault to the charges.

No one spoke. That moment of silence was all Chris needed. He knew they were bluffing. They had rushed their investigation.

They didn't know the facts; there were too many pieces of the puzzle missing. They had moved forward on too much speculation. He turned and picked up the chair. "Sorry, but no deal." He started toward the doorway but stopped abruptly and turned to face them. He pointed at Trapp. "When you sat in my living room the night of Eden's death, I knew we weren't on the same page, Detective Trapp. But I didn't realize we weren't reading from the same book. If you need to communicate with me again, bring your cuffs and call my lawyer."

They seemed stunned. He had won the first round, but the fight was just beginning; it would be a long battle.

Chapter 21

"I will not, under any circumstances, persuade my son to agree to such an outlandish suggestion." Ja'far Sa'ad Razi waved away the paper Ismail held out to him.

"They have a very strong case against Abdul and his professor, that he conspired with the professor to murder the professor's wife. They're offering a one-time, full immunity for your son if he simply signs this statement that the professor coerced him to commit murder. Some witnesses can put him within miles of the crime scene with a stack of money. They even have video footage of him with another woman who is missing. If you do not agree, your son will be extradited, prosecuted, and convicted of murder. Actually, maybe a double murder. Murder of two young, American, female citizens. What jury in the US would dare let an Arab man have a fair trial?

They want Arab blood, uncle. It could very well be Abdul's that is spilled if you don't comply." Mohammad Ismail pleaded his case.

"This issue is not about fair treatment of an Arab, Ismail, it is about right and wrong. My son says he did not kill the professor's wife and has no idea what the police are talking about. He says the professor and his wife were very good to him. He mourns her death; he mourns for the professor."

"Be reasonable, Ja'far. You thought clearly when you did not allow Abdul to go back to America. Now you must think clearly again. What is best for Abdul? The case against the professor is so strong he will likely be convicted. If you accept the deal, the professor will simply be convicted sooner, and your son will not be a part of any sort of personal attempt at prosecution. If he is innocent, as you say—"

"He is innocent."

"Since he is innocent, as you say, why should he have to go through the ordeal of extradition, an arrest, and a trial? And perhaps a … a false conviction. Just sign the deal and be done with the whole mess and eliminate any danger of a trial. Why would you risk—"

"Because it is the right thing to do."

"And just why is it the right thing to do?"

"The same reason Christ went to the cross," Ja'far said emphatically. "And for the same reason Paul had his head severed from his body. And Joseph was cast into prison. Wicked men do wicked things, and foolish men do foolish things, often at the expense of the innocent. However, the innocent must never resort to lies and deceit to save their own skins. The innocent must sometimes suffer because of the iniquitous. But if we suffer, let it be because we have done what is right, and if we are exonerated, let it not be because we did what was convenient. And only that which is right will prevail in eternity."

"But did not Paul of your Scripture say when in Rome do as the Romans do? Was he not a genius in knowing how to appease the Jewish Christians? When to eat meat and when not to eat meat. Even your Apostle Peter cursed when it was necessary to prove a point. It is a matter of being reasonable, Ja'far, not about being right or wrong." Ismail tried to use the Bible to his advantage.

"Peter also warned that evil men twist the meaning of Scriptures unto their own destruction." Ja'far remained adamant.

"Consider this scenario, Ja'far. What if Gamali Hadidi, Abdul's friend, agrees to the deal? Where does that leave your son? Still a suspect and still open to prosecution, and the deal with Gamali will implicate your son. And a sworn statement by Gamali, but no sworn statement by Abdul, will place Abdul's life in jeopardy."

"I cannot control what Gamali does."

"What if Gamali implicates Abdul? Only he will get a deal, it will be at your son's expense, and you will be the blame for the outcome," Ismail countered. It was a below-the-belt punch that he hoped would jolt Ja'far to acquiesce.

Ja'far paused and studied the golden braid attached to the front of his white robe. "I have already had this conversation with Abdul. We, not I, decided it best for him not to return to the States for his study, not until this crime is solved and his name is cleared. I did not make his decision, I merely counseled him. We have discussed the possibility of such a scenario like this. He has decided for himself. He did not kill anyone. He does not believe his professor killed his wife. He has put his fate in God's hands. If he is extradited, he will simply speak the truth."

"I know how proud you are that Abdul has followed your religious persuasions. I also realize that Abdul desires to please you. Such parental expectations can sometimes blind us to the truth. And such pressure to please can sometimes provoke a child to lie. I hope this is not the case, for if it is, you have rejected the only deal that can save your son."

"The only deal he desires is the one his Lord made for him at Calvary."

"That deal did not save Jesus," Ismail countered.

"But it accomplished what Jesus intended. It saved mankind. And God's gift is extended to all, and that includes you, Ismail."

"I have no need of a dead savior," Ismail said. He closed his briefcase and stood to leave. "You are as stubborn as Abraham. And you threaten your own son's life, just as he did. I pray God will be as merciful to you as He was to him." Ismail had done his job. He was finished, and he was clean of Abdul's blood, whose fate now rested squarely upon the shoulders of his father.

Chapter 22

One phone call changed the game plan. It was a shot in the dark, but the call revealed that Sherri Carpenter may well be alive. Jane Powers gladly agreed to travel with Detective Scott Davis to identify her cousin. Evidently, Sherri had amnesia and couldn't tell the medical personnel in Huntington, West Virginia, who she was or what had happened to her. A trip to West Virginia seemed the quickest way to prove or disprove the identity of Miss Jane Doe. Scott Davis wanted answers to his theory, and he didn't want to wait another day.

Traffic was heavy as they crept along I-64 toward Lexington. Once out of Louisville traffic, Jane's anxiety-level dropped as Davis took to the left lane and basically pushed everyone else to the right as he eased the speedometer to eighty-five and set the cruise.

"I appreciate your helping us out, Ms. Powers." Davis broke the silence.

"It's a long trip, Detective Davis, so you can call me Jane … just not Jane Doe."

"Okay, Jane." He chuckled. The humor did him good. "How long have you known Sherri?"

"Since we were kids. She's my cousin, so we grew up together. I moved away to work in New York right after college. Moved back home two years ago. Sherri never left the area. Lived in Louisville all her life."

"But she worked across the river in Clarksville. Do you know why she took that job?"

"Just a part-time job, a second job. Good girl, Sherri. She wanted to go back and finish her schooling. She worked at St. Matthews also, but you probably already knew that."

"Yes, I did. Found that out in my investigation."

The hum of the tires created a not so melodious tune.

"You a drummer?" She asked.

"Back in the day." He smiled, becoming aware that he was tapping the steering wheel with his thumbs. He'd been a drummer during high school days and never lost the impulse to keep time with the ever-playing tune in his head. "What did you do in New York?" He redirected the attention away from himself.

"Worked as a consultant for a large firm."

"So, you moved back before or after the tragedy?"

"Right after."

"Were you close to the towers?"

"I worked beside the towers. Maybe the thing that saved me was a cold. I called in sick that day. Never curse the darkness, Detective Davis."

"Wow! So you lost friends?"

"Yes." She stared out the window. "After the tragedy, the corporate office transferred me back to the downtown Louisville office … where I met you … the day I reported Sherri missing."

"I couldn't believe my eyes when I first saw—"

"I'm not that ugly, detective, am I?"

"Oh, no … I didn't mean that … what I meant—"

She interrupted him by laughing at her own joke.

"I meant I couldn't believe my eyes when I sat staring at the TV monitor in the office and saw the towers tumble to the ground." Davis slowed for a car in the left lane.

"I'm sorry. I shouldn't tease. It's not something for which joking is appropriate," she said. "I hope I didn't offend you, but lightheartedness somehow helps me cope with the reality of that day."

The conversation ended rather abruptly, for what do you say about such a tragic event? They drove on in silence. Davis remained in the left lane as blinkers flashed and drivers eased into the right lane when they realized an unmarked cruiser rode their bumper. He led a pack of cars that stayed far enough back as not to draw the wrath of a cop, while taking advantage of driving in the passing lane at breakneck speed.

"King of the road, huh," she said. "Do you have any idea how intimidating it is when a police cruiser pulls up behind you on the expressway?"

"That's why we do it." He laughed.

"Really?"

"Now, I'm teasing, Ms. Jane."

She stared out the window at the gorge where the Kentucky River horseshoed around the capitol at Frankfort. The view vanished as a wall of stone appeared on both sides of the expressway. When the road had been built, the bridge crossing the Kentucky River was much lower than the hill adjoining the river on the east side, so workers had to cut deep into the hillside. The incline was still a steep grade, and traffic slowed. As they topped the hill, the cliffs vanished, and picturesque scenes of verdant fields stretched for miles. As they approached Lexington, more and more horses grazed in wooden-fenced pastures that bordered the expressway.

"Isn't Kentucky landscape beautiful?" Davis broke the silence.

"Yes. I missed it when I worked in New York," she said. "Of course, upstate New York is beautiful. And Central Park is almost like a wonder of the world. What awesome planning on someone's part! Though I don't rightly know who had that much foresight. But so many people live there it takes the fun out of it."

"And sometimes a dangerous place," he said, "at least that's how it is in the movies." He chuckled.

"When did you find out about Sherri … if it is her?" Jane asked.

"No more than three hours ago. Right before my office called you. Thanks for going on such short notice. The department owes you one. I owe you."

She did not respond.

"Mind if I turn on some music?" Davis asked.

"Not at all," she said.

It was a slow song, with an extended piano intro. He tapped the steering wheel to the timing. "You know the song?"

"Not really. Not much into music," she said.

"You'll like this one," he said, as Billy Joel began singing *New York State of Mind*. "How ironic is that!" Davis said.

She laughed. "I may go back for a visit someday but never to live."

"I never lived outside Kentucky. Vacationed in a few beautiful places, but I'm always glad to come home to the bluegrass state."

"Family?" Jane asked.

"Parents born and raised near Louisville. Met my wife at U of L. How about you?"

"Large family scattered mostly throughout Kentucky, some in Indiana. Grandparents on my daddy's side moved here from Eastern Kentucky in the fifties. Mother's family has been here as far back as I know. Mind if I crack the window? I'm so anxious, I can barely breathe."

"Sorry, I can turn down the air."

"Thank you." She cracked the window slightly.

They drove on in silence. Jane stared out the window. She finally spoke. "How do you deal with all the crime that goes on all the time … without losing your marbles?"

"I'm usually okay, but I'm finding it difficult to sleep at night … this one has caught my heart … and the Stone murder … you know, the young lady killed in Clarksville. They seem connected."

"And you're hoping Sherri can give you information about the Stone case?"

"Yes, eventually, if she makes it." The words slipped out before his mind engaged.

"What do you mean, if she makes it?"

Scott paused before he answered. "I don't know how to break this to you gently, Jane. The officer who called you, evidently he didn't tell you details."

"Like what?"

"We're not sure Sherri Carpenter … if it is Sherri … will make it. She has been in a coma since they found her. It took them a while to locate the car … it's registered to Sherri, and they finally found it in a deep, West Virginia ravine. We assume it is Sherri in the hospital since it's her car they found, but someone could have stolen the car. So that is why I needed you to come along … to identify her … if it is Sherri."

"No, he didn't tell me any of that. I just thought she had some kind of amnesia." Tears coursed her cheeks, she looked away and wiped at them with the back of her hand.

Davis reached into the glove box and retrieved a handful of McDonald's napkins and handed them to her. That was the best he could do, for words seemed inadequate at this time.

Chapter 23

Juan Santos made the cross-country trip in three days, probably less if he hadn't spent a few hours in Vegas. He took I-15 north out of Vegas, headed east on I-70 in Utah, took the southern loop around St. Louis, where he picked up I-64 toward Louisville. The weather cooperated, so he made excellent time on his cycle, taking naps at rest areas along the way. He missed the I-265 loop at New Albany and crossed the Ohio River into downtown Louisville by mistake, so he crossed the river back into Indiana via the I-65 Kennedy Memorial Bridge. The Holiday Inn in Clarksville was a welcomed sight, where he registered under a fictitious name.

His assignment was specific: either confirm the gringo is already dead, or else finish the job and skip town immediately. He was given no details regarding how to accomplish the assignment. That pleased Juan.

A long, hot bath, followed by a tepid shower, refreshed him. He decided to keep his three-day beard for identity protection. He would resume his clean-shaven look after he completed the assignment. His plans were basic: a good night's sleep and start his surveillance before dawn. He unpacked his Canon EOS Rebel camera with its EF-S zoom lens and laid it on the bed. He then removed his Kel-Tec P32 automatic pistol from a concealed compartment in the bottom of the camera case. He walked to the bathroom and retrieved a small, glass bottle from his shaving kit. It contained a clear liquid of sulfuric acid of which he poured a small amount into a drinking glass and mixed in a little water. The combined liquids reacted instantly, as if boiling. A splash on his hand stung immediately.

His initial contribution to the Santos family was his degree in chemistry. From college, Chico assigned him to their laboratory, where he focused on drug manufacturing. With an evil yet calm nature, he rose quickly within the ranks of the family. Being a Santos family member, and because of his loyalty, he had become a trusted protector of the immediate family. And because they had been so kind to him, he became a terminator of the family's enemies: one they could trust to get the job done. He was an expert in improvised explosive devices. They should have sent him on this assignment in the first place, instead of his no-good cousin, Carlos.

A host of common household chemicals can be used to create IEDs. One of Juan's favorites was sulfuric acid, and he had used it on several occasions, mainly as a means of deterrence for would be enemies: news traveled fast in the underworld regarding his victims. The acid was cheap, easy to acquire, and cleaned up nicely: just add water, but slowly.

Though sulfuric acid is considered a pollutant, it's a common household product found in soaps and detergents. Further, it is used as a preservative for fruits and vegetables. Though few could imagine, it is the bleaching agent in flour. He smirked and shook his head as he considered the household uses. If only the consumers knew, there'd be an outcry. This common chemical had become his lethal weapon. His illegal actions on society were swift and sure; in contrast, the manufacturers' legal harm to unsuspecting customers was slow and undetected. Both his illegal activities and their legal actions played a toll on society. His swift and sure method of damage had only harmed a few people. Ironically, hundreds of thousands of customers have been affected adversely—only God knows to what extent—by the manufacturer using this lethal chemical in small quantities in and on their products. He disfigured a face or put out an eye of a few who were a menace to society, but cancer effected lives indiscriminately and attacked the innocent masses. The screams and a few disfigured faces still haunted him in dreams, so he sought ways to justify his actions. The time and energy he spent in confession booths didn't sooth his conscience, though he'd followed the priests' directives for atonement. And he didn't trust psychologists, for they played with your mind. He had narrowed his options for emotional help.

Concentrated sulfuric acid, when coming into contact with the moisture on the human body, can do severe damage to the skin, as its temperature instantly rises to a boiling point. When it mixes with the water contained on the surface of the eyes, it quickly burns the tissue, causing blindness. It is similar to the burning sensation one gets when peeling an onion, but the pain and harm is on a much more severe scale. The gases in an onion, released while being peeled, mixes with the water on the eye surface and produces a small amount of sulfuric acid that causes the eye to burn. Concentrated sulfuric acid tossed into the eyes of one's enemy increases the pain and damage multiple times over.

Juan withdrew a small, high-tech water pistol from his satchel, unscrewed a cap from the handle, and delicately poured some of the sulfuric acid from the bottle into the opening in the handle. He screwed the lid back on, aimed the pistol into the sink, and pulled the trigger. The acid shot from the pistol into the sink. It worked perfectly. He wiped the gun clean with a washcloth, placed it on the night-stand beside his real pistol, and tossed the washcloth into the waste can. On second thought, he retrieved the washcloth and stuck it inside his satchel. He was a stickler for leaving a clean crime scene.

The digital clock on the nightstand flashed 8:30 pm, and though daylight still peeped through the partially-closed venetian blinds, he felt extremely tired. He had slept little the past three days. He pulled back the bed covers and inspected the sheets before climbing into bed and turning out the light.

For a long while, Juan stared into the darkness. Luis Héctor Santos had once again entrusted him with a top assignment: another chance to climb in the family organization. He must not fail. He mentally rehearsed the plan: the street address, the prepared route retrieved from MapQuest, and the manner of attack. He was eager for this assignment. It was more than for the family: it was personal.

Chapter 24

Christopher Stone's circle of friends had definitely shrunk, primarily because he had no desire to engage in social events. Since Eden's death, his only guests were mostly those working on the investigation. He had made a few trips to see his father, but other than that and going to work, he mostly stayed home. Neighbors respected his privacy, for they appeared to understand his need to mourn. In what seemed like ages ago, he and Eden had enjoyed working alongside each other in their yard, as she mostly charmed the neighbors with her kindness. Since then he had become somewhat a hermit, for he no longer enjoyed the yard work: it had become just another chore.

Further, he withdrew because he tired of answering the same question: "How are you doing?" He also tired of the unmarked police cars that parked in various locations up and down his street: a couple neighbors were his unofficial informants, for they were curious as to why these stakeouts persisted. Shopworn of offering explanations, hibernation became his modus operandi.

He stepped onto the front porch and lingered in the morning sun, soaking in its warmth. A black sedan, tinted windows, parked half a block away, stuck out like a sore thumb among the otherwise family vehicles parked in driveways. He assumed it was an unmarked cruiser. The Feds or Clarksville Police Department? He wasn't sure, nor did he care.

A neighbor's cat scampered off his porch, startling him. He studied its retreat tactics, wondering which house it would claim. His Courier-Journal had landed again in the holly bush by the steps. He was almost certain the paper-boy aimed at the bush on purpose, knowing the prickly leaves could do damage to an intruder's hand. The Courier was the area's largest newspaper, and it served both Louisville and southern Indiana. Overwhelmed by the multiple articles regarding Eden's death, with hints that he was a suspect, he considered canceling his subscription. Why pay for his own defamation of character? He knew he was overreacting, but still, he wanted his privacy back.

He heard the motorcycle a good way off before it reached him, so he could tell it was traveling at a slow rate of speed. Chris waved to the driver as if he knew him, even though a shaded visor of the helmet concealed the face. He could recall only one neighbor having a motorcycle, a Harley, so the black Kawasaki was new to the area. The stranger returned his wave with a thumbs-up, and Chris extended a smile to the unknown biker. Southern Indiana folks were close enough to Kentucky that "friendliness" was next to godliness as much so as the proverbial "cleanliness." The only difference between Kentuckians and southern Hoosiers was a river that divided their properties. Most folks in southern Indiana had come from the Kentucky side of the river seeking employment, or they were the descendants of someone who had crossed before them.

Southern Hoosiers were split in their loyalties, and many rooted for the UK Wildcats instead of the rival team in Bloomington. Adolph Rupp had made basketball the sport of choice in Kentucky, and it made him a legend. Though the legendary coach lagged behind IU's Bobby Knight in wins, the twenty-three thousand plus seat Rupp Arena had enshrined Adolph Rupp forever in the hearts of the fans. And he wasn't fired; rather, he was forced into retirement after forty-one years of coaching—because of a mandatory seventy-year-old retirement rule for the college's faculty. Assembly Hall in Bloomington had soon forgotten its legend and moved on. In the eight-year span since Bob Knight left, they had gone through three coaches. The current Tom Crean held some promise for a comeback to days of glory, but his style as a fast break coach had not won him many games, for he was working with a depleted roster. But Indiana was known for its basketball, and Crean was a recruiter. Perhaps there were better days ahead.

Chris did his best to blend in with the community. He purchased a UK cap and an IU cap. But he did not necessarily root for either in private. And he abhorred the Kinsey Institute at the IU campus. He was convinced Alfred Kinsey was a fraud whose faulty research on human sexuality should have been tossed in the trash years ago. For some reason IU administration saw it differently, and for Chris, that was to their discredit as a research school.

The motorcycle did a slow U-turn, pulled in front of Chris' house, and stopped. The rider cut the engine, engaged the kickstand, and lifted a leg over the handlebars to disembark.

"Good morning," he said, as he took off his helmet, balanced it atop the seat, and retrieved a pair of dark-shaded sunglasses from his side-satchel.

Chris detected a somewhat camouflaged Latino accent, and his features underneath the facial hair were obviously Latino, something that had become surprisingly commonplace in the area.

The Hispanic community in Louisville had swelled to around twenty-thousand. In a city known for horse racing, baseball bats, and bourbon, it had more recently become a haven for immigrants from Cuba. This group made up a high percentage of the Spanish speaking community.

"Wondering if you could give a lost fella some directions," the stranger said, ever so politely.

"I'll certainly try," Chris said, as he walked toward the street. "Where do you need to go?"

"I have the address right here." He pulled a folded paper from his shirt pocket and handed it toward Chris.

As Chris reached for the paper, it slipped from the man's hand. Chris stooped and picked it up, but when he stood, the stranger held a small revolver aimed at his face.

"Hello, *amigo*," a familiar voice said. "Long time no see."

Chris knew immediately who it was, but too late, and before he could react, he saw Juan pull the trigger, immediately sending excruciating pain into both his eyes. He involuntarily cried out in agony, fell to his knees, and rubbed his clinched eyes with both hands.

From a distance, someone yelled. "Police! Stop!"

Retreating footsteps stopped with the revving of the Kawasaki, more shouting, and a single gunshot. The unmistakable sound of a crash ended with the cycle skidding across the pavement and clanging into a car. The engine sputtered into silence, followed by a moan, a volley of commands, and a string of cursing.

The pain in Chris' eyes dulled any concern that would have been a normal response of the ensuing scene around him. He endured his solo battle with pain, much aware of what had just transpired. Footsteps made their way toward him. In the midst of the pandemonium, he mentally berated himself for allowing this to happen, then again, perhaps this would end it all. He braced himself for another attack, feebly fighting off the invisible attacker. A hand touched his shoulder. He knocked it away, slapping indiscriminately at the air.

"Professor Stone, I'm a policeman. I'm not going to harm you."

Chris involuntarily grabbed the officer's hands as he touched his face.

"I need to examine your wounds," the officer pleaded.

Chris did not respond to his directions but continued to grip the officer's hands.

"It's okay, Professor. I'm a policeman. Can you hear me?"

"Yes!" He gritted his teeth in pain. "I hear you … but the pain … ."

"Did he throw something into your eyes?

"Yes, he … he squirted … some kind of acid … both eyes."

"May I check?"

"No, they're burning like fire," he screamed and squeezed the officer's hands tighter. "Call an ambulance, please … please … ." Chris tried to envision the activity around him, make out the conversations, wondering if Juan got away, but the pain blocked all other senses. He collapsed onto the pavement, fought against the urge to scream, and wished it could all end.

Chapter 25

In an introductory to psychology class, Chris had studied Elisabeth Kubler Ross' stages of grief in dealing with death. He had definitely experienced the symptoms when his mother passed, but with the passing of Eden, the stages seemed all garbled, like something had gone wrong with what should have been predictable stages. He knew he was emotionally out of whack, but he just didn't care anymore, and even if he cared, he didn't know what to do about it.

When his mother died, he had college to occupy his mind, and so it seemed a linear path took him through denial, anger, bargaining, depression, and ultimately to acceptance of her death. In dealing with his mother's death, he didn't fight against Mrs. Ross' philosophy regarding accepting death, and he readily accepted what he felt was the inevitable: life followed death. And his faith in God was still in tack back then, though his attendance at the synagogue had tapered off drastically. She had lived a long life and believed in life after death, so her attitude toward death brought him an element of comfort and strength. And his concern for his father's loss somewhat lessened his personal grief. In fact, Chris was a bit surprised how difficult things became for his father who had always been a tower of strength to him. Chris was beginning to see things clearer regarding his father's dealing with death and why he had moved to a new location and started over.

With Eden's death, Chris seemed to leap over denial and straight into anger. And that anger had kept him going strong. And it lingered. He refused anything other than anger. It became his friend and inspired him during the long, sleepless nights. Anger greeted him with each dawning morning. It motivated him throughout the day and kept him on the job for long hours. Busyness became his antidote for loneliness, and anger fed his busyness. Though his faith was in shambles, he sometimes found himself talking with God, other times screaming at God, and mostly questioning God. God did not answer. Not one word. He debated God's existence, since his prayers went unanswered, but then again, perhaps God did not align Himself with man's desire for vengeance. Were such thoughts some form of Ross' bargaining stage? If so, he was a long way from acceptance of Eden's death.

Lately, it seemed his blindness had caused his anger to subside, but he was not sure that was progress, for another emotion had supplanted the anger: despair. It became apparent to him that the stages of grief were not necessarily linear; instead, for him they were more like a pinball, bouncing around, not knowing what the next stage might be. He wanted the anger back, for it gave him reason to go on living. But all seemed hopeless, for, in his darkened world, life was a struggle to maneuver across the room, let alone avenge an enemy. He had no reason to get out of bed, and sleep was his only escape from the dull emotions that held him captive and made life meaningless. He wanted to die, but something within held him back. He could not pinpoint what that something was that kept him going. Was it the teaching of the rabbi echoing in his head, or the Sabbath prayers of his mother, whose faith in God never wavered?

Her mother, as a child, had lost everything at the hands of Hitler's deranged henchmen, that is, everything except her faith in God. She passed that faith to her only child, his mother. "*Gam meh yaavor,*" she often quoted, in times of difficulty. "This too shall pass." The phrase was made popular in English literature by Edward Fitzgerald in one of his poems, but the folklore actually had Jewish roots, for scholars attributed the saying to the wise King Solomon. Though many use the phrase as one of blessing (the bad shall eventually give way to good), it was originally intended to be more inclusive, for even the most joyous of times will also come to an end. This too shall pass, both the times of sorrow and the times of bliss. Job of old somewhat had a handle on the two. He proclaimed, "If I accept God's blessing, shall I not graciously accept His burden?"

Chris reflected upon a sermon he had heard at the synagogue. The rabbi described life as being like a set of train tracks. One track represents the good happening in your life, while the other represents the bad. The two always run parallel. You don't have the one without the other, but together, if you stay on track, they lead you to your destination. And that is where you find God.

Solomon certainly embraced a more balanced meaning of "this too shall pass" when he wrote, "To every thing there is a season, and a time to every purpose under the heaven: a time to be born and a time to die … ."

Why death? Why would a loving God allow death? Especially to the innocent like Eden. She had never made an enemy in her life, yet someone viciously snuffed out her life. With this thought, anger immediately resurfaced, but this time, it was God's seemingly absence that was its target. Why had not God intervened? But something else dawned with the idea that God was absent in his plight. If he was angry at God for being absent, then his belief in God's existence had not entirely stopped. He was still a believer, though ever so detached from God, but he was an angry believer. But how could he believe in God and still have no hope, no reason to go on, no desire to go on? Wasn't that God's job? To give hope.

He scratched at the whiskers on his chin and ran his fingers through his thick, wavy hair, dismayed at the oil his hair produced.

Wiping his hands on his robe, he wondered aloud what Eden would think of him. "I'm sorry, dear, it's just that I … ." Could she see him? Hear him? He hoped she could not. He had smashed the mirror in the bathroom and had not bothered to get it fixed. Nothing mattered, so why go to the bother of trying to fix things. A neighbor offered to clean his house, but he had declined her kindness. He didn't want pity from anyone.

The local jail held his nemesis, Juan, without bail. The court perceived him as a flight risk, but even that brought Chris no consolation. Nor was he angry at Chico Santos, though he was sure he had ordered the hit on him. Juan would not have acted on his own. It was planned, probably from the day he saw the Santos cartel member at the racetrack. They had found him, and he understood their anger toward himself, but were they also responsible for Eden's death? Surely, they would not have purposefully killed her, and evidently, they had not figured out the details. Did they even know they had killed his wife? Was Eden simply what they considered collateral damage: the wrong person at the wrong place at the wrong time.

Some details of the bombing still troubled him, but mostly details eluded him. He relieved the scene a thousand times, straining for the truth, wondering if he could have prevented it. Did he leave the door unlocked? Did they enter an unlocked window? But he knew those were ridiculous questions, for an assassin could gain entrance and leave without detection. He remembered kissing Eden goodnight as she sat in the living room crocheting. It was a hobby she had taken up, having taught herself from courses available on the Internet. It gave her something to do in her alone time, while he lectured at the seminary. She made a dozen baby-booties before she was pleased enough to keep one. "For our first child," she said, as she held up the blue booties for him to admire. "What if it's a girl," he had challenged. "It will be a boy. I can tell," she had assured him.

He could not remember where he had stored her crocheting tools, nor any of the items she had made. But that did not matter now, for all was lost. There would never be a child.

Why would anyone kill Eden? If the bombing had been a Santos attack, he was the intended target. He had seen their butchery first hand. Who else would have reason to kill him? Perhaps he had made more enemies than he realized.

He had kept all her clothes, and he often retrieved the hat she had worn at the racetrack and held it to his heart. The fragrance still lingered: Angel, that was her favorite. This gave him some sense of comfort, but the ache in his heart never diminished. It remained a dull pressure that sometimes created a moan of despair. Such groans were a soul-deep, desperate effort to change the past, a fruitless quest to wake up from a nightmare of hopelessness into the life he once relished with Eden. Eden, the garden of God. She was his paradise. Was this how Adam felt after the expulsion from the garden, always trying to rewind the picture and make it play out differently? Adam was never able to do so. Nor was he. How long could he go on trying before something snapped inside?

Chapter 26

Abdul, accompanied by his father and Ismail, landed at the Louisville International Airport and went straight to the office of a criminal defense lawyer Ismail had retained. Paul Palmer with *Roberts, Hall, and Palmer* had argued cases all the way to the Supreme Court, and his success rate was impressive. Further, he was noted for his defense in civil rights cases. Plus, he was a practicing Christian, something Ja'far had insisted upon, contrary, of course, to Ismail's advice. "Get an attorney who isn't bound by moral convictions," Ismail had argued. "Lying is justified in self-defense, a part of the American Constitution, the right not to incriminate oneself. Your Christian lawyer will sell you down the road on some moral technicality." But Ja'far simply reminded him of Abdul's innocence and that God would protect him, something of which Ismail seemed unconvinced.

The *Roberts, Hall, and Palmer* offices are located in a refurbished building around the corner from downtown Louisville's historic Whiskey Row. The offices occupy the top two floors. A receptionist led them into an exceptionally-large conference room where a massive, mahogany table surrounded with eighteen high-back chairs made a favorable first impression. A wall of glass twelve feet tall allowed for a spectacular view of the Ohio River with the Falls of the Ohio visible to the northwest. The city of Clarksville, home to Indiana's historic Colgate Clock, faced them from across the river.

"Quite an impressive timepiece," Ismail said, pointing at the clock.

"Yes," the receptionist answered. Her face emulated an I'm-glad-you-noticed smile, whereupon she entered into a monologue of the clock's history.

The clock, located in front of the former Colgate-Palmolive factory, owns claim to being one of the largest clocks in the world. The factory had originally been an Indiana State prison, but after a fire in 1919, the state officials determined it too costly to restore the building as a prison. So, the state sold the facility to the expanding soap company. Prior to the transition, the prison inmates worked on the restoration by day and slept in their cells by night. They were eventually transferred to a new prison facility in Pendleton, Indiana, a small town northeast of Indianapolis, much more centralized than the extreme southern location of the Clarksville facility.

Colgate moved the clock from their Jersey City, New Jersey, plant in 1924, and it has been showing the time ever sense for locals as far as a mile away. The world renown company, with hundreds of properties in North America and elsewhere, recently abandoned the local facility and moved the operations to Tennessee and Mexico. The Historic Landmarks Foundation of Indiana placed the building on their endangered landmarks list, but Colgate refuses to place the facility on the National Register of Historic Places, making the building and the clock's future uncertain.

Double side-doors to the conference room opened and three men entered. The first one extended a hand. "Good morning, gentlemen. Paul Palmer. My associates." He motioned toward the two others, much younger than he. "Sorry to keep you waiting, but I was on the phone with Steve Beshear." When no one commented, he added, "Governor Beshear … at the state house."

After introductions, they got down to business. Ismail related the same information he had previously shared by email, with interruptions from Ja'far and corroborated by Abdul. Palmer's associates took notes.

After an hour of back and forth dialog, Palmer stood. "I have spoken with the investigative officers and have requested information on their investigation. They are reluctant to share their case at this time, but I believe that is a good thing. This is not a slam dunk, as we say here in basketball country, but you were absolutely right in not accepting the deal offered by the Feds. They are simply tossing around threats and pleas because they are convinced the professor murdered his wife. They may try to implicate Abdul in the murder, but with the timeline of events, the need for a motive, and the fact that money was not the slightest motive for Abdul to get involved in a murder scheme, they don't have a case. And a more recent event, the attack on the professor by a member of a drug ring, makes me think that Abdul will be eliminated as a suspect within a matter of time—"

"Professor Stone, was attacked? Was he killed?" Abdul asked. The tone in his words reflected his deep respect for the professor.

"Yes, he was attacked, but no, he was not killed. However, the attack places grave suspicion that he is involved in some sort of drug deal gone bad. One of the investigators mentioned a son of the Santos family cartel visited him some time back… ." Palmer paused and turned his gaze toward the window. A tugboat slowly churned at the water, leaving a massive wake behind, as it pushed upstream four barges lashed to its bow. "That visit by the Santos fellow was right before the murder. Now, after the murder, he is attacked by another Santos member."

"So how is Professor Stone doing?" Abdul asked.

"He is well other than the attack left him blind."

"I must go to him, Father," Abdul pleaded.

Ja'far looked at Ismail and then at Palmer. "What do you think?"

"Not a good idea," Ismail said. "Stay far from the skunk, or you might get sprayed."

"Mr. Palmer, what do you advise?" Ja'far asked.

"I see Ismail's point. At this time, we are not sure about the professor's innocence or guilt, so—"

"I must see him, Father," Abdul pleaded.

"It may not be the right thing to do from a … a logistical viewpoint … or it may not be the legally prudent thing to do, but it is the Christian thing to do," Ja'far said.

"It was Christ who proclaimed, 'I was in prison, and you visited me not.' Will not Jesus challenge us on judgment day for such neglect?" Abdul added.

The room grew silent. Palmer's associates stared at him, awaiting his response.

"You are a practicing Christian, no, Mr. Palmer?" Ja'far broke the tense silence.

"Yes, I am a Christian," Palmer said.

"Then for a moment, if you would please, just for a moment, lay aside your books of law and what you know about the legal system in America and answer the question only from your perspective as a Christian. What should we do?" Ja'far reached across the table and placed his hand on that of Palmer. "What would Christ do?"

Palmer took Ja'far's hand in both of his, pursed his lips for a few moments before responding, prefaced by a deep breath which he slowly released. "As a Christian, I must say that your son is right. It is the Christian thing to do."

"Against my objections," Ismail said, as he pushed his chair backward and walked to the window as if to reflect upon his thoughts, but the disgust on his face reflected off the window.

"Then we will do the Christian thing," Ja'far said. He rose from his seat and extended a hand across the table to each of the attorneys. "Thank you for your time. We are finished for today. I must rest from the long journey." He slightly bowed his head and turned to leave.

"Mr. Razi, one more thing before you leave," Palmer said.

Ja'far turned to face Palmer. "And that is?"

"Your son is innocent. I now know that, and I will do everything within my power to defend him."

"Thank you, sir." Ja'far again bowed his head.

"Mr. Palmer, you are an influential man in this community, no?" Ismail said.

"Well, I know a few—"

"Then make sure the soap company does not destroy that magnificent clock across the river. That is a historic landmark that needs to be preserved. Does not your Bible say something about not removing the ancient landmarks?" Ismail smiled for the first time since the meeting.

"Indeed, it does, sir. I'll see what I can do about that."

Chapter 27

Courier-Journal headlines first broke the news to the public. The Kentuckiana joint-crime investigation of Eden Stone's murder had begun to unravel from the neatly woven case they had built around supposition and assumption. An Arab family had hired one of the largest law firms in the area to represent their son, who turned out to be innocent. Sherri Carpenter's abduction and possible murder—to hide her suspicion toward two suspected Arab assassins—turned out to be way off target. She had been found unconscious on the brim of I-64 in West Virginia, identified by her cousin, had recently recovered from her coma, and had given the full account of the night of her disappearance. Her story blew a hole in the waterline of one of the investigation team flotilla's primary frigates: she had not been kidnapped by two Arab university students. To the contrary, their car had broken down at St. Matthews Mall. They were about to miss their flight, so they needed to call a taxi. Sherri Carpenter was using the phone booth they desperately needed to call a taxi, so when they recognized her from the Applebee's Bar and Grill where she worked part-time as a waiter, they graciously offered her two Benjamin Franklin bills to drive them to the airport. The unexpected money made it possible for an unplanned visit to see her ailing grandma in West Virginia. Sadly, the late-night trip ended in a near fatality. She was still recuperating in the Huntington Hospital in West Virginia, with a favorable prognosis. Her recovery from the coma had necessitated another trip by Detective Davis, and Jane Powers again accompanied him on the trip as a calming face for the investigation.

Sherri Carpenter's story had taken a one-eighty turn from the phone call she had made incognito. Her initial suspicions had been completely wrong, and her chance meeting with them at St. Matthews had proven so. She had found the two men to be cordial and very calm other than their anxiety over being about to miss their plane and their excitement about going home for a few days. They showed no indication of fleeing a crime and even offered an explanation as to why they were in Clarksville the night of the murder. They were shopping in the Green Tree Mall at Dillards. With further investigation, the video camera at Dillards showed the two suspected students in the men's department at the proposed time of the murder. A male clerk identified their picture as the two men for which he had made a phone call to the Dillard's at St. Matthews to affirm they had particular sizes in their line of Gold Label shirts, the sizes requested by the two suspected students. A clerk at St. Matthews Mall identified a picture of the two students as the same two who had purchased shirts, minutes before the video footage of them at the phone booth.

Detective Tony Trapp slammed the newspaper onto his desktop. "This makes us look like the Gestapo," he shouted.

He was the one who had to make the phone call to attorney Mohammad Ismail Hajbi, explaining that his client was no longer under investigation. He was careful to include that it was his department's detailed investigation that had exonerated Ismail's client. He had to endure the tirade of threats that ensued, but he was used to such. He had endured half-a-dozen lawsuits in his lifetime, so he was accustomed to that. What bothered him the most was that he had traveled too far down a dead-end street on this investigation, and he knew that lost time meant lost and distorted evidence. He did not want this case to end up in some cold case file, a file that would have his fingerprints all over it. And it bugged him to no end that Professor Christopher Stone might walk completely free, when he knew deep down that Stone was in some way responsible for the death of his wife. Maybe not murder, but he was into something criminal that caused her murder. There were too many trails that led from the professor's doorsteps to those of the Santos' empire. Trapp just couldn't connect the dots, but he would keep trying.

The Feds had to backpedal with the Jordanian officials regarding their push for extradition, or a plea bargain with a Jordanian citizen, but they offered no explanation other than they were dropping their investigation. An official letter that followed did use the words "sorry, inconvenience, and kindest regards," but there was no admittance of any wrongdoing whatsoever toward the Jordanian citizens. And a copy of the report that landed on Trapp's desk hinted of the local authorities misleading the federal investigators: the local authorities, of course, would be him.

Trapp was convinced the Professor was the sole target of an assassination attempt, evidently by the Santos cartel, and he did not think the wife's murder was a part of the plan. She was truly collateral damage. But why did they want the professor dead? The answer to that question would probably be reason enough for Stone to be guilty of something, and Stones' guilt of something else was reason enough for him to journey down that path. The second attack on Chris Stone left Trapp with a bit of consternation. Why did the hitman blind Stone instead of killing him?

Trapp did not like to admit that he was wrong, but it gave him some pleasure that Stone may well not have murdered his wife. He didn't necessarily like the guy, but there was something about Stone that he admired. He had not bowed against their intense pressure. Trapp's department had thrown a lot of pitches at him, but he refused to flinch at the plate. He had guts, but then again, so do psychopaths. As much as he hated to admit it, Stone could—by some stretch of the imagination—be innocent, but Trapp's job was not to prove a suspect innocent; rather, he was to prove someone guilty. And he wasn't near ready to wash his hands of the professor, for some things just did not compute. Too much unaccounted-for money flowed through his hands. There was a crime somewhere, perhaps deep in his past, and he had to be dirty, for too much filthy lucre had his prints on it.

Trapp reflected that he once spent an entire Christmas holiday trying to put together a five-thousand-piece puzzle, only to find in the end that the puzzle, from the factory, consisted of two different scenes: both outdoor scenes, but they were two different landscapes. Was it a mechanical accident? Highly unlikely. Did someone purposefully create the ruse? Probably. The longer he considered that puzzle, the more something about Christopher Stone troubled him. He was a Melchizedek conundrum: without father or mother. It was as if he wasn't, and then he was. He had almost mysteriously appeared in Clarksville without a documented past: a red flag at best. The man not only had no relatives in the Clarksville area, he had no known living relatives anywhere. There are few explanations for that, but he was unsure of what to suspect him. The options were limited.

It seemed obvious that the Santos family hated Christopher Stone. Why? Juan Santos was not talking. Fernándo Leoncio Santos, the *Capos* of the Santos cartel was insulated from any wrongdoing by the prison walls that confined him. He was closely monitored, but nothing associated with criminal activity had been documented, though observations of his visitors were carefully scrutinized. The hit was probably approved by the Santos' lieutenant, Luis Héctor Santos, the only surviving brother not in prison, and who had recently visited the prison. The Santos cartel had all but dissembled a few years back when the CIA somehow got an informant into the organization. But was that recent visit to the prison an indication the cartel was back in business?

The one question that plagued Trapp—during the long hours of sleepless nights—remained unanswered. What was Christopher Stones' association with the Santos organization? Friend or foe? A friend turned foe seemed more likely a logical explanation.

The detective sat in his office staring at an enlarged photograph of Christopher Stone, another of the charred body of Eden Stone, and one of Mrs. Stone from the recent running of the derby. Stone had given the department the photograph at their request. The photograph needed to be returned to him. That would give Trapp cause for another visit without suspicion of it being an interrogation.

"Rogers?" He called into the common office area.

"Yes, sir."

"Come in here."

Trapp repeatedly clicked the top of an ink pen with his thumb, an unconscious maneuver he did while he contemplated the unknown. "We don't know Christopher Stone."

"Uh … sure we do, sir, he—"

"That wasn't a question, Rogers, that was a statement. We've approached this entire investigation like school-kids accepting whatever the teacher says. We haven't challenged the obvious; we've simply accepted it. We've believed everything the computer spits out about Christopher Stone without checking its source. But the Internet only spits out what someone has put in. We've never personally interviewed anyone that knew him five years ago. Where did this man come from? What did he do for a living before he came to Clarksville? Have we showed a picture of this man to anyone who was supposed to have known him before he became a professor at the seminary?"

"No, sir, we have not."

"Then it's time we do so. Get on it right away. Find out everything you can about Christopher Stone before he moved here. And you know what?"

"Can't say that I do."

"You're gonna find that Christopher Stone didn't exist five years ago, at least not the Christopher Stone that matches this picture."

"An illegal?"

"That's one option, but it's not the only one."

"The witness protection program?" Rogers asked.

"That's a possibility, Rogers. But I doubt that's the case. He just doesn't fit the profile … too many red flags of questionable activity."

Trapp tossed his pen onto the desk. "He could have stopped this investigation weeks ago by simply telling us he was in some sort of protective program. So why didn't he? That rules out the witness program … don't you think?"

"Seems to. Why not talk to the Feds?"

"Might as well ask this pen." Trapp stared at the pen as if he might just ask it. "He's illegal, probably true Spanish descent, especially by the looks of him … kind of … I see a conquistador physique." He studied the picture. "Don't you think so?"

"Could be," Rogers answered.

"And he's probably tied in with Mexican drugs coming over the border. I think he's on the payroll of a rival of the Santos clan. But if we bring in the Feds, he'll be shipped off to a federal holding camp and maybe even shipped back across the border. We need to nail him before the fact. If he's in the witness program, they're tight as a drum about their informants, so they're not going to admit anything, at least to us small town cops. We're going to have to figure this out on our own or it'll become a cold case on our books. I don't like that."

"Where's our evidence?" Rogers asked.

"The money transfers. Follow the money, and it'll lead us to the door of Mr. Stone's past."

"So, the money transfers into his account are probably drug related, you think?" Rogers, true to his style, made his point with a question.

"Probably drugs," Trapp said. "And God knows we don't need his kind around southern Indiana. We have too many kids overdosing already."

"Or, maybe he could be on the Federal payroll?" Rogers made another statement with a question. "An undercover cop for the Feds right here in our own backyard and us not told?"

"I'd say he's illegal." Trapp seemed to ignore Rogers. "Not your typical Mexican illegal, and like I said, he's more of true Spanish descent … darker complexion … black, wavy hair—"

"You really think so?" Rogers asked.

"I'm not sure, Rogers. Just thinking out loud. We need to leave all options on the table."

"But if it's the witness protection program or an undercover cop, why doesn't Stone tell us? That leads me to believe he may be a rival of the Santos' cartel. Don't you think?" Rogers asked.

"Not sure, Rogers, but we'll find out. One thing still troubles me regarding him being a rival of the Santos cartel, and I'm … ." His words trailed off and he went back to clicking his pen.

"The money he paid to the young Santos?" Rogers seemed pleased with his remembrance of that one detail.

"Yes. Why would he write a check to a Santos if he was their enemy? And something else. What is the other organization in Mexico that he sent money to every month? Did we find out?"

"No, it dead-ends at the post office. The police down there aren't inclined to find out for us, and I can't find a person in their postal department that speaks English. But if you want me to research further, I'm on it."

"Yes, please do. And one more thing. Find out who signed the checks. Christopher Stone or his wife?" He picked up the photo of Eden Stone and studied the small diamond-studded cross that hung over her creme-colored top. The light-colored dress accentuated her almond complexion. Was she of Hispanic descent? Why was she clutching it in her hand the night of the bombing? That was probably the only reason it survived the blast unharmed. He tossed the picture onto the desk, picked up his pen, and spun it on the desk as if it was a top.

Turning to his computer, Trapp pulled up the obituary of Mrs. Stone and slowly read the details: age, date of death, wife of Christopher Stone who survives, officiating clergyman, and place of internment, but no mention of any living relatives. No father. No mother. No siblings. Why?

He picked up his ink-pen and made some notations, then settled into the incessant clicking of the pen. Something was definitely amiss. And he had missed the obvious in his investigation. "Who are you folks and what have you been up to the past few years?" He tossed the pen onto his desk and sighed. Time to redo this investigation from the beginning.

Chapter 28

Unusual neighborhood activity awakened Chris sometime after midnight, and he could not get back to sleep. He was hoping his recent purchase, an inexpensive Tel-Time wristwatch, would help him return to a daily routine, something he needed to improve since his loss of sight, for his biological clock wasn't working well. The seminary had graciously decided for him to return to work in the fall semester, but of course, their decision could have been predicated upon the fact that they knew they could not discriminate against a blind professor. Either way, gracious or forced, he was appreciative, and he hoped work would help him return to some sense of normality. His doctor had strongly urged him to return to his teaching job and suggested he learn Braille, so he had signed a contract with the seminary, but he wasn't convinced he wanted to go back to school as a student to learn Braille.

He got out of bed and felt his way through the house, checking the doors to make sure he had locked them, but mentally scolding himself for his obsessive-compulsive behavior. After an hour or so of wondering what the commotion might be, he scanned the local news sources, but nothing of any significance seemed to have happened. He turned off the news and dozed sometime around four but awakened at around ten to the slamming of car doors in his neighbor's driveway. Cars came and went for the next few hours, and the obvious dawned.

The neighborhood had been kind to him with the passing of Eden, but the news that he was a suspect in her murder had caused some tongues to wag, and the food trays had stopped coming. After he had been attacked and left blinded, the rumors seemed to have subsided. Once the newspaper article all but vindicated him with the public, the neighborly kindnesses returned, but he often did not make it to the door in time to see who it was that left a Tupperware container with a piece of red velvet cake or a slice of apple pie topped with a scoop of ice-cream.

The neighbors to the east of his house were in their eighties and a little on the nosy side, but Eden had loved to converse with them over the backyard fence, and she talked to them at length about their world travels, especially their trip to Mexico. It was obvious to Chris what had happened during the night, so, though void of details, he made his way across the front yard and slowly ascended the three steps to the wide veranda that ran the width of his neighbor's house. He didn't know what to say, but he would figure that out soon enough. Like Eden and their conversation about Mexico, he now had something in common with them, he just didn't know with which one he would be speaking. He wished he had not withdrawn from them the last few months, but he didn't consider one would pass so quickly. If only he had known, perhaps he could have sent a message to Eden, to tell her how very much he missed her, but that he was doing okay. Did it work that way? He wasn't sure, but he hoped death was not the end, that life did go on in Heaven. If only he knew how to get there. He didn't want to miss out on that opportunity, but he definitely wasn't prepared.

Chapter 29

As of late, Chris found himself reflecting upon the ancient sage and king, Solomon. Known as the wisest man who ever lived, Solomon wrote many proverbs that made their way into the Hebrew Bible. Called *Tanakh* by those of Judaism, the Christians refer to these same writings as the Old Testament of their Bible. The Hebrews came up with this term, *Tanakh,* by combining the first letters of the three main sections of their Holy Book: *Torah* or *Pentateuch*, also referred to as the five Books of Moses; the *Nevi'im*, also called the Prophets; and the *Ketuvim*, or Writings, which include Solomon's Book of Proverbs and Ecclesiastics.

"To every thing there is a season, and a time to every purpose under the heaven ..." Solomon had written. Chris well understood the changes of life compared to the changing seasons, but he wasn't sure the writer of Ecclesiastes had meant for situations to change as rapidly as they had for him. Take for example the simplest of situations, such as the ringing of the doorbell. His emotions regarding the doorbell had gone through a myriad of changes the past few months, that if charted, the graph would be a weird combination of instability, up and down, up and down. When Eden was alive, he considered the doorbell a nuisance. It mostly interrupted whatever projects they were doing, though Eden never seemed to mind, for she experienced some loneliness from being dislocated from her family and friends. After her death, the doorbell became very annoying for Chris, for it meant another neighbor had come to offer some meaningful, yet shallow, words of comfort. He tired of the visits and seldom answered the door. The ongoing investigation of Eden's death, especially after he became the target, brought visits that left him with indignation and a desire for retaliation, but deep down he knew the detectives were simply doing their job, so he should not take it personally.

After the second attack and his loss of sight, the ringing of the doorbell shot adrenalin throughout his body. He often stood at the locked door and carried on a conversation with whoever stood outside, making excuse for not opening the door. But now, the doorbell was a welcomed sound, for it meant someone to talk with. He had come full circle from the day of Eden's death to hoping for a visit that would abate his loneliness. So, Abdul's visit was manna from heaven.

Professor and student talked into the night. The conversation ranged from apology on the professor's part for considering Abdul a person of interest in the death of Eden, to elation that Abdul's name had been cleared by the insightful work of the Louisville and Clarksville PD investigative teams. The near-death experience of Sherri Carpenter had been Abdul's salvation: her testimony helped the detectives trace Abdul's activities the entire evening of Eden's death and the evening of Sherri's disappearance. He had not killed Eden, and he had not kidnapped Sherri Carpenter.

The conversation turned to why Abdul risked his freedom by returning to the States. That was a gamble he could have easily lost.

"My Christian duty, Professor" Abdul responded.

"But all this time I thought you were of the Muslim religion," Chris said.

"No, my family converted to Christianity when I was young, so I was raised in the Christian faith from my teen years."

"And how did that happen, if you don't mind my asking?"

"It started with a trip to Jerusalem, to visit the Dome of the Rock, and to pray at the Al-Aqsa Mosque. You spoke of its history and significance in class. Do you recall?"

"Yes, but I am surprised you did not share with the class that you had been there," Chris said.

"I did not want to be considered bragging, for our King Hussein had donated money to have the dome's covering refurbished. And though a wonderful trip, it is now considered somewhat a contentious trip for us, since the rest of my father and mother's family are still Muslim. And we have to be cautious about sharing our Christian faith. Many in our country would persecute us severely for openly promoting Christ."

"I understand," Chris said.

Abdul continued, "The week of our visit to Jerusalem, tensions were heated between the Jews and Arabs, and during a street skirmish between Jerusalem police and some Palestinian protesters, we slipped inside a church building to avoid the conflict. Once inside, we heard joyful singing coming from the sanctuary, so we instinctively followed the sound. What we saw set us aback. For the first time in our lives, we experienced Jews and Arabs sitting peacefully in the same house of worship, singing unto Christ, and praying together in the name of Jesus. They had found a faith that transcended their religion of birth: the Christian faith. A husband and wife team who had left the security of the United States of America to go to Israel and share their Christian faith were in charge of the service. Roger and Becky, two wonderfully caring Christians, are from the Louisville area. That is why I came here to the seminary, on their suggestion. They shared with my father their testimony and answered his questions regarding Christ, and how His love united hearts of different faiths into a family of Christian believers. My father could hardly believe that such a miracle could happen. Afterward, we studied the

Holy Bible, and we concluded the God of Scripture, not just the Old Testament, but also the New Testament, was a God of love, not of violence. We determined to serve that God."

"But the God of the Old Testament was a violent God," Chris protested. "You may recall that I taught that in class, citing multiple examples," Chris challenged Abdul.

"True, at times He was a God of vengeance, but the psalmist explained, '… the judgments of the Lord are true and righteous altogether.' The God of creation, Whose judgments are always right, has the responsibility to judge and to punish when necessary. If that were not so, the world would be more chaotic than it is. Don't you agree?"

"I was raised Jewish, so the God I served in my youth was definitely a God of vengeance, and I accepted that … I suppose I accepted it because He was supposed to be on our side. But as I became older, I could not justify how God sent my people to wipe out entire nations in the so-called Promised Land. Conversely, later in our history, the same God supposedly sent a wicked and idolatrous nation to take my people into captivity. Those actions don't seem like a God of love. And in His dealings with my people, He seemed cruel in some of the punishment. Like having a man stoned for picking up sticks on the Sabbath. And how many thousands have been killed because of religion."

"I have considered those arguments," Abdul said, deliberately, "and I have come to believe that the God of Scripture is a just God. Yes, thousands have been killed because of religion, but in comparison, millions have been killed by atheistic despots and anti-religion governments. I speak of Marxism, Communism, Fascism, and Nazism. And as for God giving your people the Promised Land while destroying the inhabitants, it was not as unjust as you propose. While your people waited in Egypt, part of the time in slavery, God gave the people that inhabited Canaan some four hundred years to change from their polytheistic beliefs and to stop committing unspeakable atrocities: like murdering their own children as a sacrifice to their false gods. Four hundred years is a long time for a nation to have to repent, to change. But they did neither. And as for your people to have experienced the wrath of God, they had a choice as to accept or reject the covenant God shared with them, and they accepted the covenant, knowing full well they were under the threat of judgment if they broke it: Mount Gerizim and Mount Ebal. Am I correct, Professor?"

"You are correct. Moses did take a vote and the yeas won out overwhelmingly. So, I suppose we have no excuse for our idolatry … which our rabbis say ultimately brought God's punishment."

"And the man picking up sticks on the Sabbath was an isolated case: God punished him in order to set an example to your people right after they had agreed to the covenant. We never see that happening again in Scripture. True?"

"Right, again," Chris said.

"From my observation of Scripture, God is overwhelmingly a God of love and compassion, 'not willing that any should perish,' the Bible says. I believe the God of the Old Testament, your God, came to earth in what we Christians call the Incarnation. God became a man in Christ Jesus and died for the sins of all mankind, expressing His great love for all humanity. My family experienced this love when we accepted the Christian faith."

"But that is simply your explanation of the Scripture, Abdul. We Jews have our explanation. Muslims have their take. It's a matter of debate."

"I must respectfully disagree, sir. We, my family and I, did not just read the Scripture and call ourselves Christians. We experienced Christ … the breath of His Spirit entered us. We experienced the New Birth that Christ talked about with Nicodemus and that the apostles experienced and preached. Christ changed our hate—for those we considered infidels—into love. That is what the Holy Scripture says, you will have love one for another, and that is what we experienced. I do not mean to speak condescendingly to you, my Professor, for I have deep admiration for you, but I do pray that you will consider my words."

Chris did not answer Abdul, for he did not know how to respond. He wanted to believe Abdul's experience was real, that Christianity was truly of God, more than a man-made religion, but he still struggled with the history of the church. How could Christianity be right when you consider all the wickedness of the church?

"I will speak no more of my experience unless you request it of me." Abdul interrupted his thoughts. He paused, but Chris did not respond. "So, in the meantime, I have obtained permission from the seminary president to be your escort, to be your eyes, sir."

"Wonderful! A stubborn Jew being led around by a former Muslim turned Christian." Chris chuckled. "This is going to be quite the trip."

"I'm sure God knows what He is doing." Abdul placed a hand on Chris' shoulder.

"I hope they are paying you well for such a daunting task."

"They are not paying me, sir. I volunteered for the job. It is my delight."

Chris wanted to believe he had just experienced the first altruistic act of his entire life. He was, however, a skeptic by nature. Time would tell. "I need a favor, Abdul," he said.

"With all my heart, I will help if I can, sir. What is it that you need me to do?"

"I have lost something of meaning … somewhere in this house … I've misplaced something that … something Eden made. She taught herself to crochet, and she made booties that … ." He paused.

"Booty, sir? *Aljawarib* … stolen goods? I don't understand." Abdul said.

"No, not booty … booties … baby shoes … crocheted by Eden." He made an awkward motion, trying to mimic someone hooking yard with the end of a hooked needle. "Booties … socks … baby socks … for whenever we had a child. We had planned … ." His words trailed off.

"Yes, I understand. I am sorry. I will look for the booties. Do you have any idea where they might be?"

"The night of the bombing, she had been crocheting in this room … on the couch … so I think I would have put them in the guest bedroom where she kept her hobbies. She liked to paint … so there is some artwork there … and I think that's where I would have stored the booties."

A thorough search of the guest room turned up no booties and no crocheting needles, only a basket of yarn. They walked from room to room, Abdul searching every drawer, every closet, Chris offering instructions and asking questions. Nothing.

"It must have been destroyed in the fire," perhaps taken away with the debris," Chris said. He took a deep breath and breathed out slowly. "It's okay, Abdul. They're gone."

"I see that finding these mean very much to you. I will pray they turn up somewhere, my Professor."

"And if they do, I will have witnessed another miracle in the wilderness," Chris said.

Like the manna from heaven … like the water from the rock … like the parting of the sea."

Abdul's enthusiasm could not be seen, but Chris perceived it from his voice. "Yes, like all the above," he said.

"Like the star of Bethlehem," Abdul added.

Chris did not answer.

"Sorry, Professor, I got a bit carried away with all the miracles of Scripture."

"It's okay, Abdul. I'll take any miracle I can get."

Chapter 30

Tony Trapp had never visited Mexico. In fact, he had never been out of the country, but he was determined to solve the biggest mystery of his more than thirty years of police work. So, this trip was two-fold: he wanted to find evidence of Christopher Stone having lived in Mexico, and he was going to find out who owned the PO Box to which the Stones had mailed a regular monthly payment. Two things Rogers had already discovered: the checks were signed by Eden Stone, and the recipient had no checking account. The checks were cashed by a local bank, but they were tight-lipped in a telephone conversation regarding the person who cashed the checks. Probably the friend of a friend, and a high percentage of the money would be divided by all the friends. Trapp decided he needed to have a face-to-face encounter with those involved in any way with the money.

José Santos had vanished into thin air, so they were not able to question him. With his dad in prison, was an organization the young Santos now ran the recipient of the checks? If so, what was the connection between Christopher and Eden Stone and José Santos? And why was ten grand given to him? That was a missing piece to the puzzle that had to be answered. It definitely pointed to some kind of ongoing drug deal, but it was a deal gone south that ended in Eden Stone's death.

Rogers was convinced the Feds needed to be consulted regarding Stone's true identity. Trapp held out from a pigheaded idea that Stone might be sent back across the border and escape punishment for an abhorrent crime he was somewhat responsible for that was committed in Clarksville, Indiana. And that was Trapp's city, and it was on his watch, a blotch he didn't want on his record. He certainly didn't want it on his conscience. He was concerned that Stone would sneak out in the night and vanish, but the department had cut back finances on surveillance, so he worked feverishly trying to put the pieces together. This trip was authorized only because he had paid the plane ticket out of his own pocket.

Three days into the trip he hit the mother lode. After staking out the post office for two days, at noon on the second day a priest arrived in a beat-up Chevy van and picked up mail from the PO Box. Trapp tailed the padre to a small community about fifty kilometers from Mexico City, to a fenced compound of adobe, bunk-style buildings that housed a few dozen orphans.

Father Alejandro Rafael Francisco Gallardo was a kind man, and he shared with Trapp over a cup of strong coffee. The meeting went surprisingly well. At first, they made small talk: Trapp complimenting the padre on his excellent English, learning that he had attended college in Cincinnati, and discovering that he enjoyed soccer. The conversation eventually turned to Trapp's purpose for being in Mexico: money sent to the orphanage from Eden Stone. Father Gallardo was surprised and disappointed that the funding had abruptly stopped, and the loss of the funds had made it difficult for the orphanage. Recently the checks had started up again, and he was very grateful. And yes, Christopher Stone was the benefactor. The priest refused to share the maiden name of Eden Stone, "… even if I did know it," he said, "I would not share it," which meant he knew her maiden name. So the kind man was covering up something.

Father Gallardo had assumed Eden had gotten married, or her name change was for some kind of protection, but she had never shared her personal life. He did not bother to ask, for her letters assured him she was well. Still, she had begged him not to reveal her new identity to anyone, especially her family. Being of a confidential profession, Father Gallardo had no problem keeping her secret. And the humble manner in which he lived suggested he was of the martyr type, a man who would have died to keep his silence, since, as he had explained, that was the wishes of the sweet, young lady who used to live in the hacienda overlooking their valley, and who cared as much for the children as he did. He was obviously brokenhearted when Trapp shared the news of her death.

Trapp suspicioned Father Gallardo was hiding something, but his subtle threats to the padre didn't garnish any new information, so he finally told him the full gory details of Eden's death: she had been brutally murdered and her husband was a suspect in the investigation. Though devastated, the padre remained committed to his stonewalling regarding her identity. Her murder, he assumed, was the obvious reason the money had ceased.

"But why did it start up again if her husband was a murderer?" the padre asked.

"To make himself look innocent," Trapp explained.

Father Gallardo's speculation regarding Eden's death offered some additional information for Trapp. At the beginning of Eden's relationship with the orphanage, she came often to visit, always with a bodyguard and in a chauffeured, black Mercedes entourage. Father Gallardo did not pry into her personal life, and she did not voluntarily give such. So, that was how it remained for a couple years, special visits from an angel out of the blue who assisted them financially. Her visits bolstered his resolve that he was doing the right thing, though ever so humble, in caring for the children. Her visits ceased about three years ago, and a few months later the first of many checks arrived in a nondescript envelope with no return address, but stamped with United States postage, at first from Virginia, then from Ohio, Indiana, and sometimes Kentucky. The checks were drawn from a bank in Puerto Rico. Father Gallardo, again, refused to share her identity before she married Christopher Stone. And no, he had never met her husband.

Trapp retrieved his handkerchief and wiped at the sweat that trickled down his face and soaked his collar. "Thank you, Father. I so much want to find her killer."

"I wish I could have been more helpful, sir, but I have taken an oath of confidentiality regarding what parishioners, or even strangers, share with me. You understand, no?"

"I understand," Trapp said, but it angered him that a priest would remain mum when someone had been murdered.

"I wish you well. She did not deserve to die that way, but I do not understand how … ." The priest fought back tears.

"No, she did not. You take care, Padre."

"Bless you, my son."

"Thank you." Trapp attempted a reverend expression of appreciation. It didn't come easy for a seasoned detective that had heard every excuse in the book for a witness to protect the guilty. "Oh, here's my card. If you think of anything else that might be helpful, please get in touch with me."

Trapp relied on body language as much as he did verbal responses. The priest hesitated in taking the card, like it was poisonous, or a snake coiled to strike. Was he being put in danger by this visit? That didn't seem fair to him. But then again, he was a minister, and ministers were supposed to live sacrificially. Didn't the Scripture say something about if you take up a serpent, or drink anything deadly, they won't harm you? His Sunday School days were coming in handy again.

The priest walked him to his car. Trapp scanned the scene around him. A group of boys chased a soccer ball across a scorched field of grass to the right of the buildings. A little girl cradled her doll as she wandered aimlessly around the yard, near enough to Trapp for him to be moved by the large, brown eyes that stared at him through the dilapidated, wire fence. This group of orphans was but the tip of the iceberg in Mexico City. These were the fortunate ones, for they had three meals a day and a roof over their heads. He had read the stats: somewhere near forty-thousand homeless children wander the streets of Mexico City, finding cover wherever they can, fending for food however they can. It was part of a world epidemic. This small facility was crowded, but the children looked cared for. And loved.

Trapp corralled his wandering thoughts. "You have been helpful to me, Father, so is there any way I can repay you?"

"God always provides our needs, not necessarily our wants. Our biggest desire is to have our own well, but it is very expensive, for they must drill deep to find water in our community, and the need never fits into our budget. But God does send the rain periodically, and we have a cistern that catches and stores it, but the water sometimes stagnates. We had been saving for a well, but there always seems to be another pressing need, another child dropped off—"

"This isn't much," Trapp said, as he thumbed through a money clip stuffed with cash, "but please use it as you see fit." He handed the priest a hundred-dollar bill and was immediately rewarded by the expression of gratitude.

"Bless you, sir."

Trapp backed the car onto the road. He observed the priest gazing after him, so he drove a few hundred yards before he stopped and unfolded his map. He drew a circle around the location of the orphanage, and using his index finger as a pointer, he studied the surrounding community, looking for an area with sparse roads, perhaps an elevated location. "I'm looking for the home of a young lady who used to live in a hacienda overlooking the padre's valley." He smiled. "You've been more helpful than you can imagine, Father Gallardo. And I'm going to find your friend's killer if it's the last thing I do as a detective."

Chapter 31

After a couple hours of crisscrossing, back-tracking, and traveling in what seemed an endless circle, Trapp stopped his rented and banged-up Ford Taurus in front of a set of twin, old-world, wrought iron gates. The matching fencing stretched in both directions for what seemed a mile or more. A grim-faced, swarthy-skinned guard, packing a large, leather-holstered pistol, stuck his head from the guardhouse and walked slowly toward him.

"Afraid I'm lost," Trapp said, faking a frown.

"*Yo no hablo inglés*," the man said in a guttural tone that was supposed to scare Trapp.

Sure you don't, Trapp wanted to say, and that's how you know I was speaking English? "*Me ... estoy ... perdido* … ." Trapp stuck the map out the window and pointed to Mexico City. "I need directions to Mexico City." Trapp found himself talking loud and slow as if that would help a guard who did not understand English. "Mexico City," he repeated, jabbing his finger onto the map.

"Ah …" the guard said. "*Esa dirección.*" He pointed in the direction from which Trapp had just come. "*Giro de vuelta* … turn, turn, turn … ." He motioned in a circle with his hand as he barked out the command.

"Thank you … *gracias, señor* … thank you." Trapp placed the Taurus in reverse and backed slowly from the driveway. He mentally smiled but purposefully hid his pleasure from the guard. On the archway above the twin gates, in bold letters, a familiar name leaped out at him: *El Santos Rancho.* "Bingo," he muttered to himself. "You're a genius, Trapp, but just to be safe, I'm gonna visit the padre one more time."

The fifteen-minute trip back to the mission gave him time to formulate his thoughts. It was obvious the priest operated under a vow of confidentiality, so he had to phrase his question just right. He reached back into his memory of investigations of the past. He recalled the time he had disqualified a minister's character witness of a parishioner accused of murder by one simple question. "When was the first time it entered your mind that the parishioner might have committed the crime?" Without thinking through his answer, the minister responded, "I'm not exactly sure the first time." Wrong answer. The answer should have been, I never suspected him of committing the crime, but the subconscious mind ofttimes answers for the person before they can process the outcome of their answer.

The priest met him in the driveway, obviously surprised he had returned so soon.

"I got turned around somewhere. But I did have one more question I need to ask. And I understand confidentiality … respect you for it … but I really need to solve the murder of a mutual friend. So, I'll just ask one question, and if the answer is yes, I don't want you to answer."

"I don't like games, *señor*," he said. "Please leave and don't—"

"Is Eden Stone a member of the Santos family who owns the ranch down the road?"

"I am sorry, *mi amigo*, but this is unfair. I cannot answer your questions," he protested, his hands waving for Trapp to stop with his interrogation. "I cannot answer—"

"You just did, Padre. But you don't have to worry. No one will ever know, except you, me, and the good Lord in heaven. And I think He doesn't mind you helping me find the killer of one of his children."

Chapter 32

A package arrived at Chris' home on Eden's birthday. A young lady who identified herself as being from the Clarksville Police Department hand-delivered the package, requesting a signature. Chris signed for it, curious as to what he was signing for, but the carrier knew little about the contents, or else she purposefully played the role well of not knowing.

When he opened the container and touched its contents, his heart flooded with emotions, and he could not contain his tears. It was Eden's necklace, and arriving on her birthday made it even more emotional. Was that coincidental? Providence? Or a rude reminder by the cops that she was dead. He tried to dismiss the ugly thoughts and focus only on a past filled with pleasant memories of Eden.

The necklace offered him some comfort as he held it for long periods of time, touching each diamond as if it were a rosary. He would press the cross to his lips and kiss it gently, over and over.

It was the only piece of jewelry Eden cherished. She had shared with him the history of the necklace. It was a gift from her father on her fifteenth birthday. The traditional *fiesta de quinceañera* had taken place at the family ranch, and relatives came from near and far to participate. It was during this celebration that her father presented her with this one-of-a-kind necklace. Twenty-four small diamonds, set in a gold cross, were cut from a singular, colorless, and rare diamond of perfect clarity. Her father had purchased the diamond at an auction in Dubai and hired a diamantaire in Surat, India to cut and polish the single stone into twenty-four symmetrical squares that were mounted in the perfectly molded, gold cross he had purchased in Madrid. The delicately designed cross was three inches in length and was attached to a strand of basket-weave, 24 karat gold links, designed by an artisan in Bali, who used their centuries-old techniques passed down through generations.

Eden was not into jewelry, and she acknowledged the necklace was somewhat gaudy, but she cherished the cross, not only because of the thoughtfulness of her father but because of what it represented: her Savior. But she was careful to always acknowledge that it was a mere representation of the manner in which her Lord died, and she also acknowledged that there was no spiritual magic in the emblem. Her relationship with her God far exceeded the rituals of religion. The cross was a mere symbol; her relationship was real.

Chris reflected on Eden's thoughts regarding the necklace. Had he gotten things crisscrossed in his Jewish faith? Had he equated symbols of Judaism as equality with the God of Judaism? Had the symbolic supplanted a relationship? Did the artificial suffice for the genuine? Had the Menorah, symbolic of wisdom, been sufficient for his need of a relationship with the God of light? Moses had not settled for a burning-bush experience, he left the burning bush to find and follow the God of the fire.

A Scripture from the Christian Bible had often intrigued Chris: it was a reference to the Tabernacle of David in regard to worship.

Why would not the Jewish Christians have referenced the Tabernacle of Moses? Or the Temple of Solomon? Chris assumed it had something to do with the traditional worship performed by the priests in the Tabernacle of Moses versus the heartfelt worship of the young King David as he danced before God "with all his might," and he later erected a tent to house the Ark of God and organized and arranged singers and musicians for continual worship. Did not God make it clear to David that His presence preferred a tent of sincerity over a cathedral of ritual?

Chris slid his index finger across the sparkling diamonds and reflected upon his mental image of Eden wearing the necklace. The artifact was insignificant compared to the person who wore it, and in her heart, it paled in importance to her Savior who hung upon a wooden cross.

The necklace's value was in what it represented, not what a buyer was willing to pay. So, they had never considered getting an appraisal, for she would have had difficulty in parting with the cherished relic, though an appraisal should have been done for insurance purposes. So the recent appraisal set Chris aback. Half a million dollars would go a long way for what he had planned. Now to discretely find a buyer.

Chapter 33

Chris made plans to meet José Santos at Fountain Square in Cincinnati, located in the heart of the city at the intersection of Fifth and Vine Streets. The meeting had been arranged via an old code Chris had created for the cartel to make drops, pickups, and whatever else they deemed needed secrecy. He arrived early and occupied a designated spot beside the fountain, where he waited for José to find him.

Chris enjoyed the continual sound of the splashing of the cascading fountain. He tried to invasion the fountain as he had seen it with Eden on a weekend visit to the city. The forty-three-foot fountain was a memorial from businessman Henry Probasco for his brother-in-law and business partner, Tyler Davidson. Probasco, a hardware magnate, went to Munich, Germany, and bought the fountain. He shipped it in sections to downtown Cincinnati where it was reassembled in the middle of Fifth Street, a centerpiece in the city since 1871. The area was later reconfigured to accommodate a large square plaza, where hundreds of people congregate daily, and businesses vie for the surrounding storefronts that face the square.

Also called "The Lady" and "The Cincinnati Angel," the bronze fountain sets on a green granite base of giant proportion. A nine-feet high female stands atop the fountain, whose outstretched hands produce a continual rain of water onto the multiple human and animal figures proportionately attached to the fountain and overflowing from the multiple basins. Each of the figures resemble a story associated with water. The fountain, symbolic of man's daily need of water, represents how the city of Cincinnati was blessed with an abundance of such, as the mighty Ohio River curves along the southern borders of the city and separates it from the sister cities across the river in what transplanted Appalachians call Canaan Land, in contrast to Ohio.

From eleven in the morning until two in the afternoon on Thursdays, the crowds gather to purchase lunch from various food trucks that line the streets along the square. The Santos cartel had invested heavily in one of those vendors, including a few restaurants scattered throughout the Ohio Valley, so José Santos was no stranger to the area. The community was centrally located for easy access by car, rail, plane, and boat, so it had been a profitable adventure. There had been some concern for this rendezvous, that José might be recognized, but with the imprisonment of Chico, the Santos cartel had liquidated its assets in the area and moved associates elsewhere. José didn't have to worry about his identity being compromised by someone from his past.

The middle of the day presented an excellent opportunity for their meeting to go unnoticed. The area was crowded with merchants and customers and the curious from all across the area, who converged on downtown Cincinnati during the day. A wide variety of colors and languages created an almost carnival atmosphere every Thursday, without the rowdy sort that mainly attends evening events.

José was finishing his second year at Xavier, a Jesuit Catholic university founded in 1831 in the northern edge of Cincinnati.

Its name honored the Roman Catholic Missionary, Saint Francis Xavier. He was born in 1506, Francisco de Jasso y Azpilicueta, to a wealthy family in the Kingdom of Navarre, which is present-day Spain. Saint Xavier was co-founder of the Society of Jesus, a highly educated society of priests called Jesuits. Taking a vow of poverty, they were instrumental in spreading the Roman Catholic faith to multiple countries outside of Europe. Some are saying that a present-day Jesuit, Jorge Mario Bergoglio, has the attention of Rome, and should he ever become pope, he would be the first Jesuit priest to do so.

José was doing well at the university. A priest close to the Santos family had a longstanding history with the university, and it was his guidance that prompted José to pursue the Xavier University program, majoring in business. Ever of the analytical mindset, Chris had shown little enthusiasm toward José attending Xavier. It is said that Saint Francis proposed the Goa Inquisition, which lasted almost three centuries, and persecuted Catholic Hindus in South Asia, for their supposed cryptic-Hinduism, a secret practice of Hinduism while professing Catholicism. Such knowledge remained Chris' fodder for castigating Roman Catholicism when he lectured his class on the evils carried out against other religions, of course, in the name of religion.

As of late, Chris had been evaluating his critical attitude regarding Christianity. He reflected upon Abdul's account of his conversion to Christianity: an experience that unified converts from other faiths instead of dividing them. Perhaps he had been looking in the wrong places to formulate his negative outlook regarding Christianity. And why had he not considered Eden's faith? Her love and tenderness toward humanity trumped all corruption perpetrated by evil men veiled in robes of righteous pretension.

Abdul had driven Chris the two-hour trip from Clarksville. He left Chris sitting at the fountain while he toured Cincinnati's relatively new Great American Ball Park that housed the renowned Cincinnati Reds franchise. Dusty Baker had just finished his third season as manager, as the 2010 season ended with the Phillies sweeping them in the National League Division Series.

Chris sat along the base of the fountain, assimilating the sounds into a visual display of a life he could only remember. He had first visited Fountain Square on a mission while living in Mexico, and he had twice visited with Eden. They had sat by the fountain eating from cups of ice-cream purchased from Graeter's, a quaint shop on the square.

José found him promptly. It was an emotional meeting, the first since Eden's death. The continual spray and overflowing of the multiple basins offered an excellent cover-up for their conversation. They had a lot to talk about, a lot of catching up to do. After an hour or so of reminiscing, Chris got down to business. He pulled a small, wooden box from his pocket and handed it to José, who hesitated to open it. When José finally looked inside, his silence reflected his thoughts.

Chris broke the silence. "You remember she wore it at the wedding? One of the few times."

"It's one of a kind, Chris, a gift from her father. You knew that?"

"Yes." Chris paused. "Are you aware of the value?"

"No, but I'm sure it is expensive. How much?"

"Half a million."

"Wow!"

From the tone of José's voice, Chris assumed he had no previous idea of its value. "I want to sell it," he said. "I hope you understand."

"Not my call, Chris. It's yours to do as you like."

"I need your help." Chris placed a hand on José's shoulder.

"What do you mean?" José asked.

"If I seek a buyer, it may bring too much suspicion toward me. I can't risk that. It's a family heirloom, so it's no strange thing that you should have it. I need you to sell it for me. My future is uncertain, so I want you to have part of the money … to make sure you can finish your schooling. I was thinking a hundred thousand for you to keep."

"I can't accept—"

"Not from me, José, from Eden. She spoke often about you, and she cared for you, and what better way is there for me to honor her memory than making sure someone she cared for gets a good education."

José started to protest, but Chris silenced him with a "shush."

"Thank you," he said, hesitantly. "But how do I get the rest of the money to you without drawing suspicion?"

"You don't give me any of the money. You invest it."

"Where? How?"

"The same way we've invested money for the last three years. An investment that gives fantastic returns." Chris smiled and turned his face toward the fountain, sensing the spray of mist that flowed from the outstretched arms of the giant, bronze lady. "Fountain Square is such a unique place. Some call it 'The Genius of Water.' The renovation of this fountain cost over forty-million dollars, yet no one is allowed to borrow water from it, bathe in it, or drink from it. And I dare say there are a few hundred homeless people living within walking distance from its refreshing waters. Though I must acknowledge it had drinking fountains dispersed around it the last time I visited. Are they still there?"

"Yes, but most people I see drinking are doing so from bottled water."

"So, the fountain is mostly for show, no make-a-difference purpose … simply a reminder that a hundred years or so ago a man's friend died. And yet I doubt five people in this square know that, and those that do, don't care. Yet what value it could be in the right place. Let's make an investment in something that will bring us many returns."

José did not answer, for he was in the presence of a modern-day Samson, blind and speaking in riddles with veiled meanings, but José well understood what Chris Stone had in mind. And he was more than willing to cooperate.

Chapter 34

Chris held onto Abdul's right arm as they followed the tight-knit crowd that slowly maneuvered along the narrow corridor. The crowd quickly split into smaller factions when they stepped inside the visitors' gallery. Chris and Abdul had talked at length of this meeting, and needless to say, they were apprehensive, yet they were convinced this needed to happen. Now they were here, locked behind the same walls that incarcerated Chico Santos, not knowing what to expect. The tap-tap of the cane against the concrete floor echoed off the block walls, unique from the myriad of other sounds: voices, chairs scraping against concrete, and children squealing as they rushed across the room. It was the presence of the children that captured Chris' attention, that out-of-place sound in this world of criminals. Nothing seemed normal for a child to be here: their short-lived delight, their inability to comprehend, their having to depart without their father. Or grandfather. He followed Abdul's nudging: twenty steps and they stopped. With his cane, he traced the outline of a park-like table, settled onto the bench, and propped the cane against the end of the table.

Abdul settled onto the bench across from Chris. Neither spoke, and it seemed an unusually long wait. Was this a mistake? Had they wasted time and money making this trip? Would the old man visit with them?

After several minutes passed, the door for the prisoners' entrance squeaked open, and Abdul placed a hand gently on Chris' arm.

"Is it him?" Chris' mouth seemed dry, and his tongue stuck to the roof of his mouth as he tried to swallow. It was not fear, for he had known and dealt with fear more times than he cared to recall. So, what was it? Regrets? Doubt?

"From the picture you showed me, I believe so," Abdul said.

Adrenalin shot through Chris' body, and he instinctively braced himself for the confrontation. The shuffling of feet surprised him, and his emotions calmed. He tried to envision Chico, but his mental imagery did not match the sounds of the approaching footsteps. The last time he saw him, Chico was strong, determined, and though in chains, his spirit was still very much unshackled.

The shuffling stopped beside Chris. He rose to his feet and swiveled to face his avowed enemy.

"Mr. Santos." He held out his hand without much expectation.

Silence.

Sensing the penetrating eyes of Fernándo "Chico" Santos, Chris lowered his hand. He well knew that stare, and he tried to counter it with his own, but he had lost some control of his eye movements. His dark sunglasses offered a cover-up to his emotional pain. The last time Chris had seen him, Chico had never diverted his stare when Chris sat on the witness stand testifying against him and the Santos family. In a single hour of testimony he revealed names, dates, places, acts of violence, laws broken, and lives taken. Chico, every five feet of him filled with anger and hate, stared at him throughout the entire testimony. In the end, when Chris walked from the stand

and past the defendant's table, Chico launched at him. As the guards struggled to contain him, he screamed, "You are a dead man, *Senõr* Drew, or whatever your name is," and he went into a tirade of profanities. The threat echoed in Chris' mind as he walked from the courtroom and into the care of the witness protection program: a new name, new life, and new purpose.

In retrospect, Chico was right: he was a dead man. Hate and the sweet nectar of revenge had kept him going after Eden's death, but the loss of eyesight stole not only his vision but his hope of avenging Eden's death. He was here to complete his final purpose in life.

Chico shuffled to the opposite side of the table and sat directly across from Chris. "A little privacy, if you don't mind," he gruffly demanded. Footsteps echoed in the concrete, bunker-like room as the guard retreated to the far side.

"Thank you for seeing me, Mr. Santos."

"I did not expect to see you alive again. It looks like I may have to finish the job myself when I get out of this hothouse."

Chico may have weakened physically, but his voice was still as demanding as when he ruled over the Santos dynasty. He seemed to have some difficulty breathing, and he had a slight rattle as his breath came in short gasps.

"Oh, but I am a dead man, Mr. Santos."

"No, *Senõr* Drew, you are not yet dead. Rotting away in this hot hole is death. But soon, like *Cristo*, I will resurrect and be out of here, and when I do, I will find you. Our first man failed to kill you, and Juan only wounded you, but I want you dead. I have not forgotten your deception, and I have not forgotten my promise. You destroyed my life."

"It was nothing personal, just doing what I was supposed—"

"No. You deceived me. I trusted you as a son. I allowed you into my confidence, my home, to eat at my table. And what appreciation did I get? You turned your back on me."

"I was only doing my job, sir, a job I swore to uphold, to enforce the law of the land. You broke the law, Mr. Santos, and you were convicted for those crimes by your peers, not me. Your organization is responsible for hundreds of deaths and thousands of ruined lives.

And you show not one regret for all the crimes you have committed, so I do not feel sorry for you now." Chris had not intended to say these things. That was not his purpose for this meeting. His purpose was more meaningful, almost sacred. But the bottled thoughts erupted unconsciously, and he did not regret saying them.

Chico breathed heavily. He had been an avid smoker, cigars from Cuba being his preference. He was now denied this luxury, and every vice has its cost.

"I have one regret, *Senõr* Verco Drew, and it is that I cannot kill you here, right now!" he screamed.

Chris wiped at the spittle that sprayed his face. He removed his sunglasses but paused before he spoke. "This is not living." He gestured toward his eyes. "I walk among the tombs of the dead, visiting the grave of the love of my life. You hurt me far worse than you planned when your goon killed my wife."

"He killed your wife? Then perhaps that is better than I planned." Chico laughed. "You lost your wife, and now you are blind, a man who will never see a beautiful woman again. Was she pretty, *Senõr* Drew, your wife? I promised I would get even with you that day you testified against me. I did not forget. Do you remember?"

Chris fought to control his emotions.

"Oh, but this is more than I planned. Are we even now, *Señor* Verco Drew? We no longer owe each other anything. Me in a prison without the light of the sunshine and separated from my family, and you, separated from your wife, forever, and blind. An eye for an eye justice, that's what I call it."

Chris did not respond.

"No, it is still not even between you and me, for you took too much from me. You still owe me, *Señor* Drew."

"That is why I've come to see you, Mr. Santos. I felt I owed it to you."

"You owe me more than you can ever pay. And I always demand payment. Do not come in here and give me some sad story, expecting me to forget. I am glad to hear that my man killed your wife. Very glad. It gives me much pleasure. My heart is not touched.

Did you love her very much *Senõr* Drew … to love much is to hurt much, so I hope you truly loved her. Do you still love her?"

"Yes, I do."

"So, it is sweet revenge for the old man. You young fools never learn … you have not lived long enough—"

"The woman you killed, Mr. Santos, we … both of us … we love her very much." Tears streamed down his cheeks.

"What are you talking about, *Senõr* Drew. You are loco in your head. I never even met your wife."

"Oh, but you have."

"When? Where? At the trial? I don't remember seeing her."

"At her birth, over thirty years ago. You held her in your arms. You christened her Eden. She … Eden … my wife is your daughter, Mr. Santos. I married your daughter."

Chico did not answer. Chris sensed his attempt to ascertain what had happened, of what he had done when he gave the order to kill Verco Drew.

Chico rose to his feet but fell back onto the bench. "You lie. You try and deceive me again. Up to your old deceitful tricks. What do you want now?" The command had gone from his voice, replaced by a quiver of uncertainty. "You know my daughter has been kidnapped … yet you have no respect … no respect … for me. Please, *Senõr* Drew, though I hate you with all my whole heart, please honor the wish of a loving father. Do you know who kidnapped my Eden? Where is she?"

Chris did not answer, for he knew how unreasonable the old man was when he got something stuck in his head.

"You … you are a beast. No, you are worse than a beast. You are *Diablo* incarnate."

"No, Mr. Santos, I am no beast. I am a broken piece of humanity trying to make it through life, hoping each day is the last for me. And I am not deceiving you now. Your daughter, Eden, was not kidnapped. She left with me the day my assignment ended. We had fallen in love … even you must admit you did not object at the time … but I had a job to do … and I did it … and your daughter made her own decision for what she did. She became my wife."

The table slammed into Chris' stomach as Chico lurched at him.

Abdul struggled to contain him. "Please, Mr. Santos," Abdul pleaded.

Footsteps rushed toward them.

"Settle down, Santos, or you're back in your cell before visiting hours are over," a guard threatened.

"We're okay, sir." The calming voice of Abdul defused the situation.

The struggling stopped, and Chico fell back onto the bench, wheezing. The guards retreated to their station.

Chico's wheezing slowly subsided.

"Professor Stone, *Senõr* Drew as you know him, is being truthful, Mr. Santos. He and Eden were married," Abdul said.

"And who are you? What business do you have with me?" Chico scowled.

"My name is Abdul, a student at the university where Professor Stone teaches … ."

Chico listened as Abdul, ever so gently, told the account of Eden's death.

The moaning was uncontrollable, and it came like incessant waves that would never cease, as Chico rocked back and forth, his fists pressed against his brow. It seemed the focus of the room turned toward them. Even a blind man could see the anguish, made clear by the deep groaning. No one spoke, for what do you say at a time like this? Moments passed before the sounds around them took up again, and Chris was glad the focus had turned from them. He had hoped for some closure with the old man, who, after all, was his father-in-law. He owed it to him to share the news, but he had hoped for a better outcome, for some form of acceptance of him as the son-in-law.

Chico finally stopped his groaning. "You married my daughter? How can this be?" Chico pleaded for this to make sense.

"When I infiltrated your organization, I didn't plan to fall in love. I should have prevented it from happening, for it could never work out. But Eden and I did fall in love, and it did work out, for a while. She had your wife's temperament, your wife's faith. She wanted out, away from the crime, the constant uncertainty, and away from the guilt of a lavish lifestyle at the expense of so many."

"I don't need a lecture," Chico said. Prison had not robbed him of his spunk.

"Sorry, sir, but I didn't mean my comments to reprimand. I was only speaking the truth as I know it regarding Eden's heart."

After a long pause, Chico spoke. "Please, continue. I want to know the truth about my Eden."

"I fulfilled your daughter's wish to find a different life. The day I testified against your family, she waited for me outside the courtroom. We married that same day and have lived an alias life together ever since. You must believe me, Mr. Santos, I love your daughter, and I was devoted to her. We were happy together, unbelievably happy."

"And why tell me now, to try and hurt me, or to make me feel sorry for you?"

"No, this is not to hurt you, and I do not need your sympathy. I simply want you to know where she rests. She is buried in Clarksville, Indiana, where we have lived the last three years. Every father deserves to know where his child is buried."

For a long time, Chico did not speak. Chris wanted to comfort him, for Eden's sake, but he could not find the words. And there was a part of his psyche that would not relinquish itself to pity for a criminal.

Chico broke the silence. "My son, José, he was so close to Eden. We assumed he was abducted by our enemies, just like we assumed Eden had been taken. Could he possibly be alive? Do you have any idea where he might be?"

"Yes, I do. Eden and I have taken care of José for the past few years. Like Eden, he simply did not want the lifestyle of crime. He's a student here in the States. We met a few days ago. He is well."

"It is good that he is well. Do you think he would come and visit me?"

"I'm not sure. I'll ask him. Your family still has lots of enemies. It's important that he remains in hiding, at least for a while."

"I understand. Thank you for caring for him."

Chico seemed sincere. Chris had a mental picture of the Chico of yesterday, proud and intimidating. He sensed the contrast now, his shoulders stooped, head bowed, staring at the gray concrete floor. Chris did not regret putting Chico behind bars. His life sowed a harvest of havoc. Now he reaped from the law of the harvest. But Chris wondered how he had personally reaped such a bountiful harvest, though ever so short, as having been married to Eden. Still, now he reaped a different harvest. Emptiness. Loneliness. Meaninglessness of life. Who was really imprisoned? Chico? Or himself? How ironic this criminal had become his father-in-law! After a long silence, Chico stood to leave. Chris needed to say something conciliatory, for Eden's sake.

"She loved you, sir," Chris said.

"I know, but how can I ever forgive myself for … ." He started to walk away.

Chris stood. "Thanks for seeing me, Mr. Santos. I wish you well."

Chico stopped and shuffled back to him. He spoke slowly, his voice quivering. "*Senõr* Drew, please forgive me. I have lived a very selfish life, that even my own child does not feel at liberty to visit me."

Chris did not answer.

"If you will not forgive me, then pray to God that at least He will forgive me."

"I'm sorry, Mr. Santos, but I don't know God, especially your God, so how can I pray to Him on your behalf?"

Chapter 35

Chris followed the ophthalmologist's instructions: he looked straight up, up to the right, straight right, down at the toes: he knew the routine. Doctor Cameron Mansfield, a former special ops agent, had a lot in common with Chris. Cam had been a member of the Navy's Special Amphibious Reconnaissance Corpsman, and as a SARC he had run missions off the coast of Mexico. That's where their paths had crossed, where they had developed a friendship, but they had gone separate ways until recently. The two had a lot of catching up to do, so Chris' visits consisted of professionalism and pleasure as they took time to reflect upon old times.

After deciding he didn't want a military career, Cam used his GI Bill to complete Med School and eight additional years of advanced training as an eye specialist, able to treat all eye diseases and perform eye surgery. After college, he did a brief stint at Mayo and then started his private practice in Louisville, where he also helped at the VA hospital as a service to those he held in high esteem. It was Chris's accident that brought them back together, a chance appointment at the Louisville VA Medical Center. Chris had to confide in him regarding the witness protection program since it was obvious he was going by a different name. But Chris had no concerns of disloyalty. The two had previously bonded in life and death experiences battling organized crime attempting to invade their country.

Chris' follow-up visits were at Cam's private practice. After each examination, they talked about their past, and how their lives had crossed. They talked at length about Chris' activities as an undercover agent in the DEA's war on drugs. They talked about how his infiltration into the Santos' cartel had gained him fame within the department, but also, how it made enemies that do not forget, nor do they forgive.

Cam loved to travel, and every year included some new adventure. His more recent plans included Mt. Everest. He had never married, but he insisted he was married to his work and hobbies. Cam broached the subject of how Chris had met his wife. And the office visit turned into a therapy session. It was the most deep-seated thoughts Chris had shared with anyone since her death.

Chris had never intended to fall in love, for his life was too precarious to include a wife and family and to do so without making drastic changes would be a crime to a family. But he did fall in love. And he still was amazed at how it happened. Eden had lived in the midst of a world of affluence, with maids at her beck and call, and armed guards protecting her every movement. And it was also an environment of atrocities against humanity, which spared no one who dared stand in the way, whether child or the aged. In a five-hundred-acre estate, surrounded by poverty and squalor in all directions, the Santos family reigned among a handful of cartels, working together when it suited their cause, but each always vying for the top. Every day was like a working vacation of sorts, with pleasure galore, and guests staying for days, entertained beyond measure. In this hedonistic environment, Eden's angelic innocence stood out like a rosebud in the corner of a pigpen. She did not belong, and she wanted out.

Chico really liked Chris, promoted him in the organization, and provided opportunities for him and Eden to be together. He planned matrimony, but more. It seemed Chico planned on him assuming the leadership, so he allowed Chris liberties he did not allow other associates.

Chris and Eden spent many moonlit nights alone, walking the grounds of the estate, and over time these walks created a bond, and Eden slowly shared her dreams, dreams of a life she could never have as a hostage to the Santos' estate. Her yearning stirred a longing for a life he had left behind, free of the deceit and danger. Her caring words and kind mannerisms ran opposite the self-centered environment of pleasure seeking, greed, and butchery that dominated her environment. And Chris saw in her eyes the plea to be rescued from a world she despised but could not escape on her own. He risked his life and endangered his career when he allowed her into his secret world.

As a perceived member of the Santos inner circle, the family accepted him as one of their own, and he played the role well. He was with them in dealings with the scum of the earth, and he advised them on operations—from the information fed him by the DEA—on when to move and when to take cover. And though the department made all decisions under which Chris had to operate, he still lived with an element of guilt because of the outcome of many of those decisions. While smaller empires crumbled and fell, the Santos empire flourished, all because the DEA had a bigger fish in mind. They had their sights set on the Zetas operation, but they had been unable to infiltrate their organization. The Santos family was merely a stepping stone. For this to happen, Chris needed the Santos family to believe in him, to share their inner structure, to reveal their secrets. And they did.

The plan involved Chris buying large shipments of drugs from the Santos, a shipment that went directly into a DEA warehouse. This made the Santos family an immediate threat to the powers that controlled the Mexican market, but it also created a door for Chris to enter into the Santos' inner structure. Within months he was a constant guest at the Santos' family gatherings, always seated next to Eden. His association with the Santos family went beyond the dinner table. Within the year he sat at their planning table, and he coached them on the market across the border, his insight making them boatloads of money. But all the while, he baited the trap for their demise.

Chris' charm was his greatest weapon. The only member of the family that did not take a liking to him was Juan, but that was not because he suspected Chris' disloyalty to the cartel; it was merely the tale of two men in love with the same girl. Since Chico orchestrated the match of Chris and Eden, to challenge the old man's decisions would have brought his wrath. Though Juan could do nothing to prevent the old man's wishes, he gave Chris a cold shoulder in protest. He worked harder for the family business than anyone else did, trying to acquire the old man's favor. And it was no pretense, for he truly was loyal to a fault to Chico, more so than most of the Santos members, though they reminded Juan that he was just a distant cousin. But his loyalty paid off, for, in the end, he got his revenge when Luis approved him to put the hurt on Chris. But revenge comes with a price. Juan's trial was coming up soon. He would follow the many cartel members already in prison, some incarcerated because of Chris' infiltration, and the biggest fish in the Santos pond, Chico, incarcerated for life.

"Hmm."

Doctor Mansfield's familiar "hmm" brought Chris upright in his seat. "I don't like the sound of that, Doc," Chris said.

"No, not anything bad, Chris. I'm not sure what to think of it, and I don't want to get your hopes up until we are sure, but your eyes are responding somewhat to light. As the scars heal, light is able to penetrate the cornea, and the retina is responding."

"Which means?"

"Which means, in layman's terms, there's still life in the eye. The optic nerves are still alive, still sending messages to the occipital area of the brain. And where there is life, there is hope."

"But I thought the damage was permanent, that I am blind for life, especially since you said there's no way to do an eye transplant," Chris said. He expressed himself with little emotion because he had little emotion left in his heart. Even the recovery of sight could not restore his greatest loss, so why become excited about the possibility of seeing again. He had slowly accepted the fact that he would never see a portrait of Eden, so his memory had to suffice. Her facial features were etched in his mind. He wanted them captured forever, like Rushmore's images of the past etched in stone. Her innocent smile. The occasional frown if he didn't compliment her on a meal she prepared. One memory gave him regret. It was the lonely stare that sometimes surfaced when they walked the blacktop pathway along the state park at the Falls of the Ohio as the sun set over the distant hills of southern Indiana. The moment seemed to resurrect a memory of some distant past she could never have but still longed for. He had transplanted her to a distant land and culture, and this move isolated her from making deep friendships. Theirs was a life that had to maintain boundaries. Still, not once did she ever complain.

A familiar song, by Diamond Rio, played softly over the office sound system: *One More Day.* He couldn't prevent the tears.

Doctor Mansfield handed him a tissue. "Not the best choice of songs. Sorry, my friend."

"No, it's okay." All he had left was a past. Memory had to suffice for any resemblance of pleasure, but pleasant memories also resurrected the pain of his loss.

Doctor Mansfield repositioned his ophthalmoscope and moved uncomfortably close to Chris. "I thought your condition was irreversible also. And it may still be, depending upon the extent of damage, which we're still assessing. That's why I hesitate. When I said we can't do an eye transplant, I was speaking of the entire eye. My statement was only partially true. We can't do an entire transplant, for the optic nerve, that connects the retina to the brain, has about a million nerve fibers, so it is an impossibility to reconnect a new eye to the brain. It's actually a part of the central nervous system instead of the peripheral … stimulus to the eye goes straight to the brain …

very technical. Doctors did their first heart transplant back in '67, but the biggest challenge was connecting the blood vessels. They've even done an entire face transplant, but not the eyes. Too complex, though we are still working on it. But … ."

"But what?"

"Do you believe in miracles, Chris?"

"No. I believe in logic, in a reasonable explanation for everything that happens."

"Well … ."

Cam Mansfield way overused that word. And the long pauses that followed irritated Chris to high heaven. Why can't a man just speak what he's thinking without all the drawn-out drama?

"I do believe in miracles," Dr. Mansfield said, "for I have seen a few in my lifetime, and I may be witnessing another. Look straight ahead … into the light."

Light! How many times had that word played a key role in the Hebrew Bible? "Let there be light," are the words the book of beginnings records as the first spoken words of God to a world shrouded in darkness. Chris had memorized the stories from the *Tanakh* at a young age. That single word, light, seemed to be a golden strand woven into the tapestry of Jewish existence. When darkness covered the land of Egypt for three days, the Jewish community had light. Once they departed from four centuries of slavery, a pillar of fire stood as a barrier that protected them from Pharaoh's army that chased after them. That same pillar of fire warmed them by night as they wandered in the wilderness. Seven lamps gave continual light in the tabernacle of worship erected during their journey. And God commissioned a young lad by the name of Samuel to preserve the dimming light in that same tent as the sins of the sons of Eli the priest dulled the illumination of those golden candlesticks, almost to the point of extinction. And Gideon, with a mere three hundred men carrying torches, defeated an army of multiple thousands. The psalmist described the Bible as a light to show one the pathway. And did not the sun stand still over Mount Gibeon, so Joshua could finish the battle against the Amorites? And a star over Bethlehem? That thought surprised him. He was Jewish by birth, and they still awaited the Messiah. But Eden professed to possess the Messiah in her heart. And Chris believed in her more than life itself. Could the Christmas story be so? And Saul, a Jewish scholar who was alive when Christ lived, saw a great—

"Chris!"

"Oh, sorry Doc."

"I need you to look straight into the light for me."

For a blind man, the ritual was more difficult than one would think. So much about the physical man is associated with sight: balance, emotions, coordination. It took mental effort to move his eyes in conjunction with the doctor's commands. The examination ended, and Doctor Mansfield rolled his chair across the room, but the click for the overhead light made no difference to Chris' perspective. His was a world of darkness. The sounds of instruments being placed into cases seemed to take way too much time. For a man who ran special ops back in the day, Cam seemed way too deliberate, but then again, perhaps that's why he was alive.

Chris broke the silence. "What's the verdict, Doc? Any hope?"

"Well … ."

There he goes again.

"As the scarring heals, I am encouraged. The burn is not as deep as originally thought, the damage not as severe."

"Which means?"

"Possibilities. If the optic nerves to the brain have not been damaged, we can do a cornea transplant, or an iris transplant if necessary. We still have some possibilities."

Chris had forgotten how happiness felt, but for a moment he remembered. That surprised him.

Chapter 36

Trapp's trip to Mexico paid dividends much higher than he had anticipated. The corner pieces of the investigation puzzle were now in place. Eden Stone was a member of the Santos family, but in what capacity he did not yet know. That would be a project for Rogers. Chris Stone had probably been a member of the Santos cartel, but he may have crossed them. Stone was probably the target of the bomb that killed his wife; therefore, he was not the killer of his wife. And recent information that Stone had visited Chico Santos revealed he was still a viable part of the Santos organization. That bit of information affirmed Trapp's gut feeling: Eden Stone's murder was collateral damage of a rival cartel seeking retaliation for Stone's activities with the Santos cartel. The second attack, by Juan Santos, was probably a personal vendetta Juan had against Stone. Personal struggles for power within cartel organizations are very common.

And it sent a strong message to others that might not be loyal within the organization. Since Juan purposefully blinded the professor instead of killing him, Trapp was sure about one thing: the bombing that killed Eden Stone, and Juan's attack on Christopher Stone, were relatively unrelated. The only connection between the two was that both were somehow linked with Mexican drug cartels.

With no proof other than a gut feeling, Trapp suspected that Los Zetas, Mexico's most powerful cartel, was behind the attempted assassination of Stone. Los Zetas was a member of the confederation known as the Gulf Cartel. It had become the dominant influence under the leadership of Heriberto Lazcano, its longtime leader. Many of the members were deserters from the elite arm of the Mexican military, reportedly trained in commando warfare by both U.S. and Israeli Special Forces Units. More recently, Miguel Treviño Morales had taken over command of Los Zetas. His tactics seemed more violent than the former leadership, and the news of a massacre in San Fernando, Mexico, was proof. Seventy-two people—fifty-eight men and fourteen women—were shot in the back of the head: execution style. Such scare tactics surely sent chills down the backs of the worst in the drug world. They would think twice before crossing Los Zetas.

Had Stone crossed Los Zetas? Was his rise in the Santos Cartel a threat to their thriving market in the States? Why did someone want him dead? Would they strike again, or would his blindness render him no longer a viable threat, and thus no longer on the hit list? But he was still at the top of Trapp's list of suspected criminals. And Stone's living in southern Indiana made things personal. Trapp did not tolerate his territory becoming the marketplace for drug dealers. Maybe Stone was not a murderer, but his activities in the Mexican drug market had brought about the death of his wife, and that was a crime. Trapp was sure he was getting closer to solving it, which he assumed would open up an investigation into a long-overdue war on drugs. And he was smack-dab in the middle of it. And that pleased him.

Chapter 37

Detective Tony Trapp had two qualities that caused him to solve most cases that landed on his desk: tenacious as a bulldog and stubborn as a mule. When he caught a lead, he would not let go until all angles were thoroughly examined. Though the recent evidence proved differently than his previous hypothesis, he would revisit it just in case he missed something. He sometimes pushed the limit drawn by superiors, especially if he thought he was right.

His trip to Mexico linked Eden Stone with the Santos clan, but he was not sure in what capacity. Rogers was working on the details. Trapp derided himself for not putting that piece of the puzzle together from the beginning, a bit of information that might have prevented him from going on a few wild-goose chases. Eden Stone's murder now took second place to the current ongoing crime: Christopher Stone was heavily involved in drug trafficking. Evidently, his wife had been complicit, and it was this criminal activity that got her killed. The illegal activity had not ceased, but it would soon, for Trapp had figured out the players, and he would eventually bring them down. This would include José Santos, evidently a relative of Eden. José's visits to the Louisville area now made sense; they corroborated Trapp's suspicions regarding Stone's involvement with the Santos clan.

A good cop sometimes has to operate on instinct until he can produce the proof he needs to get a conviction. Such intuition had steered him through the fog of uncertainty. And today was no different, as Trapp followed a new hunch. He had not sought approval from his superior for this second day trip to Cincinnati, nor did he give a heads-up to the Cincinnati PD regarding his investigation in their city. He'd take care of that small oversight after he was confident of his investigation. He didn't mind sharing the glory for the arrests, but he didn't want his investigation bogged down in the red-tape necessary with inter-state cooperation. He'd do that once he confirmed his suspicions. "Better to ask forgiveness than get permission," he muttered.

An implanted GPS—in the small box containing the necklace of the deceased—had taken Trapp to downtown Cincinnati, where he witnessed Stone meeting with José Santos, son of the kingpin of the Santos organization. Further, the GPS trace of the necklace led to an Over-the-Rhine jewelry shop. Today, Trapp would have a talk with the owner of that shop, for the tiny box had not moved from the location since the day someone, probably José Santos, left it there. He had some questions that the jeweler needed to answer.

The Over-The-Rhine community, a few blocks north of downtown Cincinnati, was once a thriving German community. It prided itself in German-speaking churches, schools, shops, and newspapers. The distinctively German breweries transported their wares via multiple tunnels that wound their way underneath the city. But the anti-German fury during WWI sent most of the residents scurrying to communities outside the city, where some of them, in an attempt to hide their identity—out of fear of reprisal for their ancestry—forsook their German names and adopted more American sounding names. So, with this flight of its founders, the community went through a series of transitions during the next few generations. Scots-Irish Appalachian folks from Kentucky, Tennessee, and West Virginia filled the vacuum created by this mass exodus of German founders. Later, the razing of the west-side of Cincinnati—for the construction of I-75 that cut through the heart of the city—brought an influx of blacks into the area. This happened somewhat simultaneously as the Appalachian folks gradually moved out of the inner city for single-family housing that dotted the hillsides of the surrounding communities. Over time, most of the buildings fell into disrepair. But this inner-city architectural jewel of nineteenth-century Italianate and German Revival buildings somehow survived virtually as it had been originally built. When newly built government housing projects consumed city blocks in other areas of Cincinnati, this historic district made it into the twenty-first century, one of the few communities to do so in the United States.

The German immigrants had nicknamed their community Over-The-Rhine, and the name had stuck. To an outsider, the name didn't make much sense, but the name had piqued Trapp's curiosity. The Lake Erie Canal system once reached all the way to the Ohio River, so residents of the community had to cross over that canal to get to their places of employment in downtown Cincinnati. The German residents called the canal the Rhine, after the river in their motherland. So the phrase, "I'm headed over the Rhine" became daily casual conversation. In time, Over-The-Rhine became the name of the community, and the name survived all the other changes that happened to the city.

Though many of the buildings were abandoned and in disarray, the structures were as reliable as the day they were built. There was talk about revitalization, but the crime rate discouraged developers. One website that listed crime rates of cities—for the sake of insurance companies who offered insurance to businesses—recently listed Over-The-Rhine as the most dangerous neighborhood in the nation.

Trapp instinctively touched his sidearm as he stepped from his unmarked car and scanned the street in both directions. A construction crew had half the sidewalk blocked with plastic, orange fencing. All the windows had been removed from a series of adjoining buildings, their roofs exposed all the way to the walls, and workers were hoisting long, timber joists to the top, quite an impressive undertaking.

A bell jingled as he opened the door to the jewelry shop. A small-framed man, not much more than five feet tall and probably above eighty in age, quickly emerged from a back room. He climbed a barstool and leaned against the ornate glass counter that ran the width of the store. A magnifying lens attached to a black, eyeglass frame perched atop his forehead.

"May I help you, sir?" the man asked.

The accent was probably that of a German holdout from the old days, one of the stubborn ones who refused to leave. Or he could have been an Italian from Newport or Covington, twin cities just across the river but separated by the Licking River that flowed into the Ohio. Italian store owners had moved into the area when the Germans left. Trapp wanted to ask his nationality, but he assumed that would not be a positive way to begin the conversation.

"Yes, I'm Tony Trapp. I'm the lead detective in an investigation of a death."

"Another murder?" His expression feigned innocence before Trapp even hinted of implication to a crime.

"Yes, a young lady was killed. She was wearing a necklace … a small, diamond-studded, cross necklace about this big." He used his thumb and index finger as a ruler. He didn't bother with the true details—that the charred body of a young woman clutched the necklace in her hand—for the less info he shared about the crime the better. "I've traced the necklace to your shop, and I was hoping you could help my investigation by answering a few questions."

"I need from you an identification," the man protested.

"Oh, sure. Sorry, Mr. —"

"García … Miguel García."

The name surprised Trapp. Spanish? Certainly not German. "I should have shown that, to begin with." Trapp flashed his badge.

"May I see up close, please?"

Trapp reluctantly moved his shield closer and cringed as the man studied it. "I'm actually from across the state line … Indiana, to be exact."

"And why do you not tell me that to begin with? Never mind, it is okay. I have the necklace … it is beautiful … and I could not pass on such a beautiful masterpiece. I had no idea it was a part of an investigation. Oh, well, I have lost money before, but I'm an old man, and what is money anyway. Just paper … but diamonds, that is something much more important. It is so beautiful … and a beautiful story behind the necklace."

"What do you mean by a beautiful story?"

"It belonged to a young woman, Eden, such a beautiful child. She wore it only on three occasions … special occasions … the night of her *fiesta de quinceañera*, that was her fifteenth birthday when her father … he gave it to her. She wore it the day of her wedding, and she made the necklace beautiful. And she wore it on a visit to the Kentucky Derby. How exciting for her … the race … the beautiful horses! She used to own a beautiful horse in Mexico." He paused.

How could this man know all these facts—assuming they were all true? Some were, for Trapp had already figured them out. But this man knew too many details not to be a part of her life.

"You know an awful lot about the young woman who wore—"

"I hope I have done nothing wrong by having the necklace in my possession. I did not believe it was stolen."

"No, nothing wrong with possessing … unless it was stolen." That should shake him up some, Trapp thought. "I just have some questions about the person who sold it to you."

"He did not sell it to me. To the contrary, I am selling it for the owner. What do you need to know?" He sighed.

"Did you get the name of the person who sold ... who gave you the necklace to sell for them?"

"I did not need to get his name, for I know him."

"Professor Christopher Stone?"

"No, José Santos."

"José Santos?" This is incredulous, Trapp thought. Stone is blatantly dealing with the Santos cartel.

"Yes. A fine young man. He attends the university here. Xavier. Do you know it, the University?"

"Yes, I hear they have a decent basketball program," Trapp said, trying the casual approach.

"Perhaps. I follow little sports … soccer sometimes."

"So, how do you know José Santos?" This conversation was gaining momentum, and Trapp wanted to ride the wave as long as he could.

"I am his *padrino*."

"I don't understand—"

"Godfather … *padrino*. That's what brought me to Cincinnati. I am obligated to protect him, to guide him spiritually … and … I want that he can get a good education."

"So, you're related to the Santos family?"

"From his mother's side. Please do not judge me … and do not judge José because of his family name."

"Sure, I agree, don't judge a book by its cover … not responsible for the sins of the father … I get it," Trapp said in the kindest tone his cop tactics could muster. He paused, studying the old man's face … the wrinkles … the large eye just behind the magnifying lens that had fallen from its perched position. The sight was comical, but the occasion was too serious for humor. "Then do you happen to know how the young woman by the name of Eden was associated with José Santos?"

"Eden, yes, a sweet child if ever there was one. Yes, I know it was she who was murdered. José told me some time ago." He looked out the window, a genial stare as if he could see her walking down the street. She is his sister. You did not know that?"

"Uh … no … I assumed that they were somehow related ... but not siblings" He could not believe he had missed this. And this little bit of info was a game changer. "But why were we not able to figure out Eden was Chico Santos' daughter?"

"He was very protective of her, purposefully keeping her identity as secret as possible … for her safety. Only the inner circle knew she was his daughter. I love her and José like my own children."

"I'm sorry for your loss. That's why I'm here. I believe her husband is responsible for her death. I mean to prove that. Did you know her husband?"

"Yes, but her husband did not kill her."

"And just how would you know that?" Trapp did not hide his emotions, for he was determined to convict Christopher Stone, even if it was the hardest thing he ever accomplished.

Miguel hesitated. "You don't know, do you?" The expression on his face reflected his surprise.

"Know what?" The question set Trapp aback.

"You don't know how Christopher and Eden met. How they fell in love in Mexico … while he was an undercover agent in Mexico—"

"Stone was in law enforcement?" Trapp shook his head. It had crossed his mind, but he hadn't followed through on his hunch.

"Quite an impressive one, I understand, especially since he actually infiltrated the Santos family. I never approved of the Santos occupation, *Señor* Trapp … never … nor did Eden and José … they wanted out, and Christopher rescued them. The other family members were very angry at him, and so they planned his assassination. It was a long time before they found him."

"But it doesn't make sense … her death … their own daughter? Why would they kill her?" This info created more questions for Trapp.

"You think her father purposefully had her killed?" Miguel asked, his surprise obvious.

"No, I never thought he ordered his daughter killed … of course I did not know she was Santos' daughter."

"You are right. He would never … but he did not know she had married Christopher," Miguel said. "They assumed she and her brother had been kidnapped by one of the rival drug lords. They are ruthless, you know, the cartels. Her death was totally unplanned."

The room went silent except for the rhythmic tic-tic, tic-tic of a wall clock. A siren blared in the distance. Miguel did not seem to notice. If all this was true, Trapp had been following the wrong leads for months. Chris Stone … an undercover agent? Had the Feds purposefully withheld this info from him? Had they stonewalled him to keep their game intact? That was a possibility. The various agencies were cooperating more since 9/11, but they had a long way to go in sharing info. "So, Chico Santos' hit on Christopher Stone killed his own daughter?" Trapp said, studiedly.

"It seems so. And I shall never forgive him … Chico. His impetuousness killed his only … ."

The old man wiped away his tears.

"I'm sorry, sir." Trapp placed a comforting hand on the slumping shoulder of the old man. "I truly am. I have been trying to solve her death … but I thought the professor … her husband … had brought about her death through his dealing of drugs. I did not know he was undercover … I thought greed had—"

"No, it was simply revenge … the hate of Chico for Mr. Christopher having him locked up … for being, how do you say it?" He paused. "Suckered by Christopher Stone?"

"But even good men sometimes go bad. How can I be sure Christopher Stone hasn't seized on an opportunity to advance financially … sell the necklace to purchase drugs and capitalize on the Santos' misfortune?" Trapp asked, his hands extended in a quizzical gesture.

"I can assure you with my hand upon the Holy Book, selling the necklace is not for drugs?" The old man said emphatically.

"I need more than your word, sir. I need proof," Trapp said.

"We have already made arrangements for the money to be dispersed. One hundred thousand goes to the university for José's tuition and room and board for the next two years, and … ." He paused when a black man entered the shop.

"Good mornin', amigo, special delivery for my friend." He tossed a Cincinnati Inquirer onto the counter, gave the old man a fist bump and a gold tooth grin. "See ya tomorrow."

"Thank you, Mr. Charles," Miguel said, smiling.

"Anything for you, my man." He glanced suspiciously at Trapp and exited the room. Once outside, he hesitated, peering through the window as if he might not leave the old man alone with a stranger packing a weapon. He finally picked up his bundle of papers and headed across the street, glancing back a couple times.

The old man waited until he was out of sight before he spoke. “The remaining four hundred thousand will be sent to an orphanage in—”

“Don’t tell me, an orphanage just outside Mexico City … Father Gallardo.”

“You know him?” Miguel asked, surprised.

“Yes, I visited with him sometime back, but he was mum on what he knew about this whole ordeal. I am quite impressed by his mission to the children.”

“Eden cared for the children. Now, even in death, her love will continue.” Miguel said.

“Well, Mr. García, I thank you, sir, for your help. You’ve shared more about this case in five minutes than I’ve discovered in five months.”

“I am glad I can help Eden’s husband find some peace in his storm. Too bad about his blindness. He is a good man.”

They shook hands. “Uh, you know I will have to verify all the financial transactions?” Trapp said.

“Of course.” Miguel smiled. He pulled out a drawer, retrieved a piece of paper, and handed it to Trapp. “Here is the contact *información* for the person who will be purchasing the necklace. You will find everything I have said to be the truth.”

“Thank you, sir,” Trapp said.

They shook hands again, and Trapp exited the store. He cautiously walked to his car. What if the Santos cartel knew Miguel was in Cincinnati, helping José hide from his family, and selling a family heirloom. That could bring the wrath of Chico. The old man was certainly safer living Over-The-Rhine, no matter its crime rate, than he was crossing the Santos cartel.

He sat in his car for a long moment, reflecting. One thing still troubled him: If Eden Stone only wore the necklace on special occasions, which Miguel listed as three times, why was she clutching it in her hand the night of her murder? The old man had given him much to consider.

Chapter 38

Thomas Stein sat in the living room of the home that he had moved into the year his wife died and right after his son had left for college. The move from New York to Louisville proved to be a good change for Thomas. He became acquainted with a Christian businessman who helped him through his grief and witnessed to him about the hope offered through Christ's resurrection.

At first, Thomas resisted the idea of Christianity, for to become a Christian seemed an abandonment of his Jewish faith. On the advice of his friend, he read multiple times the Bible story of the conversion of a prominent Jewish rabbi in the first century by the name of Saul. As he considered the transition of this first-century theologian from Judaism to Christianity, he found himself asking the same question that Saul had asked. "Who art thou, Lord?"

Thomas wrestled with the account of Saul's conversion, like Jacob of old wrestled all night with an unidentified angel. "Tell me, I pray thee, thy name," Jacob had pleaded for the identity of this heavenly being. The request wasn't granted Jacob, but the angel did change his name. The name change signified he was a transformed man. Further, the angel protected Jacob's life from the wrath of his angry brother, Esau. Jacob went from a name which implied "deceiver" to being called Israel: "one who strives with God." Jacob received the Lord's blessing, but not without a cost. A painful limp remained a constant reminder of his clash with Deity on that moonlit plain.

Almost two millenniums after Jacob, another Hebrew, Saul—also known by his Roman name, Paul—sought to know the identity of God, and this time God revealed His name. "I am Jesus whom thou persecutest." The answer surprised Saul, but he accepted it. And like Jacob, Saul's encounter with God had its cost, for he had a "thorn in his flesh" that remained the rest of his life.

Saul became a missionary, and using his Roman name, Paul, preached the message of the Jewish Messiah to the Gentiles, and he raised up multiple congregations across Asia Minor all the way to Rome. In one of his several letters to the churches, he mentioned his "thorn in the flesh." The Scripture doesn't precisely define what Paul's thorn happened to be. Some speculate it was lingering impaired vision caused by the bright light that shown from heaven and left him blind until a Christian minister prayed for him to receive his sight.

Unlike Jacob and Saul, Thomas Stein could identify no lingering physical impairment as a result of his spiritual journey, but he could identify with them in their quest for God's identity. He eventually realized that Jesus of Nazareth was much more than a prophet, or a good man, or an anointed teacher. He was God Incarnate, God in human form: Immanuel, God with us, is how the Prophet Isaiah described the coming Messiah. And the angel's announcement to Joseph reiterated such. The God of the *Tanakh* became a man in Christ and became the Savior of the world. In becoming a Christian,

Thomas Stein wasn't rejecting the God of Judaism; he was accepting the promised Messiah of Israel.

Things worked out well when the protective witness program decided to send Chris Stone to Clarksville, Indiana, just across the river from where his father lived. The agency never knew his father had moved from New York to Louisville, and Chris never bothered to tell them. He had been able to introduce Eden to his father, and they infrequently met at restaurants around the area.

"I wish you could have gotten to know Eden better." Chris broke the silence.

"I do too, son. And you know what else I wish for?"

"What's that?"

"I wish you can get to know her God and Savior."

"You're speaking of Jesus?"

"Yes."

"The way she adored her God, I wish I could know him too, but with all that's happened, I'm rather confused about God, and Jesus, and Judaism, and Christianity. Nothing makes sense to me. Why would a loving God … ?" He did not finish his question, but he could not prevent the complete question in his thoughts. And he could not dull the pain it aroused in his heart.

"There was a Jewish man a long time ago who became confused about the identity of God." Thomas Stein spoke slowly. He had not seen his son for weeks. It was good to be together again, and surprisingly, it was somewhat comfortable for them to speak about God. This had been a closed door in the past couple of years.

"You're referring to Saul of Tarsus?"

"Yes. You've heard about him?"

"Of course, I've heard of Saul, Dad! I'm a religions professor. Remember?"

"Sorry, I didn't mean to sound condescending."

"And I was over responding. Eden tried to get me to believe the story, but as much as I adored her, I never put much stock in the stories from the Christian Bible. So I never really took time to consider Saul's story."

"Do you mind if I share it, from my perspective, and how it has helped me?" Thomas asked.

"Can't hurt." Chris knew his heart was softening toward Christianity. In the past, he would not have wasted his time with such a conversation. He somewhat regretted he had not read from Eden's Bible, for that would have created another memory of her. But that was a part of her life which he did not share.

Thomas' enthusiasm spilled over into his New York accent. "Saul was a dyed-in-the-wool Jew. He could have been among the crowd demanding Christ's death. And we know, from his own testimony, that he violently persecuted Christians, incarcerating many, dividing families, even responsible for the death of some. But God saw his heart, a heart convinced he did God service by fighting against apostasy. So God personally challenged his acts, struck him to the ground, blinded him, and demanded an answer as to what he was doing. And that is how Saul came to be a Christian, and ultimately he became one of Christ's apostles."

"And let's suppose for a moment that I believe the account actually happened. How did Saul, being Jewish, conclude that Jesus was God? How did he bypass the basic of *Shema*, 'Hear oh Israel, the Lord our God is one?'"

"At first Saul was confused, since he thought he was on the side of God, but it was obvious he was fighting against God. So, he inquired as to the identity of this Divine interruption, for indeed it was a Divine interruption: a voice, a force that struck him to the ground, and a light so bright it blinded him. After that, God responded, 'I am Jesus.' So the answer to your question of how Saul found out who Jesus was is that he asked Him." The sound of Thomas' teacup as he set it on the glass-covered end-table seemed to punctuate the statement.

"He asked? He just asked? That's it?" Chris questioned emphatically.

"Yes."

Chris didn't try to conceal his sarcasm. "But I am no Saul, and to the contrary, I'm far from being a religious man." Chris reached slowly for his own cup of tea.

"In a way, you are like Saul?"

Chris sipped his tea contemplatively. "How's that?" He couldn't suppress a smile. This was the father he remembered, the salesman.

"Jewish by birth. Youthful zealousness. Confusion regarding religion. Blindness."

Chris did not respond.

"I'm not trying to make a sell, David. I'm simply being honest with you regarding my newfound faith."

His father was the only person alive who called him David. Something about the sound of it gave him a sense of belonging. He had been adrift too long. Eden had been his anchor.

"I suppose, in a way, you're right, Dad. Don't forget the name change. Saul started using his Roman name as a missionary to the Gentiles. Right?" Chris chuckled.

"Yes, especially the name change. I think you know more about this story than you're letting on."

The room grew silent, except for the ticking of the family heirloom, a grandfather clock Thomas purchased from an antique dealer in the old city of Jerusalem. A momentary clang of the clock startled Chris, but his heart had relaxed by the tenth dong. He had heard the old chimes for almost two decades, and the commonness of its tolls almost rendered it meaningless to tell time. Blindness had done something to him, for him. He listened more intently, purposefully, and in so doing, nothing of sound escaped his ears, and most everything of significance made its unique sound, and every sound carried meaning.

It had been a good evening, special, even though religion could cause rifts in his relationship with his father, but he was no longer offended by his dad's persuasive means. Still, his heart remained unchanged. He was hopelessly cast into an emotionless, religious abyss, and religion left him with more questions than answers.

The recliner moaned as his dad disengaged the footrest. "And speaking of name changes," Thomas said, "don't you think it's about time you start using your real name? Your secret is blown anyway. And I doubt the Santos family will pursue revenge now. I don't want you leaving me again and taking on another identity. I want you to come home, David. Reclaim your identity. You're a Stein, David Stein, not Chris Stone. I still can't believe they allowed you to use Stone for your new identity. Did you choose it?"

"Yes, I thought it rather clever." Chris gently placed his cup on the end-table, making sure it was away from the edge. "I best be going. Will you call a cab for me?" He stood and reached for his cane.

Thomas rose from his chair, wrapped his arms around Chris, and held him tightly. "They probably never had a clue your Jewish name actually meant stone. Did you ever tell them it's meaning?"

"No, never did."

Thomas released his grip and nudged Chris to the window. "We used to view the stars together when you were a little tyke. You were fascinated by the night sky."

"I remember, but that seems a long time ago."

"Look, there's Sirius, the brightest of stars, standing out among many." Thomas paused, realizing his mistake. "I'm sorry son, I can't imagine being blind, for light is God's gift to us. He needs no light to see, for He is light, so the lights He created are for our benefit. Our story began when God first said, 'Let there be light.' It was a star that led the wise men to Jesus. It was a bright light that caused Saul to question his life and search out the truths of God, instead of following the traditions of men. Without Christ's light, there is no life, for 'In Him was life; and the life was the light of men.'"

There was a long silence before Chris spoke. "I feel like I'm not only living in physical darkness, I'm in spiritual darkness regarding God. Do you think He'll ever show me the way, show me who He really is?"

"Why not ask Him and see?"

"Is it really that simple?"

"It worked for Saul."

The conversation fell silent, amplifying Thomas' footsteps on the hardwood floor as he made his way across the room and dialed a cab. Chris stared intently into the darkness of the night and into the endless blackness that shrouded his soul. A flash of light startled him. It was a flash akin to an eye condition he had experienced years before, caused by a tiny retina tear in his right eye. He blinked.

Another flash of light. And another. Hope momentarily arose in his heart. And though ever so slightly, it was, for the first time in a long time, a ray of hope. For some unknown reason, he mentally recited a Scripture he recalled from Paul's letter to the church at Corinth, a verse that his father had sent him when explaining his conversion to Christianity. "For God, who commanded the light to shine out of darkness, hath shined in our hearts, to give the light of the knowledge of the glory of God in the face of Jesus Christ."

If only that light could shine in his heart.

Chapter 39

The contact gave no time for discussion. He established the dollar amount at half a million, the time and place for the rendezvous, and hung up in the middle of the first question. Chris immediately dialed José Santos and made arrangements to fly out of Louisville International. He ended the conversation emphatically: "*Vamos!*"

Chapter 40

Tony Trapp's case had unraveled quicker than a kitten attacking a roll of toilet paper. What a terrible mistake in judgment regarding Christopher Stone hiring two Arabs to assassinate his wife! His new theory—Trapp as an undercover agent whose wife was simply collateral damage—likewise left him high and dry. The Feds wouldn't return his call to verify that Stone was in their witness protective program, leaving him on a dead-end street. Further, Miguel Garcías's story wasn't panning out. Trapp had been gullible and swallowed the bait hook, line, and sinker. He weighed the evidence he had compiled regarding the necklace and the recent turn of events. He had used the jewelry in an attempt to track and trap Christopher Stone in some criminal act. The ruse had terribly backfired. Whether planned or as an afterthought, he could not be sure why things had gone south, but half a million dollars can cause the best of men to quickly sour.

The contact information for the buyers of the necklace—the old man in Cincinnati had given the info to him—could not be verified, as multiple phone calls and messages went unanswered. He now believed Miguel García had lied to him. A third trip to Cincinnati found a "closed" sign in the window of the jewelry store. A trace on the old man confirmed through Mexico customs that a Miguel García, traveling with José Santos, and Christopher Stone had entered the country, but they had no idea of their whereabouts. They had entered the country legally, all with passports, so the authorities didn't seem too concerned.

He had been duped: by an eighty-year-old man. And Stone and José Santos and the old man had disappeared into the Mexican underworld, probably never to be seen or heard from again. The Mexican government would not cooperate with a small-time cop, so he now had to take this mess to his superior. He'd rather write his resignation and be gone from the department, but he was no quitter, so he would take his reprimand on the chin and get back to work. He had to admit, this was the most perplexing crime that had ever come across his desk.

To further mystify the case, an overnight package arrived via Federal Express from Father Gallardo with a note that didn't make any sense.

> *You asked that I contact you if I had any information to share. This may be of interest to you. I received the enclosed items in the mail. Not sure what this means. Perhaps it is a veiled threat to the orphanage. I am not sure, but I am concerned.*

The package also contained a pair of baby booties. Was this some kind of joke? In a matter of a week he'd let go of a diamond necklace of considerable worth, and he now had a pair of fifty-cent baby booties to replace it. But he now had a new lead—if you call a pair of baby booties a lead—and he had a lot of explaining to do to his superiors. As for the note from Father Gallardo, multiple calls to the orphanage went unanswered. He had no idea what the letter meant, and he could only surmise that the padre was now in danger, thanks to him, or was up to his neck in some kind of Mexican corruption. And the only thing Trapp had to show for five months of investigation was a pair of baby booties. He studied the booties, turning them in his hand.

In the past, when a case stumped Trapp, though he had never divulged his secret to anyone, he sometimes used a routine as simple as an elementary reading class. He decided it time to revert to his child-like logic. He turned to a blank page on a yellow, legal pad and drew a pentagon. In each section of the five points, he wrote one of five different words: who, when, where, what, and why. In the middle of the diagram, he wrote a single word: story. Called a story star, he used the sketch to focus on all the known points of the case. He slowly went from point to point, answering each of the five questions with as much detail as possible. He kept returning to the "what" category. He had missed something. He scribbled a single word and circled it a couple times. What could baby booties have to do with a murder? An hour into this routine, he slammed his pencil onto the notepad.

"Rogers," he barked, "book me a flight to Mexico City. On second thought, book two tickets. Is your passport up-to-date?"

"Yes, sir," Rogers responded, a grin spreading across his face as transparent as a Red Delicious apple wrapped in cellophane. "When?"

"Yesterday," Trapp said. "We should have been there yesterday."

Chapter 41

A tired Trapp fell asleep before the landing gear retracted and slept through snack-time, but his biological clock woke him before dawn. He stared out the window at the soul-stirring sight taking place in the distant horizon. The six-hour, red-eye flight floated parallel to the bright-orange sphere glowing in the eastern skyline.

A thousand-million lights flickered out in the vast valley that sprawled below them. Mexico City is the most densely populated capitol in America, with well over eight million people, and the metro area has as many as twenty million, making it the most populated metropolis in the Western Hemisphere. It boasts as being the most populated Spanish-speaking city in the world. And at over seven thousand feet in elevation, it is the seventh tallest capitol city in the world.

The ancient city was built on an island in the midst of Lake Texcoco, the largest lake of a multi-lake system that inundated the Valley of Mexico. The lakes were eventually drained for city expansion, but due to the heavily saturated clay of the former lake bottoms, in some locations of the modern city, the land had sunk as much as thirty feet. To further complicate the lives of its citizens, the city is vulnerable to earthquakes, and the people have experienced many devastating quakes.

The plane skirted the edge of the metropolis as they approached the international airport, located on the east side of Mexico City. In centuries past, minus the smog of a hundred-thousand cook stoves, the sun rose brightly over the ancient city, illuminating the *Templo Mayor.* This "Main Temple" area used to be the Aztec's capitol city, Tenochtitlan. This thirteenth century Aztec temple complex is now a favorite tourist attraction, though its location had been lost for centuries, buried beneath the sprawling city. The conquering Spaniards tore the temple apart around the fifteen hundreds, and they built their own cathedral atop the sprawling site. The buried ruins were discovered early in the twentieth century, and extensive archaeology digs have reconfigured the ancient site.

Dedicated to the god of war and also the god of agriculture, the temple complex had dominated the lives of the ancient people with strange rituals. In one such ceremony, designed for personal communication with the gods, individuals perforated parts of the body: lips, tongue, earlobes, chest, and God knows what else. Strange how history repeats itself, how religious rituals resurrect and dominate later societies, often with little if any understanding of the origin. The purpose of such ancient rituals and their places of worship stood in contrast to what present-day, civilized societies' modus operandi is supposed to be. Still, some of the considerations of social and moral development that qualified some people of the past as being uncivilized, seem to be present in so-called civilized societies of today.

Since his last trip to Mexico, Trapp had read a couple books on Aztec history, of which he was both intrigued and appalled. The craftsmanship of the ancient temples fascinated him: erected of massive stones, symmetrically designed, using ancient tools and what should have been limited math skills. And multiple sites remain. Still, the appalling rituals that took place in the Aztec temples were difficult for him to comprehend. How does a society stoop to human sacrifice? How do you destroy that which you value the most? Life! Can one truly value something and terminate it at the same time. But somehow—in a distorted way, no, it was more than distorted, it was a debased and perverted mindset—mankind imagines that the gods demand the most cherished. Trapp well understood why priests of these ancient rituals wore masks. He wondered about the expressions on the faces of modern doctors as they tear from their mothers the tiny body parts of the unborn, who moments before had beating hearts, active brainwaves, and instincts such as sucking their thumbs. To what cause are these infants sacrificed? Convenience? Secrecy? Ambition? Selfishness? Or is it just that the pro-choice movement has successfully brainwashed a society?

He contrasted Christianity—which celebrated the sacrifice of Christ on the cross—to the religions that offered humans as a sacrifice to the gods. How did it differ? The God of Christianity didn't demand from the humans one of their own; instead, God came in human form to be their sacrifice. Trapp reflected upon the ancient proclamation of Abraham of Scripture: "God shall prepare Himself a sacrifice." He had not been to church for months, but childhood memory verses popped into his head involuntarily.

The plane touched down and made its way to the newest of the two terminals. Detectives Diego Quinones and Samuel Ortega, plain clothes detectives, met them inside the terminal and flashed their badges to by-pass customs. Once outside, they crowded into a Volkswagen Beetle parked illegally alongside the pickup curb.

With their luggage tied to the top of the Beetle, they weaved in and out of morning rush-hour, and an hour later pulled up to the driveway of the orphanage Trapp had previously visited. The children were at play inside the fenced compound. Some stopped what they were doing and rushed to the fence, where they peered at the strangers, their huge, dark eyes reflecting the message of their empty stomachs, fodder for those pushing hard against Mexico's strict abortion laws. A worker, in a black uniform and tattered, white tennis shoes strolled to the fence and redirected the children back to their morning activities.

A black Mercedes-Benz SUV blocked the entrance to the driveway. The driver exited the vehicle and walked toward the Beetle, his concealed gun bulging from his left side. Trapp instinctively reached for his own sidearm, but quickly remembered he was a stranger in a foreign land, entirely dependent upon the two detectives in the front seat.

"That's Santiago," Detective Quinones whispered.

Quinones was a thirty-year veteran in the anti-drug war that dominated Mexico's police activities. He rolled down his window and waited, his Glock 9-millimeter resting on his knee. When the driver reached the window, Quinones snatched up his Glock, pointed it at Santiago's chest, and calmly said, "Hello, Santiago. We've been looking for you for a long time. Looks like you are up to no good. Now slowly, extend your hands and place them on the door. One word from you and I will split your skull like a dropped, overripe melon."

Quinones cuffed Santiago's left wrist to the steering wheel, slipped his gun from its holster, and tossed it to Trapp. "*Vamos, amigos.* Let's go. *Señor* Rogers, check the SUV and see if you can find another gun."

As Quinones exited the Beetle, Santiago slammed the door into him. Quinones pushed back against Santiago, maneuvered from the car, and whacked him against the side of his head. Santiago fell hard to the ground, his left arm dangling awkwardly at the end of the cuff: blood gushed from the gash in his head.

Detective Samuel Ortega hastened toward the main entrance of the compound. Trapp and Quinones quickly joined him. Quinones eased the door ajar to see the backs of two suited men, thumbing bills from a stuffed briefcase that sat on a table in the middle of the foyer. Trapp saw their pistols laying on the table. How lucky can a cop get!

Father Gallardo stood to the left of the room, his eyes seemingly riveted on Trapp, to which Trapp motioned for him to look away. He quickly complied. The old man from Cincinnati stood to the right, perplexity and fear scrawled across his face. José Santos, sat in a high-back, wooden chair, his eyes darting from the perpetrators to the briefcase as if any moment he would rush them. Trapp touched an index finger to his lips, and shook his head, hoping José could read his gestures, and if so, would obey them. A young and frightened woman, her eyes bloodshot and her face flushed, sat on a worn and stained purple, velveteen chair, her hands gripped together in her lap. Professor Stone, wearing dark sunglasses, stood behind her, his hands resting consolingly on her shoulders.

A lopsided fan oscillated in the corner, it's annoying rattle sufficient enough to muffle their entrance. Detective Quinones tiptoed across the room and pressed his pistol against one of the perps, who froze in mid-count of a stack of bills. "Make a wrong move, and you are a dead man, *Señor* Fernando." Fernando dropped the stack of bills into the briefcase and slowly raised his hands.

As if on cue, Rogers entered from a rear door, welding some sort of assault weapon with a pistol grip, just as Trapp rushed to the other man and stuck his confiscated gun against his spine. The man started for his gun, but Detective Quinones whacked his pistol against his bald head. The man crumpled to the floor, knocking the briefcase off the table, and the fan sent bills flying in all directions.

Father Gallardo fell to his knees, hands clasped against his chest, face upward, eyes closed, mouthing a prayer. José Santos rushed to the young woman who collapsed into his arms. The old man dropped to his knees and started gathering up the bills and placing them back into the briefcase. Chris Stone showed little emotion behind the dark glasses, that is until the young woman turned to him and pulled him close, gently stroking his wavy-black hair. Months of constrained emotions broke forth in heavy sobs as tears flooded his cheeks and fell onto her cream-colored, silk blouse.

Detective Tony Trapp shook his head in disbelief as he observed in one sweeping motion the scene before him. The last of the puzzle pieces had fallen into place, and the picture was completely different then he had ever imagined, but it was the most beautiful outcome in all his years of police work. He had just witnessed, not a drug deal, but a ransom plot foiled by sheer conjecture, and he had participated in a last-minute rescue of five innocent people from the hands of a cruel and calculating drug cartel. But more amazing than this, it slowly dawned on him that he had witnessed the resurrection of Eden Stone. Never in all his wildest dreams would he have pictured this outcome for the most difficult case of his career. "Only God," he whispered, "only God."

Chapter 42

Trapp and Rogers met at the Jeffersonville, Indiana, waterfront near the John F. Kennedy Memorial Bridge, at a local restaurant called Kingfish. They gathered to celebrate their victory in what they considered the most extraordinary case in their law-enforcement career. Trapp said so himself, with the flair resembling the speech of a coach to his celebrating team after a comeback victory. Their special guests sat across from them: Chris and Eden Stone.

Kingfish was a locally owned restaurant that had been a landmark in the Kentuckiana area for over sixty years. It opened in 1948 on Derby Day, and it served up its delicious seafood seven days a week to hungry locals who appreciate the finest in seafood and service. The original two owners named the restaurant after a character in the famous radio program called *Amos and Andy*—Kingfish. The new owners chose to keep the classic name. And through the years the management worked hard to maintain their proud reputation for great seafood and excellent service.

Their table faced the waterfront, offering a perfect view of the Louisville skyline through a wall of glass. A tugboat pushed a flotilla of barges upstream, struggling against the formidable tide of the Ohio. The captain had just maneuvered the strait that by-passed—by a few dozen yards—the treacherous Falls of the Ohio. This area was where Lewis and Clark met a little over two-hundred years ago and began their trek westward. Their camp on the island near the falls served two purposes: protection from Indians and the prevention of deserters. Their goal was to explore beyond the continental divide, all the way to the Pacific coast. A specific objective was to discover a waterway across the continent, for the purpose of commerce. They journeyed southwest on the Ohio to the mighty Mississippi and north to St. Louis, then northwest on the Missouri River, which they hoped would lead them to the water passage through the divide. They discovered a lot of Native American Indian tribes, and they made significant contributions to science as they cataloged and described various plants, animals, birds, and multiple never before recorded observations of this new and varied land, but they found no water passageway through the divide, for, to their disappointment, such a waterway did not exist. They carried with them recently minted silver metals, called Indian Peace Metals, which they gave as gifts to the Indian tribes along the way. The recipients wore them proudly around their necks, displaying the portrait of the white man's president, Thomas Jefferson. They had no understanding that these metals around their necks could well represent the sovereignty of the United States government over all the free-spirited Indian nations inhabiting the land, an unprecedented amount of land which President Jefferson had recently convinced Congress to purchase from Napoleon's French Republic. The purchase helped Napoleon finance what became a failed campaign in Europe, and it would displace entire indigenous nations in the western hemisphere. The cost involved far more than money; it would affect countless lives on both sides of the Atlantic. And that journey across the great divide began in Louisville.

Life is full of change: good and bad. Much of the change along a major waterway like the Ohio is caused by flooding. The latest of four major floods had affected the landscape of the area. Shortly after that flood, the owners of the Kingfish Restaurant relocated from the Kentucky side of the river in downtown Louisville to its current location in Jeffersonville, looking back across the river to where the restaurant used to be.

The last few months had brought unbelievable change to the life of Chris Stone: mostly bad. But the pendulum had swung back in his favor, and though blind, he now saw life clearer than when his eyes could see. He awkwardly tapped the table until he touched Eden's hand. She responded by clasping his hand.

"I'm living the dream," Chris said to no one in particular. He smiled.

"Yes, you are, Chris," Trapp said. "I never, in my wildest imaginations, could see this ending."

"Nor I," Chris said.

"When did the ransom demand come, Chris," Trapp asked.

"Right after your trip to Cincinnati to track the necklace." Chris hesitated before continuing. "It's like they knew we had the money from the sale of the necklace … but I think that was coincidental."

"I'm sorry, Eden, perhaps we shouldn't speak of this for a while … until you—"

"No, Detective Trapp, I am okay to speak of it. I don't think I was ever in any harm, but they didn't exactly know what to do with me. They seemed afraid to let my family know they had kidnapped me, and both I, and them, assumed Chris was dead from the bombing. So, it was like we were in a holding pattern … my father in prison … from whom could they collect a ransom? And it took them a while to figure out Chris was alive."

"And us all the time thinking you were dead," Trapp said, "so we were not looking for you."

"So, when did you figure it out, that Eden was alive?" Chris asked Trapp.

Trapp hesitated as he contemplated the question. "I really never realized she was alive, till the moment we entered the orphanage and

I saw this beautiful lady … ." He paused. "I saw this phantom … I couldn't believe my eyes, but then it all fit, like the missing pieces of a puzzle. The booties literally popped into my brain, and something clicked. The first day we met, that night sitting in your living room, Chris, you said she was crocheting before you went to bed. Remember?"

"I do." Chris nodded.

"Was that a hint for this thick-headed cop, or was that coincidental?" Trapp asked.

"No, sir, I had not yet put it together, that the crocheting material was missing, until much later," Chris answered. "I actually had a friend search my house looking for it," he added, "but even though he didn't find it, I still didn't connect the dots."

"I, Dallas and I—"

"Thank you, sir, for including me in this investigation," Rogers said. They all laughed.

"Like I was saying, Dallas and I hadn't given it much attention either. We should have challenged the missing crocheting material … followed the lead or proved you a liar. But when the package with the booties and note from Father Gallardo arrived, that got me to thinking. We had not conducted an autopsy to confirm the identity of the slain woman … since all evidence pointed it to being Eden. I wondered, could the dead person be someone else. Could Eden Stone be alive, abducted, and having taken the crochet material with her somehow … maybe stuffed in her pocket. And I thought she could be sending a message … though I must admit my faith was a bit … Peterian … if that is a word. Dallas, is that a word?"

"Doubtful," Rogers said. They all laughed.

"You know, the Apostle Peter sinking when he took his eyes off Jesus," Trapp explained.

"We got it, sir," Rogers said. "Just giving you a hard time." They laughed again.

"Of course, the question also arose, had she faked her own death for some reason to escape her marriage? Sorry, Chris, but at first I had pegged you as contributing to whatever had happened to Eden. Then we finally associated Eden with the Santos family."

Trapp breathed in and exhaled slowly. “Miguel filled in most of the blanks for me, but then he disappeared, and I thought I had been duped. Then the package arrived. It had me baffled at first, but I followed the lead … we followed the lead … Rogers would have never forgiven me if I hadn’t taken him along to Mexico.”

“Right you are, sir,” Rogers said. He held up a finger like a schoolboy needing permission to ask a question. “I have a question for Chris about—”

“Permission to ask a question granted,” Trapp said, slurping down some iced tea.

“Why didn’t you tell us you were in the witness protection program?” Rogers asked.

Chris shook his head. “I don’t really know. It was a combination of things.” He paused, reaching again for Eden’s hand, which she extended to his. “Mostly it was that my life was over. And then the anger kicked in, and I wanted to avenge her death … alone. But after my blindness … .” He paused and clasped Eden’s hand in both of his. “In retrospect, I should have told you, and we could have worked together, but my anger blinded me long before the acid did. Anger is a strong motivation, but it is rather one-dimensional, and it leaves you quite isolated.”

“Did you ever suspect she was alive, Chris?” Trapp asked. The mood turned suddenly somber.

Chris hesitated. “That’s a tough question … it may have crossed my mind … the necklace should have been the eyeopener, for she always placed the necklace in the safe, but it was found in her hand … the dead woman’s hand. But under the circumstances, I missed that part. Even after the ransom demand, I feared it was a ruse, that it would take a miracle for her to be alive. I couldn’t bring myself to hope in a miracle … to believe that … .” His words trailed off.

“And we still haven’t identified the dead woman,” Trapp said.

“I can’t help but feel sorry for her,” Eden said, “even though she was an assassin … and a thief.”

“And a kidnapper,” Trapp chimed in. “Don’t leave that little crime out.”

"But to think that no one cared enough about her to come looking for her is so sad," Eden said.

"It's the price you pay for the company you keep," Trapp said.

"But that's all behind us," Chris said. "And I think I've found it in my heart to forgive."

"Eden, I've been wondering about something. How did you get the booties to Father Gallardo?" Trapp asked.

"I begged my captors to let me send them, and one of them, who has a small child of his own, mailed them for me, but without a note, I had no idea if Father Gallardo would realize it was a plea for help."

"That was brilliant of you," Trapp said.

"No, not really. It was a package sent on a wish and a prayer. I remembered I once sent to the orphanage some booties I had crocheted, and I had explained to Father Gallardo it was a new hobby I had taken up and hoped he could use them. I only hoped ... ." She paused. "Thank you, Detective Trapp, for figuring out what Father Gallardo's note meant."

"I call it luck," Trapp responded. "I'm just glad I left Father Gallardo my contact information ... and that you thought to send him the booties ... and that the padre sent the note to me ... and—"

"That is not luck, Detective, that is an answer to prayer," Eden said.

"I'm still wondering how the cartel located you, Chris," Rogers said.

"It was probably the man I saw at the Kentucky Derby. I believe he recognized us both, and he cashed me in but determined to kidnap Eden for a ransom," Chris said.

"And the woman got greedy in the process, stole the necklace, and had it in her hand when she accidentally blew herself up trying to place the bomb under your bed," Trapp said. "That's now an ongoing investigation that is going slowly. We'll need you to help identify the man at the Derby, Chris," Trapp said. "We've got a stack of files—"

"And just how am I going to do that?" Chris chuckled.

"Sorry … I momentarily forgot about your eyes," Trapp said.

Eden gently placed a hand on Chris' forearm. "One person is missing from this table," she said, almost in a whisper, and probably a polite manner in which to change the conversation.

"Who?" Chris asked.

"Father Gallardo," she said.

"Actually two," Trapp said. "Scott Davis from the Louisville PD was accommodating in the investigation, but yes, Father Gallardo got us on track. And I'm grateful we got there in time. He must have been looking after us." Trapp pointed upward.

"So, let's settle the issue with a question for Detective Trapp," Chris said, smiling. "Did you go to Mexico to break up a drug deal or to find and rescue a kidnapped Eden Stone."

"That's two questions." Trapp laughed. "To rescue Eden, of course, Chris. I'm a pretty good detective if I must say so myself." Trapp laughed again. His laughter quickly turned to a serious tone. "I didn't really know what I would find, but I had to pursue the lead from the padre."

"Thank you for showing up," Chris said. "We shouldn't have delivered the ransom without telling you—"

"True," Trapp said, "very true. Never, ever deliver—"

"But everything worked out," Chris interrupted him. "And I'm still trying to figure out if you're a good detective or just lucky." They all laughed.

"Good and lucky," Trapp said, laughing at himself.

"And modest," Chris added.

"Christopher!" Eden scolded him.

"Just teasing him, dear. You have no idea what I had to endure at the end of his pointed questions these last few months. He's like a … ." Chris pointed at his plate. "He's like a lobster that latches on and won't let go. You have to bite off your fingers to get released."

"You were a conundrum, sir," Trapp said.

"Seriously, Detective Trapp, Detective Rogers," Chris said, as he picked up his glass, "I'm lifting my glass to you both. From the depth of my heart, thank you!" Chris held his glass of Diet Coke toward them. "You did a fantastic job figuring things out."

"Thank you, kind professor, but … ," Trapp hesitated. "I'm so sorry … for Eden and your sake … sorry that we did not figure it out sooner."

"You had no way of knowing," Chris responded.

"A simple DNA test on that dead woman's charred body would have told us a lot on day one." His tone grew somber. "But it all seemed so evident under the circumstances, a grieving husband … the crime scene itself … all the obvious evidence pointed to the lady with the diamond cross in her hand as being Eden. I really messed up on this one. But, here we are … together … celebrating. I'm lifting my glass, but this time skyward. God is good!"

"Yes, He is good," Chris said.

"Hear, hear," reverberated around the table as they all joined in affirmation.

Their table grew quiet, as if in reflection. Sounds of the room amplified: conversations, laughter, clinking of forks against plates, a baby crying and a parent shushing, Kenny Rogers' smooth voice resonating through the speakers … *I can't remember when you were not there* … . For a moment, Chris took in the sounds as if life had just returned … a fish released back into water … a caged bird set free … a prison door swung open wide. He was blind, but for the first time in his adult life, he could see clearly. Doctor Mansfield was optimistic about his vision returning, but he did not place his future on such a miracle, for he had already had his miracle, and either way, he could now see life clearer than ever. He could not see Eden sitting beside him, but though he would grow old, she would forever be young, beautiful, and innocent in his sight, for her face was etched, not only in memory but on his heart. He believed what some scientists were lately speculating: the heart is much more than an organ beating in the chest, pumping and receiving blood; it may well be a brain within itself, receiving and cherishing memories. How had the writer of Proverbs put it? *As a man thinks in his heart, so is he.* Today his heart overflowed with thankfulness, not of his own doing, but the goodness of God toward him. How could his heart speak anything from now on but good? The treasure of his life had been returned to him. He had for a while lost both Eden and God. Eden had been jerked from his life by evil men, but he had walked away from God's goodness of his own accord. Still, the goodness of God had never left him. And the goodness of God had returned her to him. The miracle of the resurrection had taken place once again, but this time it was personal for him. How could he not be a believer?

"Most excitement we've had in our career. Don't you agree, boss?" Rogers broke the silence.

"For once I'll have to agree with you, Rogers."

They all laughed at Trapp's teasing of Rogers, and Roger's respect and admiration for Trapp was obvious. They were a team, those two.

"But I'm still angry we didn't take in a bullfight," Rogers chided.

"Another day, another case, maybe another visit to Mexico just to see the bullfights," Eden said.

"Another day, but hopefully not another case like this one," Trapp responded. "And I haven't gotten to mention it before, but I think it's a wonderful thing what you two did for the orphanage … giving the money from the sale of the necklace."

"It was all Christopher's idea," Eden said.

"Might as well give it away, for I could have never gotten it back across the border," Chris said.

"How did you get it into Mexico?" Rogers asked.

"I'd rather not discuss that with a table of cops," Chris said. They all laughed. "Believe it or not, I still have some favors I've never cashed in. I did live there a few years."

"And you stole her across the border, somehow," Trapp said, pointing at Eden. The table erupted in more laughter.

"But seriously, all jokes aside, I am indebted to the two of you, a debt I can never, in a thousand lifetimes, repay," Chris said. He wiped at tears that coursed down his face.

The table grew contemplatively quiet.

Trapp broke the silence. "So, where do you go from here, Chris, if you don't mind my asking?"

Chris smiled. "First, I'm taking Eden to see her father."

"Thank you, Christopher. That will please me very much." She placed a hand on his.

"That's not as altruistic as it may sound, dear. I want to thank him for withdrawing the hit he had out on my life." Chris chuckled.

"I'm so sorry for his actions, but it is good to see you laughing, Christopher, and not hating my father."

"And," Chris continued, "I've done a lot of contemplating regarding religion and my faith. I read something the other day that makes a lot of sense, and it definitely applies to me. 'Faith—like air and water and food—is a gift of God, but you have to act on it. These three gifts are worthless unless you breathe, and drink, and eat. The same is true with faith: you must act.' So," he turned toward Eden and continued, "I told my father that you and I would like to go with him to church this Sunday."

"Something we all should give some serious consideration to, Chris," Trapp said in a resolute tone. "I for one have certainly strayed from the God of our fathers."

"And," Chris paused in contemplation, "I want to continue helping with the orphanage." He continued deliberately, not wanting to sound prideful. "I want to help Father Gallardo oversee the digging of a well." He paused and smiled. "No pun intended … oversee … a blind man overseeing something."

No one responded.

"I thought it was a little funny," Chris added.

They laughed.

"Oh, but I have a wonderful idea," Eden said excitedly. "Let's all take a trip back to Mexico when the well is finished, for the dedication of the well."

"And the fountain," Chris added.

"A fountain?" Eden asked.

"Yes, a fountain for the children," Chris said. "I think a fountain at the orphanage will be an added touch."

"Like the fountain that you took me to see in Cincinnati?" Eden asked excitedly.

"Well, not nearly that elaborate." Chris chuckled. "I was thinking more of a modest, single-spray fountain where the children can splash and play in the heat of the day."

"Oh, wonderful! The children will love that. And let's call it the Fountain of Youth … like the name of the fountain the Spanish explorer Ponce de Leon searched for," Eden said. "We will write an inscription in Spanish … *la fuente de la juventud* … for the children to read."

"That's a good name," Chris responded, "but I had something else in mind."

"Really!" Eden said. "What is that?"

Chris hesitated.

"Tell me, Christopher," Eden pleaded.

"I was thinking we'd call it the Fountain of Eden."

"Which actually means the Fountain of Delight," Rogers chimed in.

"Are you sure that's what Eden's name means, Rogers? Delight?" Trapp teased. "She's brought us a lot of headaches the last few months."

"Sure is, sir," Rogers responded, his face beaming with pleasure over his acclaim to the trivia.

"What do you think, dear?" Chris asked. "The Fountain of Eden?"

"Let's not call it the Fountain of Eden. That seems too flattering, though I thank you for the thoughtfulness. Instead, let's call it what Detective Rogers just said, Fountain of Delight." Eden mouthed the words softly before continuing. "I would like that, Chris … not for me … but for the children. I would like that very much."

Additional Books by Larry M. Arrowood

The Shenandoah Series

Book One: Bloodroot
Book Two: The Last Hemlock

Troublesome Blue

Cross Switch

Grace Faith Works, Finding the Biblical Balance
(Revised edition)

They Came to Save Us

Suffering With Purpose
(Revised edition of Surviving the Storm of Suffering)

Overcoming Temptation
(Revised edition)

Building the Home

Books by Larry Arrowood may be ordered through your preferred bookstore or online through:

Barnes and Noble

Amazon

Woodsong Publishing

www.woodsongpublishing.com

www.facebook.com/LarryArrowood

larryarrowood@mac.com

www.ingramcontent.com/pod-product-compliance
Lightning Source LLC
Chambersburg PA
CBHW070339260626
47160CB00003B/1085
* 9 7 8 0 9 9 7 9 1 4 6 9 6 *